NEMESIS

Miss Jane Marple, elderly and mild-mannered, would never have thought that anyone could consider her a *ruthless* person. Yet that was apparently how Jason Rafiel had regarded her. She remembered her Caribbean holiday some time ago, and how she had enlisted his help in solving a mysterious murder case. . . . Nemesis! That was the word she had used then. . . . Now, the wealthy Mr Rafiel has died, leaving a letter quoting that same word and asking for *her* help in solving a crime and rectifying a wrong. He doesn't specify what the crime was, but only gives her some strange instructions. In complying with these, Miss Marple finds herself on a coach tour in a part of rural England, where she is soon faced with a number of baffling problems. Was it just an *accident* that caused the death of a member of their coach party? And those unsolved mysteries from the past—two young local girls: one who had disappeared without trace and the other who was brutally murdered. . . . Was Mr Rafiel's wayward son, Michael, really responsible for either or both of these? Miss Marple's intuition, experience and tenacity are tested to the limit in seeking the answer to these and many other questions, and she realizes that Mr Rafiel was right—in fulfilling the role of Nemesis she *does* become quite ruthless! She finds, too, that in searching for the truth she places herself in an extremely perilous situation. . . .

Also by
AGATHA CHRISTIE

★

NEMESIS

★

AGATHA CHRISTIE

THE
COMPANION BOOK CLUB
LONDON

This edition, published in 1972 by
The Hamlyn Publishing Group Ltd,
is issued by arrangement with
William Collins, Sons & Co. Ltd.

THE COMPANION BOOK CLUB

The Club is not a library; all books are the
property of members. There is no entrance fee
or any payment beyond the low Club price of
each book. Details of membership will gladly
be sent on request.
Write to:
            The Companion Book Club,
            Borough Green, Sevenoaks, Kent

---

*Made and printed in Great Britain
for the Companion Book Club
by Odhams (Watford) Ltd.*

SBN 600871541
254.11.72

To
Daphne Honeybone

1. Overture

IN THE AFTERNOONS it was the custom of Miss Jane Marple to unfold her second newspaper. Two newspapers were delivered at her house every morning. The first one Miss Marple read while sipping her early morning tea, that is, if it was delivered in time. The boy who delivered the papers was notably erratic in his management of time. Frequently, too, there was either a new boy or a boy who was acting temporarily as a stand-in for the first one. And each one would have ideas of his own as to the geographical route that he should take in delivering. Perhaps it varied monotony for him. But those customers who were used to reading their paper early so that they could snap up the more saucy items in the day's news before departing for their bus, train or other means of progress to the day's work were annoyed if the papers were late, though the middle-aged and elderly ladies who resided peacefully in St Mary Mead often preferred to read a newspaper propped up on their breakfast table.

Today, Miss Marple had absorbed the front page and a few other items in the daily paper that she had nick-named 'the Daily All-Sorts', this being a slightly satirical allusion to the fact that her paper, the *Daily Newsgiver*, owing to a change of proprietor, to her own and to other of her friends' great annoyance, now provided articles on men's tailoring, women's dress, female heart-throbs, competitions for children, and complaining letters from women and had managed pretty well to shove any real news off any part of it but the front page, or to some obscure corner where it was impossible to find it. Miss Marple, being old-fashioned, preferred her newspapers to *be* newspapers and give you news.

7

In the afternoon, having finished her luncheon, treated herself to twenty minutes' nap in a specially purchased, upright armchair which catered for the demands of her rheumatic back, she had opened *The Times* which lent itself still to a more leisurely perusal. Not that *The Times* was what it used to be. The maddening thing about *The Times* was that you couldn't *find* anything any more. Instead of going through from the front page and knowing where everything else was so that you passed easily to any special articles on subjects in which you were interested, there were now extraordinary interruptions to this time-honoured programme. Two pages were suddenly devoted to travel in Capri with illustrations. Sport appeared with far more prominence than it had ever had in the old days. Court news and obituaries were a little more faithful to routine. The Births, Marriages and Deaths which had at one time occupied Miss Marple's attention first of all owing to their prominent position had migrated to a different part of *The Times*, though of late, Miss Marple noted, they had come almost permanently to rest on the back page.

Miss Marple gave her attention first to the main news on the front page. She did not linger long on that because it was equivalent to what she had already read this morning, though possibly couched in a slightly more dignified manner. She cast her eye down the table of contents. Articles, comments, science, sport; then she pursued her usual plan, turned the paper over and had a quick run down the Births, Marriages and Deaths, after which she proposed to turn to the page given to correspondence, where she nearly always found something to enjoy; from that she passed on to the Court Circular, on which page today's news from the Sale Rooms could also be found. A short article on Science was often placed there but she did not propose to read that. It seldom made sense for her.

Having turned the paper over as usual to the Births, Marriages and Deaths, Miss Marple thought to herself, as so often before——

'It's sad really, but nowadays one is only interested in the *deaths*!'

People had babies, but the people who had babies were not likely to be even known by name to Miss Marple. If there had been a column dealing with babies labelled as grandchildren, there might have been some chance of a pleasurable recognition. She might have thought to herself,

'Really, Mary Prendergast has had a *third* granddaughter!', though even that perhaps might have been a bit remote.

She skimmed down Marriages, also with not a very close survey, because most of her old friends' daughters or sons had married some years ago already. She came to the Deaths column and gave that her more serious attention. Gave it enough, in fact, so as to be sure she would not miss a name. Alloway, Angopastro, Arden, Barton, Bedshaw, Burgoweisser—(dear me, what a *German* name, but he seemed to be late of Leeds). Carpenter, Camperdown, Clegg. Clegg? Now was that one of the Cleggs she knew? No, it didn't seem to be. Janet Clegg. Somewhere in Yorkshire. McDonald, McKenzie, Nicholson. Nicholson? No. Again not a Nicholson she knew. Ogg, Ormerod, —that must be one of the aunts, she thought. Yes, probably so. Linda Ormerod. No, she hadn't known her. Quantril? Dear me, that must be Elizabeth Quantril. Eighty-five. Well, really! She had thought Elizabeth Quantril had died some years ago. Fancy her having lived so long! So delicate she'd always been, too. Nobody had expected *her* to make old bones. Race, Radley, Rafiel. Rafiel? Something stirred. That name was familiar. Rafiel. Belford Park, Maidstone. Belford Park, Maidstone. No, she couldn't recall that address. No flowers. Jason Rafiel.

Oh well, an unusual name. She supposed she'd just heard it somewhere. Ross-Perkins. Now that might be—no, it wasn't. Ryland? Emily Ryland. No. No, she'd never known an Emily Ryland. *Deeply loved by her husband and children.* Well, very nice or very sad. Whichever way you liked to look at it.

Miss Marple laid down her paper, glancing idly through the crossword while she puzzled to remember why the name Rafiel was familiar to her.

'It will come to me,' said Miss Marple, knowing from long experience the way old people's memories worked. 'It'll come to me, I have no doubt.'

She glanced out of the window towards the garden, withdrew her gaze and tried to put the garden out of her mind. Her garden had been the source of great pleasure and also a great deal of hard work to Miss Marple for many, many years. And now, owing to the fussiness of doctors, working in the garden was forbidden to her. She'd once tried to fight this ban, but had come to the conclusion that she had, after all, better do as she was told. She had arranged her chair at such an angle as not to be easy to look out in the garden unless she definitely and clearly wished to see something in particular. She sighed, picked up her knitting bag and took out a small child's woolly jacket in process of coming to a conclusion. The back was done and the front. Now she would have to get on with the sleeves. Sleeves were always boring. Two sleeves, both alike. Yes, very boring. Pretty coloured pink wool, however. Pink wool. Now wait a minute, where did that fit in? Yes—yes—it fitted in with that name she'd just read in the paper. Pink wool. A blue sea. A Caribbean sea. A sandy beach. Sunshine. Herself knitting and—why, of course, Mr Rafiel. That trip she had made to the Caribbean. The island of St Honoré. A treat from her nephew Raymond. And she remembered Joan, her niece-in-law, Raymond's wife, saying:

'Don't get mixed up in any more murders, Aunt Jane. It isn't good for you.'

Well, she hadn't *wished* to get mixed up in any murders, but it just happened. That was all. Simply because of an elderly Major with a glass eye who had insisted on telling her some very long and boring stories. Poor Major—now what was *his* name? She'd forgotten that now. Mr Rafiel and his secretary, Mrs—Mrs Walters, yes, Esther Walters, and his masseur-attendant, Jackson. It all came back. Well, well. Poor Mr Rafiel. So Mr Rafiel was dead. He had known he was going to die before very long. He had practically told her so. It seemed as though he had lasted longer than the doctors had thought. He was a strong man, an obstinate man—a very rich man.

Miss Marple remained in thought, her knitting needles working regularly, but her mind not really on her knitting. Her mind was on the late Mr Rafiel, and remembering what she could remember about him. Not an easy man to forget, really. She could conjure his appearance up mentally quite well. Yes, a very definite personality, a difficult man, an irritable man, shockingly rude sometimes. Nobody ever resented his being rude, though. She remembered that also. They didn't resent his being rude because he was so rich. Yes, he had been very rich. He had had his secretary with him and a valet attendant, a qualified masseur. He had not been able to get about very well without help.

Rather a doubtful character that nurse-attendant had been, Miss Marple thought. Mr Rafiel had been very rude to him sometimes. He had never seemed to mind. And that, again, of course was because Mr Rafiel was so rich.

'Nobody else would pay him half what I do,' Mr Rafiel had said, 'and he knows it. He's good at his job, though.'

Miss Marple wondered whether Jackson?—Johnson? had stayed on with Mr Rafiel. Stayed on for what must have been—another year? A year and three or four months. She thought probably not. Mr Rafiel was one who liked a change. He got tired of people, tired of their ways, tired of their faces, tired of their voices.

Miss Marple understood that. She had felt the same sometimes. That companion of hers, that nice, attentive, maddening woman with her cooing voice.

'Ah,' said Miss Marple, 'what a change for the better since—' oh dear, she'd forgotten *her* name now—Miss—Miss Bishop?—no, not Miss Bishop, of course not. Why had she thought of the name Bishop. Oh dear, how difficult it was.

Her mind went back to Mr Rafiel and to—no, it wasn't Johnson, it had been Jackson, Arthur Jackson.

'Oh, dear,' said Miss Marple again, 'I always get *all* the names wrong. And of course, it was Miss *Knight* I was thinking of. Not Miss *Bishop*. Why do I think of her as Miss Bishop?' The answer came to her. Chess, of course. A chess piece. A knight. A bishop.

'I shall be calling her Miss Castle next time I think of her, I suppose, or Miss Rook. Though, really, she's not the sort of person who would ever rook anybody. No, indeed. And now what was the name of that nice secretary that Mr Rafiel had. Oh yes, Esther Walters. That was right. I wonder what has happened to Esther Walters? She'd inherited money? She would probably inherit money now.'

Mr Rafiel, she remembered, had told her something about that, or she had—oh, dear, what a muddle things were when you tried to remember with any kind of exactitude. Esther Walters. It had hit her badly, that business in the Caribbean, but she would have got over it. She'd been a widow, hadn't she? Miss Marple hoped that Esther Walters had married again, some nice, kindly, reliable man. It seemed faintly unlikely. Esther Walters, she thought, had had rather a genius for liking the wrong kind of men to marry.

Miss Marple went back to thinking about Mr Rafiel. No flowers, it had said. Not that she herself would have dreamed of sending flowers to Mr Rafiel. He could buy up all the nurseries in England if he'd wanted to. And anyway, they hadn't been on those terms. They hadn't been—friends, or on terms of affection. They had been— what was the word she wanted?—allies. Yes, they had been allies for a very short time. A very exciting time. And he had been an ally worth having. She had known so. She'd known it as she had gone running through a dark, tropical night in the Caribbean and had come to him. Yes, she remembered, she'd been wearing that pink wool —what used they to call them when she was young?—a fascinator. That nice pink wool kind of shawl-scarf that she'd put round her head, and he had looked at her and laughed, and later when she had said—she smiled at the remembrance—one word she had used and he had laughed, but he hadn't laughed in the end. No, he'd done what she asked him and therefore—'Ah!' Miss Marple sighed, it had been, she had to admit it, all very exciting. And she'd never told her nephew or dear Joan about it because, after all, it was what they'd told her not to do, wasn't it? Miss Marple nodded her head. Then she murmured softly:

'Poor Mr Rafiel, I hope he didn't—suffer.'

Probably not. Probably he'd been kept by expensive doctors under sedatives, easing the end. He had suffered a great deal in those weeks in the Caribbean. He'd nearly always been in pain. A brave man.

A brave man. She was sorry he was dead because she thought that though he'd been elderly and an invalid and ill, the world had lost something through his going. She had no idea what he could have been like in business. Ruthless, she thought, and rude and over-mastering and aggressive. A great attacker. But—but a good friend, she thought. And somewhere in him a deep kind of kindness that he was very careful never to show on the surface. A man she admired and respected. Well, she was sorry he was gone and she hoped he hadn't minded too much and that his passing had been easy. And now he would be cremated no doubt and put in some large, handsome marble vault. She didn't even know if he'd been married. He had never mentioned a wife, never mentioned children. A lonely man? Or had his life been so full that he hadn't needed to feel lonely? She wondered.

She sat there quite a long time that afternoon, wondering about Mr Rafiel. She had never expected to see him again after she had returned to England and she never *had* seen him again. Yet in some queer way she could at any moment have felt she was in touch with him. If he had approached her or had suggested that they meet again, feeling perhaps a bond because of a life that had been saved between them, or of some other bond. A bond——

'Surely,' said Miss Marple, aghast at an idea that had come into her mind, 'there can't be a bond of *ruthlessness* between us?' Was she, Jane Marple—could she ever be—ruthless? 'D'you know,' said Miss Marple to herself, 'it's extraordinary, I never thought about it before. I believe, you know, I *could* be ruthless . . .'

The door opened and a dark, curly head was popped in. It was Cherry, the welcome successor to Miss Bishop—Miss Knight.

'Did you say something?' said Cherry.

'I was speaking to myself,' said Miss Marple, 'I just wondered if I could ever be ruthless.'

'What, you?' said Cherry. 'Never! You're kindness itself.'

'All the same,' said Miss Marple, 'I believe I *could* be ruthless if there was due cause.'

'What would you call due cause?'

'In the cause of justice,' said Miss Marple.

'You did have it in for little Gary Hopkins I must say,'

said Cherry. 'When you caught him torturing his cat that day. Never knew you had it in you to go for anyone like that! Scared him stiff, you did. He's never forgotten it.'

'I hope he hasn't tortured any more cats.'

'Well, he's made sure you weren't about if he did,' said Cherry. 'In fact I'm not at all sure as there isn't other boys as got scared. Seeing you with your wool and the pretty things you knits and all that—anyone would think you were gentle as a lamb. But there's times I could say you'd behave like a lion if you was goaded into it.'

Miss Marple looked a little doubtful. She could not quite see herself in the rôle in which Cherry was now casting her. Had she ever—she paused on the reflection, recalling various moments—there had been intense irritation with Miss Bishop—Knight. (Really, she must *not* forget names in this way.) But her irritation had shown itself in more or less ironical remarks. Lions, presumably, did not use irony. There was nothing ironical about a lion. It sprang. It roared. It used its claws, presumably it took large bites at its prey.

'Really,' said Miss Marple, 'I don't think I have ever behaved *quite* like that.'

Walking slowly along her garden that evening with the usual feelings of vexation rising in her, Miss Marple considered the point again. Possibly the sight of a plant of snapdragons recalled it to her mind. Really, she had *told* old George again and again that she only wanted sulphur-coloured antirrhinums, *not* that rather ugly purple shade that gardeners always seemed so fond of. 'Sulphur yellow,' said Miss Marple aloud.

Someone the other side of the railing that abutted on the lane past her house turned her head and spoke.

'I beg your pardon? You said something?'

'I was talking to myself, I'm afraid,' said Miss Marple, turning to look over the railing.

This was someone she did not know, and she knew

most people in St Mary Mead. Knew them by sight even if not personally. It was a thickset woman in a shabby but tough tweed skirt, and wearing good country shoes. She wore an emerald pullover and a knitted woollen scarf.

'I'm afraid one does at my age,' added Miss Marple.

'Nice garden you've got here,' said the other woman.

'Not particularly nice now,' said Miss Marple. 'When I could attend to it myself——'

'Oh I know. I understand just what you feel. I suppose you've got one of those—I have a lot of names for them, mostly very rude—elderly chaps who say they know all about gardening. Sometimes they do, sometimes they don't know a thing about it. They come and have a lot of cups of tea and do a little very mild weeding. They're quite nice, some of them, but all the same it does make one's temper rise.' She added, 'I'm quite a keen gardener myself.'

'Do you live here?' asked Miss Marple, with some interest.

'Well, I'm boarding with a Mrs Hastings. I think I've heard her speak of you. You're Miss Marple, aren't you?'

'Oh yes.'

'I've come as a sort of companion-gardener. My name is Bartlett, by the way. Miss Bartlett. There's not really much to do there,' said Miss Bartlett. 'She goes in for annuals and all that. Nothing you can really get your teeth into.' She opened her mouth and showed her teeth when making this remark. 'Of course I do a few odd jobs as well. Shopping, you know, and things like that. Anyway, if you want any time put in here, I could put in an hour or two for you. I'd say I might be better than any chap you've got now.'

'That would be easy,' said Miss Marple. 'I like flowers best. Don't care so much for vegetables.'

'I do vegetables for Mrs Hastings. Dull but necessary. Well, I'll be getting along.' Her eyes swept over Miss

Marple from head to foot, as though memorizing her, then she nodded cheerfully and tramped off.

Mrs Hastings? Miss Marple couldn't remember the name of any Mrs Hastings. Certainly Mrs Hastings was not an old friend. She had certainly never been a gardening chum. Ah, of course, it was probably those newly built houses at the end of Gibraltar Road. Several families had moved in in the last year. Miss Marple sighed, looked again with annoyance at the antirrhinums, saw several weeds which she yearned to root up, one or two exuberant suckers she would like to attack with her secateurs, and finally, sighing, and manfully resisting temptation, she made a detour round by the lane and returned to her house. Her mind recurred again to Mr Rafiel. They had been, he and she—what was the title of that book they used to quote so much when she was young? *Ships that pass in the night.* Rather apt it was really, when she came to think of it. Ships that pass in the night. . . . It was in the night that she had gone to him to ask—no, to demand— help. To insist, to say no time must be lost. And he had agreed, and put things in train at once! Perhaps she *had* been rather lion-like on that occasion? No. No, that was quite wrong. It had not been anger she had felt. It had been insistence on something that was absolutely imperative to be put in hand at once. And he'd understood.

Poor Mr Rafiel. The ship that had passed in the night had been an interesting ship. Once you got used to his being rude, he might have been quite an agreeable man? No! She shook her head. Mr Rafiel could never have been an agreeable man. Well, she must put Mr Rafiel out of her head.

Ships that pass in the night, and speak each other in passing;
Only a signal shown and a distant voice in the darkness.

She would probably never think of him again. She would look out perhaps to see if there was an obituary of him in *The Times*. But she did not think it was very likely. He was not a very well known character, she thought. Not famous. He had just been very rich. Of course, many people did have obituaries in the paper just because they were very rich; but she thought that Mr Rafiel's richness would possibly not have been of that kind. He had not been prominent in any great industry, he had not been a great financial genius, or a noteworthy banker. He had just all his life made enormous amounts of money. . . .

2. Code Word Nemesis

IT WAS ABOUT A WEEK OR SO after Mr Rafiel's death that Miss Marple picked up a letter from her breakfast tray, and looked at it for a moment before opening it. The other two letters that had come by this morning's post were bills, or just possibly receipts for bills. In either case they were not of any particular interest. This letter might be.

A London postmark, typewritten address, a long, good quality envelope. Miss Marple slit it neatly with the paper knife she always kept handy on her tray. It was headed, Messrs Broadribb and Schuster, Solicitors and Notaries Public, with an address in Bloomsbury. It asked her, in suitable courteous and legal phraseology, to call upon them one day in the following week, at their office, to discuss a proposition that might be to her advantage. Thursday, the 24th was suggested. If that date was not convenient, perhaps she would let them know what date she would be likely to be in London in the near future. They added that they were the solicitors to the late Mr Rafiel, with whom they understood she had been acquainted.

Miss Marple frowned in some slight puzzlement. She got up rather more slowly than usual, thinking about the letter she had received. She was escorted downstairs by Cherry, who was meticulous in hanging about in the hall so as to make sure that Miss Marple did not come to grief walking by herself down the staircase, which was of the old-fashioned kind which turned a sharp corner in the middle of its run.

'You take very good care of me, Cherry,' said Miss Marple.

'Got to,' said Cherry, in her usual idiom. 'Good people are scarce.'

'Well, thank you for the compliment,' said Miss Marple, arriving safely with her last foot on the ground floor.

'Nothing the matter, is there?' asked Cherry. 'You look a bit rattled like, if you know what I mean.'

'No, nothing's the matter,' said Miss Marple. 'I had rather an unusual letter from a firm of solicitors.'

'Nobody is suing you for anything, are they?' said Cherry, who was inclined to regard solicitors' letters as invariably associated with disaster of some kind.

'Oh no, I don't think so,' said Miss Marple. 'Nothing of that kind. They just asked me to call upon them next week in London.'

'Perhaps you've been left a fortune,' said Cherry, hopefully.

'That, I think, is *very* unlikely,' said Miss Marple.

'Well, you never know,' said Cherry.

Settling herself in her chair, and taking her knitting out of its embroidered knitting bag, Miss Marple considered the possibility of Mr Rafiel having left her a fortune. It seemed even more unlikely than when Cherry had suggested it. Mr Rafiel, she thought, was not that kind of a man.

It was not possible for her to go on the date suggested. She was attending a meeting of the Women's Institute to discuss the raising of a sum for building a small additional couple of rooms. But she wrote, naming a day in the following week. In due course her letter was answered and the appointment definitely confirmed. She wondered what Messrs Broadribb and Schuster were like. The letter had been signed by J. R. Broadribb who was, apparently, the senior partner. It was possible, Miss Marple thought, that Mr Rafiel *might* have left her some small memoir or souvenir in his will. Perhaps some book on rare flowers that had been in his library and which he thought would please an old lady who was keen on gardening. Or perhaps a cameo brooch which had belonged to some great-aunt of his. She amused herself by these fancies. They were only fancies, she thought, because in either case it would merely be a case of the Executors—if these lawyers were the Executors—forwarding her by post any such object. They would not have wanted an interview.

'Oh well,' said Miss Marple, 'I shall know next Tuesday.'

2

'Wonder what she'll be like,' said Mr Broadribb to Mr Schuster, glancing at the clock as he did so.

'She's due in a quarter of an hour,' said Mr Schuster. 'Wonder if she'll be punctual?'

'Oh, I should think so. She's elderly, I gather, and much more punctilious than the young scatter-brains of today.'

'Fat or thin, I wonder?' said Mr Schuster.

Mr Broadribb shook his head.

'Didn't Rafiel ever describe her to you?' asked Mr Schuster.

'He was extraordinarily cagey in everything he said about her.'

'The whole thing seems very odd to me,' said Mr Schuster. 'If we only knew a bit more about what it all meant. . . .'

'It might be,' said Mr Broadribb thoughtfully, 'something to do with Michael.'

'What? After all these years? Couldn't be. What put that into your head? Did he mention——'

'No, he didn't mention anything. Gave me no clue at all as to what was in his mind. Just gave me instructions.'

'Think he was getting a bit eccentric and all that towards the end?'

'Not in the least. Mentally he was as brilliant as ever.

His physical ill-health never affected his brain, anyway. In the last two months of his life he made an extra two hundred thousand pounds. Just like that.'

'He had a *flair*,' said Mr Schuster with due reverence. 'Certainly, he always had a flair.'

'A great financial brain,' said Mr Broadribb, also in a tone of reverence suitable to the sentiment. 'Not many like him, more's the pity.'

A buzzer went on the table. Mr Schuster picked up the receiver. A female voice said,

'Miss Jane Marple is here to see Mr Broadribb by appointment.'

Mr Schuster looked at his partner, raising an eyebrow for an affirmative or a negative. Mr Broadribb nodded.

'Show her up,' said Mr Schuster. And he added, 'Now we'll see.'

Miss Marple entered a room where a middle-aged gentleman with a thin, spare body and a long rather melancholy face rose to greet her. This apparently was Mr Broadribb, whose appearance somewhat contradicted his name. With him was a rather younger middle-aged gentleman of definitely more ample proportions. He had black hair, small keen eyes and a tendency to a double chin.

'My partner, Mr Schuster,' Mr Broadribb presented.

'I hope you didn't feel the stairs too much,' said Mr Schuster. 'Seventy if she is a day—nearer eighty perhaps,' he was thinking in his own mind.

'I always get a little breathless going upstairs.'

'An old-fashioned building this,' said Mr Broadribb apologetically. 'No lift. Ah well, we are a very long established firm and we don't go in for as many of the modern gadgets as perhaps our clients expect of us.'

'This room has very pleasant proportions,' said Miss Marple, politely.

She accepted the chair that Mr Broadribb drew forward

for her. Mr Schuster, in an unobtrusive sort of way, left the room.

'I hope that chair is comfortable,' said Mr Broadribb. 'I'll pull that curtain slightly, shall I? You may feel the sun a little too much in your eyes.'

'Thank you,' said Miss Marple, gratefully.

She sat there, upright as was her habit. She wore a light tweed suit, a string of pearls and a small velvet toque. To himself Mr Broadribb was saying, 'The Provincial Lady. A good type. Fluffy old girl. May be scatty—may not. Quite a shrewd eye. I wonder where Rafiel came across her. Somebody's aunt, perhaps, up from the country?' While these thoughts passed through his head, he was making the kind of introductory small talk relating to the weather, the unfortunate effects of late frosts early in the year and such other remarks as he considered suitable.

Miss Marple made the necessary responses and sat placidly awaiting the opening of preliminaries to the meeting.

'You will be wondering what all this is about,' said Mr Broadribb, shifting a few papers in front of him and giving her a suitable smile. 'You've heard, no doubt, of Mr Rafiel's death, or perhaps you saw it in the paper.'

'I saw it in the paper,' said Miss Marple.

'He was, I understand, a friend of yours.'

'I met him first just over a year ago,' said Miss Marple. 'In the West Indies,' she added.

'Ah. I remember. He went out there, I believe, for his health. It did him some good, perhaps, but he was already a very ill man, badly crippled, as you know.'

'Yes,' said Miss Marple.

'You knew him well?'

'No,' said Miss Marple, 'I would not say that. We were fellow visitors in a hotel. We had occasional conversations. I never saw him again after my return to England. I live very quietly in the country, you see, and I gather that he was completely absorbed in business.'

'He continued transacting business right up—well, I could almost say right up to the day of his death,' said Mr Broadribb. 'A very fine financial brain.'

'I am sure that was so,' said Miss Marple. 'I realized quite soon that he was a—well, a very remarkable character altogether.'

'I don't know if you have any idea—whether you've been given any idea at some time by Mr Rafiel—as to what this proposition is that I have been instructed to put up to you?'

'I cannot imagine,' said Miss Marple, 'what possible kind of proposition Mr Rafiel might have wanted to put up to me. It seems most unlikely.'

'He had a very high opinion of you.'

'That is kind of him, but hardly justified,' said Miss Marple. 'I am a very simple person.'

'As you no doubt realize, he died a very rich man. The provisions of his Will are on the whole fairly simple. He had already made dispositions of his fortune some time before his death. Trusts and other beneficiary arrangements.'

'That is, I believe, very usual procedure nowadays,' said Miss Marple, 'though I am not at all cognizant of financial matters myself.'

'The purpose of this appointment,' said Mr Broadribb, 'is that I am instructed to tell you that a sum of money has been laid aside to become yours absolutely at the end of one year, but conditional on your accepting a certain proposition, with which I am to make you acquainted.'

He took from the table in front of him a long envelope. It was sealed. He passed it across the table to her.

'It would be better, I think, that you should read for yourself of what this consists. There is no hurry. Take your time.'

Miss Marple took her time. She availed herself of a small paper-knife which Mr Broadribb handed to her, slit up the envelope, took out the enclosure, one sheet of typewriting, and read it.

She folded it up again, then she re-read it and looked at Mr Broadribb.

'This is hardly very definite. Is there no more definite elucidation of any kind?'

'Not so far as I am concerned. I was to hand you this, and tell you the amount of the legacy. The sum in question is twenty thousand pounds free of legacy duty.'

Miss Marple sat looking at him. Surprise had rendered her speechless. Mr Broadribb said no more for the moment. He was watching her closely. There was no doubt of her surprise. It was obviously the last thing Miss Marple had expected to hear. Mr Broadribb wondered what her first words would be. She looked at him with the directness, the severity that one of his own aunts might have done. When she spoke it was almost accusingly.

'That is a very large sum of money,' said Miss Marple.

'Not quite so large as it used to be,' said Mr Broadribb (and just restrained himself from saying, 'Mere chicken feed nowadays').

'I must admit,' said Miss Marple, 'that I am amazed. Frankly, quite amazed.'

She picked up the document and read it carefully through again.

'I gather you know the terms of this?' she said.

'Yes. It was dictated to me personally by Mr Rafiel.'

'Did he not give you any explanation of it?'

'No, he did not.'

'You suggested, I suppose, that it might be better if he did,' said Miss Marple. There was a slight acidity in her voice now.

Mr Broadribb smiled faintly.

'You are quite right. That is what I did. I said that

25

you might find it difficult to—oh, to understand exactly what he was driving at.'

'Very remarkable,' said Miss Marple.

'There is no need, of course,' said Mr Broadribb, 'for you to give me an answer now.'

'No,' said Miss Marple, 'I should have to reflect on it.'

'It is, as you have pointed out, quite a substantial sum of money.'

'I am old,' said Miss Marple. 'Elderly, we say, but old is a better word. Definitely old. It is both possible and indeed probable that I might not live as long as a year to earn this money, in the rather doubtful case that I *was* able to earn it.'

'Money is not to be despised at any age,' said Mr Broadribb.

'I could benefit certain charities in which I have an interest,' said Miss Marple, 'and there are always people. People whom one wishes one could do a little something for but one's own funds do not admit of it. And then I will not pretend that there are not pleasures and desires—things that one has not been able to indulge in or to afford —I think Mr Rafiel knew quite well that to be able to do so, quite unexpectedly, would give an elderly person a great deal of pleasure.'

'Yes, indeed,' said Mr Broadribb. 'A cruise abroad, perhaps? One of these excellent *tours* as arranged nowadays. Theatres, concerts—the ability to replenish one's cellars.'

'My tastes would be a little more moderate than that,' said Miss Marple. 'Partridges,' she said thoughtfully, 'it is very difficult to get partridges nowadays, and they're very expensive. I should enjoy a partridge—a whole partridge—to myself, very much. A box of *marrons glacés* are an expensive taste which I cannot often gratify. Possibly a visit to the opera. It means a car to take one to Covent Garden and back, and the expense of a night in a

26

hotel. But I must not indulge in idle chat,' she said. 'I will take this back with me and reflect upon it. Really, what on earth made Mr Rafiel—you have no idea *why* he should have suggested this particular proposition, and why he should think that I could be of service to him in any way? He must have known that it was over a year, nearly two years since he had seen me and that I might have got much more feeble than I have, and much more unable to exercise such small talents as I might have. He was taking a risk. There are other people surely much better qualified to undertake an investigation of this nature?'

'Frankly, one would think so,' said Mr Broadribb, 'but he selected *you*, Miss Marple. Forgive me if this is idle curiosity but have you had—oh, how shall I put it?—any connection with crime or the investigation of crime?'

'Strictly speaking I should say no,' said Miss Marple. 'Nothing professional, that is to say. I have never been a probation officer or indeed sat as a magistrate on a Bench or been connected in any way with a detective agency. To explain to you, Mr Broadribb, which I think is only fair for me to do and which I think Mr Rafiel ought to have done, to explain it in any way all I can say is that during our stay in the West Indies, we both, Mr Rafiel and myself, had a certain connection with a crime that took place there. A rather unlikely and perplexing murder.'

'And you and Mr Rafiel solved it?'

'I should not put it quite like that,' said Miss Marple. 'Mr Rafiel, by the force of his personality, and I, by putting together one or two obvious indications that came to my notice, were successful in preventing a second murder just as it was about to take place. I could not have done it alone, I was physically far too feeble. Mr Rafiel could not have done it alone, he was a cripple. We acted as allies, however.'

'Just one other question I should like to ask you, Miss Marple. Does the word "Nemesis" mean anything to you?'

'*Nemesis*,' said Miss Marple. It was not a question. A very slow and unexpected smile dawned on her face. 'Yes,' she said, 'it does mean something to me. It means something to me and it meant something to Mr Rafiel. I said it to him, and he was much amused by my describing myself by that name.'

Whatever Mr Broadribb had expected it was not that. He looked at Miss Marple with something of the same astonished surprise that Mr Rafiel had once felt in a bedroom by the Caribbean sea. A nice and quite intelligent old lady. But really—Nemesis!

'You feel the same, I am sure,' said Miss Marple.

She rose to her feet.

'If you should find or receive any further instructions in this matter, you will perhaps let me know, Mr Broadribb. It seems to me extraordinary that there should not be *something* of that kind. This leaves me entirely in the dark really as to what Mr Rafiel is asking me to do or try to do.'

'You are not acquainted with his family, his friends, his——'

'No. I told you. He was a fellow traveller in a foreign part of the world. We had a certain association as allies in a very mystifying matter. That is all.' As she was about to go to the door she turned suddenly and asked: 'He had a secretary, Mrs Esther Walters. Would it be infringing etiquette if I asked if Mr Rafiel left her fifty thousand pounds?'

'His bequests will appear in the press,' said Mr Broadribb. 'I can answer your question in the affirmative. Mrs Walters's name is now Mrs Anderson, by the way. She has re-married.'

'I am glad to hear that. She was a widow with one daughter, and she was a very adequate secretary, it appears. She understood Mr Rafiel very well. A nice woman. I am glad she has benefited.'

28

That evening, Miss Marple, sitting in her straight-backed chair, her feet stretched out to the fireplace where a small wood fire was burning owing to the sudden cold spell which, as is its habit, can always descend on England at any moment selected by itself, took once more from the long envelope the document delivered to her that morning. Still in a state of partial unbelief she read, murmuring the words here and there below her breath as though to impress them on her mind,

'To Miss Jane Marple, resident in the village of St Mary Mead.

This will be delivered to you after my death by the good offices of my solicitor, James Broadribb. He is the man I employ for dealing with such legal matters as fall in the field of my private affairs, not my business activities. He is a sound and trustworthy lawyer. Like the majority of the human race he is susceptible to the sin of curiosity. I have not satisfied his curiosity. In some respects this matter will remain between you and myself. Our code word, my dear lady, is Nemesis. I don't think you will have forgotten in what place and in what circumstances you first spoke that word to me. In the course of my business activities over what is now quite a long life, I have learnt one thing about a man whom I wish to employ. He has to have a flair. A flair for the particular job I want him to do. It is not knowledge, it is not experience. The only word that describes it is *flair*. A natural gift for doing a certain thing.

You, my dear, if I may call you that, have a natural *flair* for justice, and that has led to your having a natural *flair* for crime. I want you to investigate a certain crime. I have ordered a certain sum to be placed so that if you accept this request and as a result of your investigation this crime is properly elucidated, the money will become yours absolutely. I have set aside a year for you to engage on this mission. You are not young, but you are, if I may say so, tough. I think I can trust a reasonable fate to keep you alive for a year at least.

I think the work involved will not be distasteful to you. You have a natural genius, I should say, for investigation. The necessary funds for what I may describe as working capital for making this investigation will be remitted to you during that period, whenever necessary. I offer this to you as an alternative to what may be your life at present.

I envisage you sitting in a chair, a chair that is agreeable and comfortable for whatever kind or form of rheumatism from which you may suffer. All persons of your age, I consider, are likely to suffer from some form of rheumatism. If this ailment affects your knees or your back, it will not be easy for you to get about much and you will spend your time mainly in knitting. I see you, as I saw you once one night as I rose from sleep disturbed by your urgency, in a cloud of pink wool.

I envisage you knitting more jackets, head scarves and a good many other things of which I do not know the name. If you prefer to continue knitting, that is your decision. If you prefer to serve the cause of justice, I hope that you may at least find it interesting.

Let justice roll down like waters
And righteousness like an everlasting stream.

Amos.'

3. Miss Marple Takes Action

MISS MARPLE read this letter three times—then she laid it aside and sat frowning slightly while she considered the letter and its implications.

The first thought that came to her was that she was left with a surprising lack of definite information. Would there be any further information coming to her from Mr Broadribb? Almost certainly she felt that there would be no such thing. That would not have fitted in with Mr Rafiel's plan. Yet how on earth could Mr Rafiel expect her to do anything, to take any course of action in a matter about which she knew nothing. It was intriguing. After a few minutes more for consideration, she decided that Mr Rafiel had meant it to be intriguing. Her thoughts went back to him, for the brief time that she had known him. His disability, his bad temper, his flashes of brilliance, of occasional humour. He'd enjoy, she thought, teasing people. He had been enjoying, she felt, and this letter made it almost certain, baffling the natural curiosity of Mr Broadribb.

There was nothing in the letter he had written her to give her the slightest clue as to what this business was all about. It was no help to her whatsoever. Mr Rafiel, she thought, had very definitely not meant it to be of any help. He had had—how could she put it?—other ideas. All the same, she could not start out into the blue knowing nothing. This could almost be described as a crossword puzzle with no clues given. There would *have* to be clues. She would *have* to know what she was wanted to do, where she was wanted to go, whether she was to solve some problem sitting in her armchair and laying aside her knitting needles in order to concentrate better. Or did Mr

Rafiel intend her to take a plane or a boat to the West Indies or to South America or to some other specially directed spot? She would either have to find out for herself what it was she was meant to do, or else she would have to receive definite instructions. He might think she had sufficient ingenuity to guess at things, to ask questions, to find out that way? No, she couldn't quite believe *that*.

'If he does think that,' said Miss Marple aloud, 'he's gaga. I mean, he was gaga before he died.'

But she didn't think Mr Rafiel would have been gaga.

'I shall receive instructions,' said Miss Marple. 'But what instructions and when?'

It was only then that it occurred to her suddenly that without noticing it she had definitely accepted the mandate. She spoke aloud again, addressing the atmosphere.

'I believe in eternal life,' said Miss Marple. 'I don't know exactly where you are, Mr Rafiel, but I have no doubt that you are *somewhere*—I will do my best to fulfil your wishes.'

2

It was three days later when Miss Marple wrote to Mr Broadribb. It was a very short letter, keeping strictly to the point.

'Dear Mr Broadribb,

I have considered the suggestion you made to me and I am letting you know that I have decided to accept the proposal made to me by the late Mr Rafiel. I shall do my best to comply with his wishes, though I am not at all assured of success. Indeed, I hardly see how it is possible for me to be successful. I have been given no direct instructions in his letter and have not been—I think the term is briefed—*in any way*. If you have any further communication you are holding for me which sets out definite instructions, I should be glad if you will send it to me, but I imagine that as you have not done so, that is not the case.

I presume that Mr Rafiel was of sound mind and disposition when he died? I think I am justified in asking if there had been recently in his life any criminal affair in which he might possibly have been interested, either in the course of his business or in his personal relations. Has he ever expressed to you any anger or dissatisfaction with some notable miscarriage of justice about which he felt strongly? If so, I think I should be justified in asking you to let me know about it. Has any relation or connection of his suffered some hardship, lately been the victim of some unjust dealing, or what might be considered as such?

I am sure you will understand my reasons for asking these things. Indeed, Mr Rafiel himself may have expected me to do so.'

3

Mr Broadribb showed this to Mr Schuster, who leaned back in his chair and whistled.

'She's going to take it on, is she? Sporting old bean,' he said. Then he added, 'I suppose she knows something of what it's all about, does she?'

'Apparently not,' said Mr Broadribb.

'I wish we did,' said Mr Schuster. 'He was an odd cuss.'

'A difficult man,' said Mr Broadribb.

'I haven't got the least idea,' said Mr Schuster, 'have you?'

'No, I haven't,' said Mr Broadribb. He added, 'He didn't want me to have, I suppose.'

'Well, he's made things a lot more difficult by doing that. I don't see the least chance that some old pussy from the country can interpret a dead man's brain and know what fantasy was plaguing him. You don't think he was leading her up the garden path? Having her on? Sort of joke, you know. Perhaps he thinks that she thinks she's the cat's whiskers at solving village problems, but he's going to teach her a sharp lesson——'

'No,' said Mr Broadribb, 'I don't quite think that. Rafiel wasn't that type of man.'

'He was a mischievous devil sometimes,' said Mr Schuster.

'Yes, but not—I think he was serious over this. *Something* was worrying him. In fact I'm quite sure something was worrying him.'

'And he didn't tell you what it was or give you the least idea?'

'No, he didn't.'

'Then how the devil can he expect——' Schuster broke off.

'He can't really have expected anything to come of this,' said Mr Broadribb. 'I mean, how is she going to set about it?'

'A practical joke, if you ask me.'

'Twenty thousand pounds is a lot of money.'

'Yes, but if he knows she can't do it?'

'No,' said Mr Broadribb. 'He wouldn't have been as unsporting as all that. He must think she's got a chance of doing or finding out whatever it is.'

'And what do we do?'

'Wait,' said Mr Broadribb. 'Wait and see what happens next. After all, there has to be some development.'

'Got some sealed orders somewhere, have you?'

'My dear Schuster,' said Mr Broadribb, 'Mr Rafiel had implicit trust in my discretion and in my ethical conduct as a lawyer. Those sealed instructions are to be opened only under certain circumstances, none of which has yet arisen.'

'And never will,' said Mr Schuster.

That ended the subject.

4

Mr Broadribb and Mr Schuster were lucky in so much as they had a full professional life to lead. Miss Marple was not so fortunate. She knitted and she reflected and she also went out for walks, occasionally remonstrated with by Cherry for so doing.

'You know what the doctor said. You weren't to take too much exercise.'

'I walk very slowly,' said Miss Marple, 'and I am not doing anything. Digging, I mean, or weeding. I just—well, I just put one foot in front of the other and wonder about things.'

'What things?' asked Cherry, with some interest.

'I wish I knew,' said Miss Marple, and asked Cherry to bring her an extra scarf as there was a chilly wind.

'What's fidgeting her, that's what I would like to know,' said Cherry to her husband as she set before him a Chinese plate of rice and a concoction of kidneys. 'Chinese dinner,' she said.

Her husband nodded approval.

'You get a better cook every day,' he said.

'I'm worried about her,' said Cherry. 'I'm worried because she's worried a bit. She had a letter and it stirred her all up.'

'What she needs is to sit quiet,' said Cherry's husband. 'Sit quiet, take it easy, get herself new books from the library, get a friend or two to come and see her.'

'She's thinking out something,' said Cherry. 'Sort of plan. Thinking out how to tackle something, that's how I look at it.'

She broke off the conversation at this stage and took in the coffee tray and put it down by Miss Marple's side.

'Do you know a woman who lives in a new house some- where here, she's called Mrs Hastings?' asked Miss Marple. 'And someone called Miss Bartlett, I think it is, who lives with her——'

'What—do you mean the house that's been all done up and repainted at the end of the village? The people there haven't been there very long. I don't know what their names are. Why do you want to know? They're not very interesting. At least I shouldn't say they were.'

'Are they related?' asked Miss Marple.

'No. Just friends, I think.'

'I wonder why——' said Miss Marple, and broke off.

'You wondered why what?'

'Nothing,' said Miss Marple. 'Clear my little hand desk, will you, and give me my pen and the notepaper. I'm going to write a letter.'

'Who to?' said Cherry, with the natural curiosity of her kind.

'To a clergyman's sister,' said Miss Marple. 'His name is Canon Prescott.'

'That's the one you met abroad, in the West Indies, isn't it? You showed me his photo in your album.'

'Yes.'

'Not feeling bad, are you? Wanting to write to a clergyman and all that?'

'I'm feeling extremely well,' said Miss Marple, 'and I am anxious to get busy on something. It's just possible Miss Prescott might help.'

'Dear Miss Prescott,' wrote Miss Marple, 'I hope you have not forgotten me. I met you and your brother in the West Indies, if you remember, at St Honoré. I hope the dear Canon is well and did not suffer much with his asthma in the cold weather last winter.

I am writing to ask you if you can possibly let me have the address of Mrs Walters—Esther Walters— whom you may remember from the Caribbean days. She was secretary to Mr Rafiel. She did give me her address at the time, but unfortunately I have mislaid it. I was anxious to write to her as I have some horticultural information which she asked me about but which I was not able to tell her at the time. I heard in a roundabout way the other day that she had married again, but I don't think my informant was very certain of these facts. Perhaps you know more about her than I do.

I hope this is not troubling you too much. With kind regards to your brother and best wishes to yourself,

Yours sincerely,

Jane Marple.'

Miss Marple felt better when she had despatched this. 'At least,' she said, 'I've started *doing* something. Not that I hope much from this, but still it might help.'

Miss Prescott answered the letter almost by return of post. She was a most efficient woman. She wrote a pleasant letter and enclosed the address in question.

'I have not heard anything directly about Esther Walters,' she said, 'but like you I heard from a friend that they had seen a notice of her re-marriage. Her name now is, I believe, Mrs Alderson or Anderson. Her address is Winslow Lodge, near Alton, Hants. My brother sends his best wishes to you. It is sad that we live so far apart. We in the north of England and you south of London. I hope that we may meet on some occasion in the future.

Yours sincerely,

Joan Prescott.'

'Winslow Lodge, Alton,' said Miss Marple, writing it down. 'Not so far away from here, really. No. Not so far away. I could—I don't know what would be the best method—possibly one of Inch's taxis. Slightly extravagant, but if anything results from it, it could be charged as expenses quite legitimately. Now do I write to her beforehand or do I leave it to chance? I think it would be better really, to leave it to chance. Poor Esther. She could hardly remember me with any affection or kindliness.'

Miss Marple lost herself in a train of thought that arose from her thoughts. It was quite possible that her actions in the Caribbean had saved Esther Walters from being murdered in the not far distant future. At any rate, that was Miss Marple's belief, but probably Esther Walters had not believed any such thing. 'A nice woman,' said Miss Marple, uttering the words in a soft tone aloud, 'a very nice woman. The kind that would so easily marry a bad lot. In fact, the sort of woman that would marry a murderer if she were ever given half a chance. I still consider,' continued Miss Marple thoughtfully, sinking her voice still lower, 'that I probably saved her life. In fact, I am almost sure of it, but I don't think she would agree with that point of view. She probably dislikes me very much. Which makes it more difficult to use her as a source of information. Still, one can but try. It's better than sitting here, waiting, waiting, waiting.'

Was Mr Rafiel perhaps making fun of her when he had written that letter? He was not always a particularly kindly man—he could be very careless of people's feelings.

'Anyway,' said Miss Marple, glancing at the clock and deciding that she would have an early night in bed, 'when one thinks of things just before going to sleep, quite often ideas come. It may work out that way.'

'Sleep well?' asked Cherry, as she put down an early morning tea tray on the table at Miss Marple's elbow.

'I had a curious dream,' said Miss Marple.

'Nightmare?'

'No, no, nothing of that kind. I was talking to someone, not anyone I knew very well. Just talking. Then when I looked, I saw it wasn't that person at all I was talking to. It was somebody else. Very odd.'

'Bit of a mix up,' said Cherry, helpfully.

38

'It just reminded me of something,' said Miss Marple, 'or rather of someone I once knew. Order Inch for me, will you? To come here about half past eleven.'

Inch was part of Miss Marple's past. Originally the proprietor of a cab, Mr Inch had died, been succeeded by his son 'Young Inch', then aged forty-four, who had turned the family business into a garage and acquired two aged cars. On his decease the garage acquired a new owner. There had been since then Pip's Cars, James's Taxis and Arthur's Car Hire—old inhabitants still spoke of Inch.

'Not going to London, are you?'

'No, I'm not going to London. I shall have lunch perhaps in Haslemere.'

'Now what are you up to now?' said Cherry, looking at her suspiciously.

'Endeavouring to meet someone by accident and make it seem purely natural,' said Miss Marple. 'Not really very easy, but I hope that I can manage it.'

At half past eleven the taxi waited. Miss Marple instructed Cherry.

'Ring up this number, will you, Cherry? Ask if Mrs Anderson is at home. If Mrs Anderson answers or if she is going to come to the telephone, say a Mr Broadribb wants to speak to her. You,' said Miss Marple, 'are Mr Broadribb's secretary. If she's out, find out what time she will be in.'

'And if she is in and I get her?'

'Ask what day she could arrange to meet Mr Broadribb at his office in London next week. When she tells you, make a note of it and ring off.'

'The things you think of! Why all this? Why do you want *me* to do it?'

'Memory is a curious thing,' said Miss Marple. 'Sometimes one remembers a voice even if one hasn't heard it for over a year.'

39

'Well, Mrs What's-a-name won't have heard mine at any time, will she?'

'No,' said Miss Marple. 'That is why *you* are making the call.'

Cherry fulfilled her instruction. Mrs Anderson was out shopping, she learned, but would be in for lunch and all the afternoon.

'Well, that makes things easier,' said Miss Marple. 'Is Inch here? Ah yes. Good morning, Edward,' she said, to the present driver of Arthur's taxis whose actual name was George. 'Now this is where I want you to go. It ought not to take, I think, more than an hour and a half.'

The expedition set off.

4. Esther Walters

ESTHER ANDERSON came out of the Supermarket and went towards where she had parked her car. Parking grew more difficult every day, she thought. She collided with somebody, an elderly woman limping a little who was walking towards her. She apologized, and the other woman made an exclamation.

'Why, indeed, it's—surely—it's Mrs Walters, isn't it? Esther Walters? You don't remember me, I expect. Jane Marple. We met in the hotel in St Honoré, oh—quite a long time ago. A year and a half.'

'Miss Marple? So it is, of course. Fancy seeing you!'

'How very nice to see you. I am lunching with some friends near here but I have to pass back through Alton later. Will you be at home this afternoon? I should so like to have a nice chat with you. It's so nice to see an old friend.'

'Yes, of course. Any time after three o'clock.'

The arrangement was ratified.

'Old Jane Marple,' said Esther Anderson, smiling to herself. 'Fancy her turning up. I thought she'd died a long time ago.'

Miss Marple rang the bell of Winslow Lodge at 3.30 precisely. Esther opened the door to her and brought her in.

Miss Marple sat down in the chair indicated to her, fluttering a little in the restless manner that she adopted when slightly flustered. Or at any rate, when she was seeming to be slightly flustered. In this case it was misleading, since things had happened exactly as she had hoped they would happen.

'It's so nice to see you,' she said to Esther. 'So very nice to see you again. You know, I do think things are so very odd in this world. You hope you'll meet people again and you're quite sure you will. And then time passes and suddenly it's all such a surprise.'

'And then,' said Esther, 'one says it's a small world, doesn't one?'

'Yes, indeed, and I think there *is* something in that. I mean, it does *seem* a very large world and the West Indies are such a very long way away from England. Well, I mean, of course I might have met you anywhere. In London or at Harrods. On a railway station or in a bus. There are so many possibilities.'

'Yes, there are a lot of possibilities,' said Esther. 'I certainly shouldn't have expected to meet you just here because this isn't really quite your part of the world, is it?'

'No. No, it isn't. Not that you're really so very far from St Mary Mead where I live. Actually, I think it's only about twenty-five miles. But twenty-five miles in the country, when one hasn't got a car—and of course I couldn't afford a car, and anyway, I mean, I can't drive a car—so it wouldn't be much to the point, so one really only does see one's neighbours on the bus route, or else go by a taxi from the village.'

'You're looking wonderfully well,' said Esther.

'I was just going to say *you* were looking wonderfully well, my dear. I had no idea you lived in this part of the world.'

'I have only done so for a short time. Since my marriage, actually.'

'Oh, I didn't know. How interesting. I suppose I must have missed it. I always do look down the marriages.'

'I've been married four or five months,' said Esther. 'My name is Anderson now.'

'Mrs Anderson,' said Miss Marple. 'Yes. I must try and remember that. And your husband?'

It would be unnatural, she thought, if she did not ask about the husband. Old maids were notoriously inquisitive.

'He is an engineer,' said Esther. 'He runs the Time and Motion Branch. He is,' she hesitated—'a little younger than I am.'

'Much better,' said Miss Marple immediately. 'Oh, much better, my dear. In these days men age so much quicker than women. I know it used not to be said so, but actually it's true. I mean, they get more things the matter with them. I think, perhaps, they worry and work too much. And then they get high blood pressure or low blood pressure or sometimes a little heart trouble. They're rather prone to gastric ulcers, too. I don't think *we* worry so much, you know. I think we're a tougher sex.'

'Perhaps we are,' said Esther.

She smiled now at Miss Marple, and Miss Marple felt reassured. The last time she had seen Esther, Esther had looked as though she hated her and probably she had hated her at that moment. But now, well now, perhaps, she might even feel slightly grateful. She might have realized that she, herself, might even have been under a stone slab in a respectable churchyard, instead of living a presumably happy life with Mr Anderson.

'You look very well,' she said, 'and very gay.'

'So do you, Miss Marple.'

'Well, of course, I am rather older now. And one has so many ailments. I mean, not desperate ones, nothing of that kind, but I mean one has always some kind of rheumatism or some kind of ache and pain somewhere. One's feet are not what one would like feet to be. And there's usually one's back or a shoulder or painful hands. Oh, dear, one shouldn't talk about these things. What a very nice house you have.'

'Yes, we haven't been in it very long. We moved in about four months ago.'

Miss Marple looked round. She had rather thought that that was the case. She thought, too, that when they had moved in they had moved in on quite a handsome scale. The furniture was expensive, it was comfortable, comfortable and just this side of luxury. Good curtains, good covers, no particular artistic taste displayed, but then she would not have expected that. She thought she knew the reason for this appearance of prosperity. She thought it had come about on the strength of the late Mr Rafiel's handsome legacy to Esther. She was glad to think that Mr Rafiel had not changed his mind.

'I expect you saw the notice of Mr Rafiel's death,' said Esther, speaking almost as if she knew what was in Miss Marple's mind.

'Yes. Yes, indeed I did. It was about a month ago now, wasn't it? I was so sorry. Very distressed really, although, well, I suppose one knew—he almost admitted it himself, didn't he? He hinted several times that it wouldn't be very long. I think he was quite a brave man about it all, don't you?'

'Yes, he was a very brave man, and a very kind one really,' said Esther. 'He told me, you know, when I first worked for him, that he was going to give me a very good salary but that I would have to save out of it because I needn't expect to have anything more from him. Well, I certainly didn't expect to have *anything* more from him. He was very much a man of his word, wasn't he? But apparently he changed his mind.'

'Yes,' said Miss Marple. 'Yes. I am very glad of that. I thought perhaps—not that he, of course, said anything—but I wondered.'

'He left me a very big legacy,' said Esther. 'A surprisingly large sum of money. It came as a very great surprise. I could hardly believe it at first.'

'I think he wanted it to be a surprise to you. I think he was perhaps that kind of man,' said Miss Marple. She added: 'Did he leave anything to—oh, what was his name?—the man attendant, the nurse-attendant?'

'Oh, you mean Jackson? No, he didn't leave anything to Jackson, but I believe he made him some handsome presents in the last year.'

'Have you ever seen anything more of Jackson?'

'No. No, I don't think I've met him once since the time out in the islands. He didn't stay with Mr Rafiel after they got back to England. I think he went to Lord somebody who lives in Jersey or Guernsey.'

'I would like to have seen Mr Rafiel again,' said Miss Marple. 'It seems odd after we'd all been mixed up so. He and you and I and some others. And then, later, when I'd come home, when six months had passed—it occurred to me one day how closely associated we had been in our time of stress, and yet how little I really knew about Mr Rafiel. I was thinking it only the other day, after I'd seen the notice of his death. I wished I could know a little more. Where he was born, you know, and his parents. What they were like. Whether he had any children, or nephews or cousins or any family. I would so like to know.'

Esther Anderson smiled slightly. She looked at Miss Marple and her expression seemed to say 'Yes, I'm sure you always want to know everything of that kind about everyone you meet.' But she merely said:

'No, there was really only one thing that everyone *did* know about him.'

'That he was very rich,' said Miss Marple immediately. 'That's what you mean, isn't it? When you know that someone is very rich, somehow, well, you don't ask any more. I mean you don't ask to *know* any more. You say "He is very rich" or you say "He is enormously rich," and your voice just goes down a little because it's so impressive, isn't it, when you meet someone who *is* immensely rich.'

Esther laughed slightly.

'He wasn't married, was he?' asked Miss Marple. 'He never mentioned a wife.'

'He lost his wife many years ago. Quite soon after they were married, I believe. I believe she was much younger than he was—I think she died of cancer. Very sad.'

'Had he children?'

'Oh yes, two daughters and a son. One daughter is married and lives in America. The other daughter died young, I believe. I met the American one once. She wasn't at all like her father. Rather a quiet, depressed looking young woman.' She added, 'Mr Rafiel never spoke about the son. I rather think that there had been trouble there. A scandal or something of that kind. I believe he died some years ago. Anyway—his father never mentioned him.'

'Oh dear. That was very sad.'

'I think it happened quite a long time ago. I believe he took off for somewhere or other abroad and never came back—died out there, wherever it was.'

'Was Mr Rafiel very upset about it?'

'One wouldn't know with him,' said Esther. 'He was the kind of man who would always decide to cut his losses. If his son turned out to be unsatisfactory, a burden instead of a blessing, I think he would just shrug the whole thing off. Do what was necessary perhaps in the way of sending him money for support, but never thinking of him again.'

'One wonders,' said Miss Marple. 'He never spoke of him or said anything?'

'If you remember, he was a man who never said anything much about personal feelings or his own life.'

'No. No, of course not. But I thought perhaps, you having been—well, his secretary for so many years, that he might have confided any troubles to you.'

'He was not a man for confiding troubles,' said Esther. 'If he had any, which I rather doubt. He was wedded to his business, one might say. He was father to his business and his business was the only kind of son or daughter that he had that mattered, I think. He enjoyed it all, investment, making money. Business coups——'

'Call no man happy until he is dead—' murmured Miss Marple, repeating the words in the manner of one pronouncing them as a kind of slogan, which indeed they appeared to be in these days, or so she would have said.

'So there was nothing especially worrying him, was there, before his death?'

'No. Why should you think so?' Esther sounded surprised.

'Well, I didn't actually think so,' said Miss Marple, 'I just wondered because things do worry people more when they are—I won't say getting old—because he really wasn't old, but I mean things worry you more when you are laid up and can't do as much as you did and have to take things easy. Then worries just come into your mind and make themselves *felt*.'

'Yes, I know what you mean,' said Esther. 'But I don't think Mr Rafiel was like that. Anyway,' she added, 'I ceased being his secretary some time ago. Two or three months after I met Edmund.'

'Ah yes. Your husband. Mr Rafiel must have been very upset at losing you.'

'Oh I don't think so,' said Esther lightly. 'He was not one who would be upset over that sort of thing. He'd immediately get another secretary—which he did. And then if she didn't suit him he'd just get rid of her with a kindly golden handshake and get somebody else, till he found somebody who suited him. He was an intensely sensible man always.'

'Yes. Yes, I can see that. Though he could lose his temper very easily.'

'Oh, he enjoyed losing his temper,' said Esther. 'It made a bit of drama for him, I think.'

'Drama,' said Miss Marple thoughtfully. 'Do you think —I have often wondered—do you think that Mr Rafiel had any particular interest in criminology, the study of it, I mean? He—well, I don't know. . . .'

'You mean because of what happened in the Caribbean?' Esther's voice had gone suddenly hard.

Miss Marple felt doubtful of going on, and yet she must somehow or other try and get a little helpful knowledge.

'Well, no, not because of that, but afterwards, perhaps, he wondered about the psychology of these things. Or he got interested in the cases where justice had not been administered properly or—oh well . . .'

She sounded more scatty every minute.

'Why should he take the least interest in anything of that kind? And don't let's talk about that horrible business in St Honoré.'

'Oh no, I think you are *quite* right. I'm sure I'm very sorry. I was just thinking of some of the things that Mr Rafiel sometimes *said*. Queer turns of phrase, sometimes, and I just wondered if he had any theories, you know, . . . about the causes of crime?'

'His interests were always entirely financial,' said Esther shortly. 'A really clever swindle of a criminal kind might have interested him, nothing else——'

She was looking coldly still at Miss Marple.

'I am sorry,' said Miss Marple apologetically. 'I—I shouldn't have talked about distressing matters that are fortunately past. And I must be getting on my way,' she added. 'I have got my train to catch and I shall only just have time. Oh dear, what did I do with my bag—oh yes, here it is.'

She collected her bag, umbrella and a few other things, fussing away until the tension had slightly abated. As she went out of the door, she turned to Esther who was urging her to stay and have a cup of tea.

'No thank you, my dear, I'm so short of time. I'm very pleased to have seen you again and I do offer my best congratulations and hopes for a very happy life. I don't suppose you will be taking up any post again now, will you?'

'Oh, some people do. They find it interesting, they say. They get bored when they have nothing to do. But I think I shall rather enjoy living a life of leisure. I shall enjoy my legacy, too, that Mr Rafiel left me. It was very kind of him and I think he'd want me—well, to enjoy it even if I spent it in what he'd think of perhaps as a rather silly, female way! Expensive clothes and a new hair-do and all that. He'd have thought that sort of thing very silly.' She added suddenly, 'I was fond of him, you know. Yes, I was quite fond of him. I think it was because he was a sort of challenge to me. He was difficult to get on with, and therefore I enjoyed managing it.'

'And managing him?'

'Well, not quite managing him, but perhaps a little more than he knew I was.'

Miss Marple trotted away down the road. She looked back once and waved her hand—Esther Anderson was still standing on the doorstep, and she waved back cheerfully.

'I thought this might have been something to do with her or something she knew about,' said Miss Marple to herself. 'I think I'm wrong. No. I don't think she's concerned in this business, whatever it is, *in any way*. Oh dear, I feel Mr Rafiel expected me to be much *cleverer* than I am being. I think he expected me to put things together— but what things? And what do I do next, I wonder?' She shook her head.

She had to think over things very carefully. This business had been, as it were, left to her. Left to her to refuse, to accept, to understand what it was all about? Or *not* to understand anything, but to go forward and hope that some kind of guidance might be given to her. Occasionally she closed her eyes and tried to picture Mr Rafiel's face. Sitting in the garden of the hotel in the West Indies, in his

49

tropical suit; his bad-tempered corrugated face, his flashes of occasional humour. What she really wanted to know was what had been in his mind when he worked up this scheme, when he set out to bring it about. To lure her into accepting it, to persuade her to accept it, to—well, perhaps one should say—to bully her into accepting it. The third was much the most likely, knowing Mr Rafiel. And yet, take it that he had wanted something done and he had chosen her, settled upon her to do it. Why? Because she had suddenly come into his mind? But why should she have come into his mind?

She thought back to Mr Rafiel and the things that had occurred at St Honoré. Had perhaps the problem he had been considering at the time of his death sent his mind back to that visit to the West Indies? Was it in some way connected with someone who had been out there, who had taken part or been an onlooker there and was that what had put Miss Marple into his mind? Was there some link or some connection? If not, why should he suddenly think of her? What was it about her that could make her useful to him, in any way at all. She was an elderly, rather scatty, quite ordinary person, physically not very strong, mentally not nearly as alert as she used to be. What had been her special qualifications, if any? She couldn't think of any. Could it possibly have been a bit of *fun* on Mr Rafiel's part? He might have wanted to have some kind of joke.

She could not deny that Mr Rafiel could quite possibly wish to have a joke, even on his death-bed. Some ironical humour of his might be satisfied.

'I must,' said Miss Marple to herself firmly, 'I *must* have some qualification for something.' After all, since Mr Rafiel was no longer in this world, he could not enjoy his joke at first hand. What qualifications *had* she got? 'What qualities have I got that could be useful to anyone for *anything*?' said Miss Marple.

She considered herself with proper humility. She was inquisitive, she asked questions, she was the sort of age and type that could be expected to ask questions. That was one point, a possible point. You could send a private detective round to ask questions, or some psychological investigator, but it was true that you could much more easily send an elderly lady with a habit of snooping and being inquisitive, of talking too much, of wanting to find out about things, and it would seem perfectly natural.

'An old pussy,' said Miss Marple to herself. 'Yes, I can see I'm quite recognizable as an old pussy. There are so many old pussies, and they're all so much alike. And, of course, yes, I'm very ordinary. An ordinary rather scatty old lady. And that of course is very good *camouflage*. Dear me, I wonder if I'm thinking on the right lines. I do, sometimes, know what people are *like*. I mean, I know what people are like, because they remind me of certain other people I have known. So I know some of their faults and some of their virtues. I know what kind of people *they* are. There's that.'

She thought again of St Honoré and the Hotel of the Golden Palm. She had made one attempt to inquire into the possibilities of a link, by her visit to Esther Walters. That had been definitely non-productive, Miss Marple decided. There didn't seem any further link leading from there. Nothing that would tie up with his request that Miss Marple should busy herself with something, the nature of which she still had no idea!

'Dear me,' said Miss Marple, 'what a tiresome man you are, Mr Rafiel!' She said it aloud and there was definite reproach in her voice.

Later, however, as she climbed into bed and applied her cosy hot water bottle to the most painful portion of her rheumatic back, she spoke again—in what might be taken as a semi-apology.

'I've done the best I could,' she said.

She spoke aloud with the air of addressing one who might easily be in the room. It is true he might be anywhere, but even then there might be some telepathic or telephonic communication, and if so, she was going to speak definitely and to the point.

'I've done all I could. The best according to my limitations, and I must now leave it up to *you*.'

With that she settled herself more comfortably, stretched out a hand, switched off the electric light, and went to sleep.

5. Instructions From Beyond

IT WAS SOME three or four days later that a communication arrived by the second post. Miss Marple picked up the letter, did what she usually did to letters, turned it over, looked at the stamp, looked at the handwriting, decided that it wasn't a bill and opened it. It was typewritten:

'Dear Miss Marple,

By the time you read this I shall be dead and also buried. *Not* cremated, I am glad to think. It has always seemed to me unlikely that one would manage to rise up from one's handsome bronze vase full of ashes and haunt anyone if one wanted so to do! Whereas the idea of rising from one's grave and haunting anyone is quite possible.

Shall I want to do that? Who knows. I might even want to communicate with *you*.

By now my solicitors will have communicated with you and will have put a certain proposition before you. I hope you will have accepted it. If you have not accepted it, don't feel in the least remorseful. It will be your choice.

This should reach you, if my solicitors have done what they were told to do and, if the posts have done the duty they are expected to perform, on the 11th of the month. In two days from now you will receive a communication from a travel bureau in London. I hope what it proposes will not be distasteful to you. I needn't say more. I want you to have an open mind. Take care of yourself. I think you will manage to do that. You are a very shrewd person. The best of luck and may your guardian angel be at your side looking after you. You may need one.

Your affectionate friend,

J. B. Rafiel.'

'Two days!' said Miss Marple.

She found it difficult to pass the time. The Post Office did their duty and so did the Famous Houses and Gardens of Great Britain:

'Dear Miss Jane Marple,

Obeying instructions given us by the late Mr Rafiel we send you particulars of our Tour No 37 of the Famous Houses and Gardens of Great Britain which starts from London on Thursday next—the 17th.

If it should be possible for you to come to our office in London, our Mrs Sandbourne who is to accompany the tour, will be very glad to give you all particulars and to answer all questions.

Our tours last for a period of two to three weeks. This particular tour, Mr Rafiel thinks, will be particularly acceptable to you as it will visit a part of England which as far as he knows you have not yet visited, and takes in some really very attractive scenery and gardens. He has arranged for you to have the best accommodation and all the luxury available that we can provide.

Perhaps you will let us know which day would suit you to visit our office in Berkeley Street?'

Miss Marple folded up the letter, put it in her bag, noted the telephone number, thought of a few friends whom she knew, rang up two of them, one of whom had been for tours with the Famous Houses and Gardens, and spoke highly of them, the other one had not been personally on a tour but had friends who had travelled with this particular firm and who said everything was very well done, though rather expensive, and not too exhausting for the elderly. She then rang up the Berkeley Street number and said she would call upon them on the following Tuesday.

The next day she spoke to Cherry on the subject.

'I may be going away, Cherry,' she said. 'On a Tour.'

'A Tour?' said Cherry. 'One of these travel tours? You mean a package tour abroad?'

'Not abroad. In this country,' said Miss Marple. 'Mainly visiting historic buildings and gardens.'

'Do you think it's all right to do that at your age? These things can be very tiring, you know. You have to walk miles sometimes.'

'My health is really very good,' said Miss Marple, 'and I have always heard that in these tours they are careful to provide restful intervals for such people who are not particularly strong.'

'Well, be careful of yourself, that's all,' said Cherry. 'We don't want you falling down with a heart attack, even if you are looking at a particularly sumptuous fountain or something. You're a bit old, you know, to do this sort of thing. Excuse me saying it, it sounds rude, but I don't like to think of you passing out because you've done too much or anything like that.'

'I can take care of myself,' said Miss Marple, with some dignity.

'All right, but you just be careful,' said Cherry.

Miss Marple packed a suitable bag, went to London, booked a room at a modest hotel—('Ah, Bertram's Hotel,' she thought in her mind, 'what a wonderful hotel *that* was! Oh dear, I must forget all those things, the St George is quite a pleasant place.') At the appointed time she was in Berkeley Street and was shown in to the office where a pleasant woman of about thirty-five rose to meet her, explained that her name was Mrs Sandbourne and that she would be in personal charge of this particular tour.

'Am I to understand,' said Miss Marple, 'that this trip is in my case——' she hesitated.

Mrs Sandbourne, sensing slight embarrassment, said:

'Oh yes, I ought to have explained perhaps better in the letter we sent you. Mr Rafiel has paid all expenses.'

'You *do* know that he is dead?' said Miss Marple.

'Oh yes, but this was arranged before his death. He mentioned that he was in ill health but wanted to provide a treat for a very old friend of his who had not had the opportunity of travelling as much as she could have wished.'

2

Two days later, Miss Marple, carrying her small overnight bag, her new and smart suitcase surrendered to the driver, had boarded a most comfortable and luxurious coach which was taking a north-westerly route out of London; she was studying the passenger list which was attached to the inside of a handsome brochure giving details of the daily itinerary of the coach, and various information as to hotels and meals, places to be seen, and occasional alternatives on some days which, although the fact was not stressed, actually intimated that one choice of itinerary was for the young and active and that the other choice would be peculiarly suitable for the elderly, those whose feet hurt them, who suffered from arthritis or rheumatism and who would prefer to sit about and *not* walk long distances or up too many hills. It was all very tactful and well arranged.

Miss Marple read the passenger list and surveyed her fellow passengers. There was no difficulty about doing this because the other fellow passengers were doing much the same themselves. They were surveying her, amongst others, but nobody as far as Miss Marple could notice was taking any particular interest in her.

Mrs Riseley-Porter
Miss Joanna Crawford

Colonel and Mrs Walker
Mr and Mrs H. T. Butler
Miss Elizabeth Temple
Professor Wanstead
Mr Richard Jameson
Miss Lumley
Miss Bentham
Mr Caspar
Miss Cooke
Miss Barrow
Mr Emlyn Price
Miss Jane Marple

There were four elderly ladies. Miss Marple took note of them first so, as it were, to clear them out of the way. Two were travelling together. Miss Marple put them down as about seventy. They could roughly be considered as contemporaries of her own. One of them was very definitely the complaining type, one who would want to have seats at the front of the coach or else would make a point of having them at the back of the coach. Would wish to sit on the sunny side or could only bear to sit on the shady side. Who would want more fresh air, or less fresh air. They had with them travelling rugs and knitted scarves and quite an assortment of guide books. They were slightly crippled and often in pain from feet or backs or knees but were nevertheless of those whom age and ailments could not prevent from enjoying life while they still had it. Old pussies, but definitely *not* stay-at-home old pussies. Miss Marple made an entry in the little book she carried.

Fifteen passengers not including herself, or Mrs Sandbourne. And since she had been sent on this coach tour, one at least of those fifteen passengers must be of importance in some way. Either as a source of information or someone concerned with the law or a law case, or it might even be a murderer. A murderer who might have already

57

killed or one who might be preparing to kill. Anything was possible, Miss Marple thought, with Mr Rafiel! Anyway, she must make notes of these people.

On the right-hand page of her notebook, she would note down who might be worthy of attention from Mr Rafiel's point of view and on the left she would note down or cross off those who could only be of any interest if they could produce some useful information for her. Information, it might be, that they did not even know they possessed. Or rather that even if they possessed it, they did not know it could possibly be useful to her or to Mr Rafiel or to the law or to Justice with a capital 'J'. At the back of her little book, she might this evening make a note or two as to whether anyone had reminded her of characters she had known in the past at St Mary Mead and other places. Any similarities might make a useful pointer. It had done so on other occasions.

The other two elderly ladies were apparently separate travellers. Both of them were about sixty. One was a well preserved, well dressed woman of obvious social importance in her own mind, but probably in other people's minds as well. Her voice was loud and dictatorial. She appeared to have in tow a niece, a girl of about eighteen or nineteen who addressed her as Aunt Geraldine. The niece, Miss Marple noted, was obviously well accustomed to coping with Aunt Geraldine's bossiness. She was a competent girl as well as being an attractive one.

Across the aisle from Miss Marple was a big man with square shoulders and a clumsy-looking body, looking as though he had been carelessly assembled by an ambitious child out of chunky bricks. His face looked as though nature had planned it to be round but the face had rebelled at this and decided to achieve a square effect by developing a powerful jaw. He had a thick head of greyish hair and enormous bushy eyebrows which moved up and down to give point to what he was saying. His remarks seemed mainly to come out in a series of barks as though he was a talkative sheepdog. He shared his seat with a tall dark foreigner who moved restlessly in his seat and gesticulated freely. He spoke a most peculiar English, making occasional remarks in French and German. The bulky man seemed quite capable of meeting these onslaughts of foreign language, and shifted obligingly to either French or German. Taking a quick glance at them again, Miss Marple decided that the bushy eyebrows must be Professor Wanstead and the excitable foreigner was Mr Caspar.

She wondered what it was they were discussing with such animation, but was baffled by the rapidity and force of Mr Caspar's delivery.

The seat in front of them was occupied by the other woman of about sixty, a tall woman, possibly over sixty, but a woman who would have stood out in a crowd anywhere. She was still a very handsome woman with dark grey hair coiled high on her head, drawn back from a fine forehead. She had a low, clear, incisive voice. A personality, Miss Marple thought. Someone! Yes, she was decidedly someone. 'Reminds me,' she thought to herself, 'of Dame Emily Waldron.' Dame Emily Waldron had been the Principal of an Oxford College and a notable scientist, and Miss Marple, having once met her in her nephew's company, had never quite forgotten her.

Miss Marple resumed her survey of the passengers. There were two married couples, one American, middle-aged, amiable, a talkative wife and a placidly agreeing husband. They were obviously dedicated travellers and sightseers. There was also an English middle-aged couple whom Miss Marple noted down without hesitation as a retired military man and wife. She ticked them off from the list as Colonel and Mrs Walker.

In the seat behind her was a tall, thin man of about thirty with a highly technical vocabulary, clearly an architect. There were also two middle-aged ladies travelling together rather further up the coach. They were discussing the brochure and deciding what the tour was going to hold for them in the way of attractions. One was dark and thin and the other was fair and sturdily built and the latter's face seemed faintly familiar to Miss Marple. She wondered where she had seen or met her before. However, she could not recall the occasion to mind. Possibly someone she had met at a cocktail party or sat opposite to in a train. There was nothing very special about her to remember.

Only one more passenger remained for her to appraise, and this was a young man, possibly of about nineteen or twenty. He wore the appropriate clothes for his age and sex; tight black jeans, a polo-necked purple sweater, and his head was an outsize rich mop of non-disciplined black hair. He was looking with an air of interest at the bossy woman's niece, and the bossy woman's niece also, Miss Marple thought, was looking with some interest at him. In spite of the preponderance of elderly pussies and middle-aged females there were, at any rate, two *young* people among the passengers.

They stopped for lunch at a pleasant riverside hotel, and the afternoon sightseeing was given over to Blenheim. Miss Marple had already visited Blenheim twice before, so she saved her feet by limiting the amount of sightseeing indoors and coming fairly soon to the enjoyment of the gardens and the beautiful view.

By the time they arrived at the hotel where they were to stay the night, the passengers were getting to know each other. The efficient Mrs Sandbourne, still brisk and un-wearied by her duties in directing the sightseeing, did her part very well: creating little groups by adding anyone who looked as if they were left out to one or other of them, murmuring, 'You *must* make Colonel Walker describe his garden to you. Such a wonderful collection of fuchsias he has.' With such little sentences she drew people together.

Miss Marple was now able to attach names to all the passengers. Bushy eyebrows turned out to be Professor Wanstead, as she had thought, and the foreigner was Mr Caspar. The bossy woman was Mrs Riseley-Porter and her niece was called Joanna Crawford. The young man with the hair was Emlyn Price and he and Joanna Crawford appeard to be finding out that certain things in life —such as decided opinions on economics, art, general dislikes, politics and such topics—they had in common.

The two eldest pussies graduated naturally to Miss Marple as a kindred elderly pussy. They discussed happily arthritis, rheumatism, diets, new doctors, remedies both professional, patent, and reminiscences of old wives' treatments which had had success where all else failed. They discussed the many tours they had been on to foreign places in Europe; hotels, travel agencies and finally the County of Somerset where Miss Lumley and Miss Bentham lived, and where the difficulties of getting suitable gardeners could hardly be believed.

The two middle-aged ladies travelling together turned out to be Miss Cooke and Miss Barrow. Miss Marple still felt that one of these two, the fair one, Miss Cooke, was faintly familiar to her, but she still could not remember where she had seen her before. Probably it was only her fancy. It might also be just fancy but she could not help feeling that Miss Barrow and Miss Cooke appeared to be avoiding her. They seemed rather anxious to move away if she approached. That, of course, *might* be entirely her imagination.

Fifteen people, one of whom at least must matter in some way. In casual conversation that evening she introduced the name of Mr Rafiel, so as to note if anyone reacted in any way. Nobody did.

The handsome woman was identified as Miss Elizabeth Temple, who was the retired Headmistress of a famous girls' school. Nobody appeared to Miss Marple likely to be a murderer, except possibly Mr Caspar, and that was probably foreign prejudice. The thin young man was Richard Jameson, an architect.

'Perhaps I shall do better tomorrow,' said Miss Marple to herself.

3

Miss Marple went to bed definitely tired out. Sightseeing was pleasant but exhausting, and trying to study fifteen or sixteen people at once and wondering as you did so which of them could possibly be connected with a murder, was even more exhausting. It had a touch of such unreality about it that one could not, Miss Marple felt, take it seriously. These seemed to be all perfectly nice people, the sort of people who go on cruises and on tours and all the rest of it. However, she took another quick and cursory glance at the passenger list, making a few little entries in her notebook.

Mrs Riseley-Porter? *Not* connected with crime. Too social and self-centred.

Niece, Joanna Crawford? The same? But very efficient.

Mrs Riseley-Porter, however, might have information of some kind which Miss Marple might find had a bearing on matters. She must keep on agreeable terms with Mrs Riseley-Porter.

Miss Elizabeth Temple? A personality. Interesting. She did not remind Miss Marple of any murderer she'd ever known. 'In fact,' said Miss Marple to herself, 'she really radiates integrity. *If* she had committed a murder, it would be a very popular murder. Perhaps for some noble reason or for some reason that she thought noble?' But that wasn't satisfactory either. Miss Temple, she thought, would always know what she was doing and why she was doing it and would not have any silly ideas about nobility when merely evil existed. 'All the same,' said Miss Marple, 'she's *someone* and she might—she just *might* be a person Mr Rafiel wanted me to meet for some reason.' She jotted down these thoughts on the right-hand side of her notebook.

She shifted her point of view. She had been considering a possible murderer—what about a prospective victim? Who was a possible victim? No one very likely. Perhaps Mrs Riseley-Porter might qualify—rich—rather disagreeable. The efficient niece might inherit. She and the anarchistic Emlyn Price might combine in the cause of anti-capitalism. Not a very credible idea, but no other feasible murderee seemed to offer.

Professor Wanstead? An interesting man, she was sure. Kindly, too. Was he a scientist or was he medical? She was not as yet sure, but she put him down on the side of science. She herself knew nothing of science, but it seemed not at all unlikely.

Mr and Mrs Butler? She wrote them off. Nice Americans. No connections with anyone in the West Indies or anyone she had known. No, she didn't think the Butlers could be relevant.

Richard Jameson? That was the thin architect. Miss Marple didn't see how architecture could come into it, though it might, she supposed. A priest's hole, perhaps? One of the houses they were going to visit might have a priest's hole which would contain a skeleton. And Mr Jameson, being an architect, would know just where the priest's hole was. He might aid her to discover it, or she might aid him to discover it and then they would find a body. 'Oh really,' said Miss Marple, 'what nonsense I am talking and thinking.'

Miss Cooke and Miss Barrow? A perfectly ordinary pair. And yet she'd certainly seen one of them before. At least she'd seen Miss Cooke before. Oh well, it would come to her, she supposed.

Colonel and Mrs Walker? Nice people. Retired Army

63

folk. Served abroad mostly. Nice to talk to, but she didn't think there'd be anything for her there.

Miss Bentham and Miss Lumley? The elderly pussies. Unlikely to be criminals, but, being elderly pussies, they might know plenty of gossip, or have some information, or might make some illuminating remark even if it happened to come about in connection with rheumatism, arthritis or patent medicine.

Mr Caspar? Possibly a dangerous character. Very excitable. She would keep him on the list for the present.

Emlyn Price? A student presumably. Students were very violent. Would Mr Rafiel have sent her on the track of a student? Well, it would depend perhaps on what the student had done or wished to do or was going to do. A dedicated anarchist, perhaps.

'Oh dear,' said Miss Marple, suddenly exhausted, 'I *must* go to bed.' Her feet ached, her back ached and her mental reactions were not, she thought, at their best. She slept at once. Her sleep was enlivened by several dreams.

One where Professor Wanstead's bushy eyebrows fell off because they were not his own eyebrows, but false ones. As she woke again, her first impression was that which so often follows dreams, a belief that the dream in question had solved everything. 'Of course,' she thought, 'of *course*!' His eyebrows were false and that solved the whole thing. *He* was the criminal.

Sadly, it came to her that nothing was solved. Professor Wanstead's eyebrows coming off was of no help at all.

Unfortunately now, she was no longer sleepy. She sat up in bed with some determination.

She sighed and slipped on her dressing-gown, moved from her bed to an upright chair, took a slightly larger notebook from her suitcase and started work.

'The project I have undertaken,' she wrote, 'is connected certainly with crime of some kind. Mr Rafiel has distinctly stated that in his letter. He said I had a *flair* for justice and that necessarily included a flair for crime. So crime is involved, and it is presumably not espionage or fraud or robbery, because such things have never come my way and I have no connection with such things, or knowledge of them, or special skills. What Mr Rafiel knows of me is only what he knew during the period of time when we were both in St Honoré. We were connected there with a murder. Murders as reported in the press have never claimed my attention. I have never read books on criminology as a subject or really been interested in such a thing. No, it has just happened that I have found myself in the vicinity of murder rather more often than would seem normal. My attention has been directed to murders involving friends or acquaintances. These curious coincidences of connections with special subjects seem to happen to people in life. One of my aunts, I remember, was on five occasions shipwrecked and a friend of mine was what I believe is officially called accident-prone. I know some of her friends refused to ride in a taxi with her. She had been in four taxi accidents and three car accidents and two railway accidents. Things like this seem to happen to certain people for no appreciable reason. I do not like to write it down but it does appear that murders seem to happen, not to me myself, thank goodness, but seem to happen in my vicinity.'

Miss Marple paused, changed her position, put a cushion in her back, and continued:

'I must try to make as logical a survey as I can of this project which I have undertaken. My instructions, or my "briefing" as naval friends of mine put it, are so far quite inadequate. Practically non-existent. So I must ask myself one clear question. What is all this *about*? Answer! *I do not know*. Curious and interesting. An odd way for a man like Mr Rafiel to go about things, especially when he was a successful business and financial operator. He wants me to guess, to employ my instinct, to observe and to obey such directions as are given to me or are hinted to me.

'So: Point 1. Direction will be given me. Direction from a dead man. Point 2. What is involved in my problem is *justice*. Either to set right an injustice or to avenge evil by bringing it to justice. This is in accord with the code word Nemesis given to me by Mr Rafiel.

'After explanations of the principle involved, I received my first factual directive. It was arranged by Mr Rafiel before his death that I was to go on Tour No 37 of Famous Houses and Gardens. Why? That is what I have to ask myself. Is it for some geographical or territorial reason? A connection or a clue? Some particular famous house? Or something involving some particular garden or landscape connected? This seems unlikely. The more likely explanation lies in the *people* or one of the people on this particular coach party. None of them is known to me personally, but one of them at least must be connected with the riddle I have to solve. Somebody among our group is connected or concerned with a murder. Somebody has information or a special link with the victim of a crime, or someone personally is himself or herself a murderer. A murderer as yet unsuspected.'

Miss Marple stopped here suddenly. She nodded her head. She was satisfied now with her analysis so far as it went. And so to bed.

Miss Marple added to her notebook.

'Here endeth the First Day.'

6. Love

THE FOLLOWING MORNING they visited a small Queen Anne Manor House. The drive there had not been very long or tiring. It was a very charming-looking house and had an interesting history as well as a very beautiful and unusually-laid-out garden.

Richard Jameson, the architect, was full of admiration for the structural beauty of the house, and being the kind of young man who is fond of hearing his own voice, he slowed down in nearly every room that they went through, pointing out every special moulding or fireplace, and giving historical dates and references. Some of the group, appreciative at first, began to get slightly restive, as the somewhat monotonous lecturing went on. Some of them began to edge carefully away and fall behind the party. The local caretaker, who was in charge, was not himself too pleased at having his occupation usurped by one of the sightseers. He made a few efforts to get matters back into his own hands but Mr Jameson was unyielding. The caretaker made a last try.

'In this room, ladies and gentlemen, the White Parlour, folks call it, is where they found a body. A young man it was, stabbed with a dagger, lying on the hearthrug. Way back in seventeen hundred and something it was. It was said that the Lady Moffatt of that day had a lover. He came through a small side door and up a steep staircase to this room through a loose panel there was to the left of the fireplace. Sir Richard Moffatt, her husband, you see, was said to be across the seas in the Low Countries. But he came home, and in he came unexpectedly and caught 'em there together.'

He paused proudly. He was pleased at the response

from his audience, glad of a respite from the architectural details which they had been having forced down their throats.

'Why, isn't that just too romantic, Henry?' said Mrs Butler in her resonant transatlantic tones. 'Why, you know, there's quite an *atmosphere* in this room. I feel it. I certainly can feel it.'

'Mamie is very sensitive to atmospheres,' said her husband proudly to those around him. 'Why, once when we were in an old house down in Louisiana . . .'

The narrative of Mamie's special sensitivity got into its swing and Miss Marple and one or two others seized their opportunity to edge gently out of the room and down the exquisitely moulded staircase to the ground floor.

'A friend of mine,' said Miss Marple to Miss Cooke and Miss Barrow who were next to her, 'had a most nerve-racking experience only a few years ago. A dead body on their library floor one morning.'

'One of the family?' asked Miss Barrow. 'An epileptic fit?'

'Oh no, it was a murder. A strange girl in evening dress. A blonde. But her hair was dyed. She was really a brunette; and—oh . . .' Miss Marple broke off, her eyes fixed on Miss Cooke's yellow hair where it escaped from her headscarf.

It had come to her suddenly. She knew why Miss Cooke's face was familiar and she knew where she had seen her before. But when she had seen her then, Miss Cooke's hair had been dark—almost black. And now it was bright yellow.

Mrs Riseley-Porter, coming down the stairs, spoke decisively as she pushed past them and completed the staircase and turned into the hall.

'I really cannot go up and down any more of those stairs,' she declared, 'and standing around in these rooms is very tiring. I believe the gardens here, although not

68

extensive, are quite celebrated in horticultural circles. I suggest we go there without loss of time. It looks as though it might cloud over before long. I think we shall get rain before the morning is out.'

The authority with which Mrs Riseley-Porter could enforce her remarks had its usual result. All those near at hand or within hearing followed her obediently out through french doors in the dining-room into the garden. The gardens had indeed all that Mrs Riseley-Porter had claimed for them. She herself took possession firmly of Colonel Walker and set off briskly. Some of the others followed them, others took paths in the opposite direction.

Miss Marple herself made a determined bee-line for a garden seat which appeared to be of comfortable proportions as well as of artistic merit. She sank down on it with relief, and a sigh matching her own was emitted by Miss Elizabeth Temple as she followed Miss Marple and came to sit beside her on the seat.

'Going over houses is always tiring,' said Miss Temple. 'The most tiring thing in the world. Especially if you have to listen to an exhaustive lecture in each room.'

'Of course, all that we were told is very interesting,' said Miss Marple, rather doubtfully.

'Oh, do you think so?' said Miss Temple. Her head turned slightly and her eyes met those of Miss Marple. Something passed between the two women, a kind of *rapport*—of understanding tinged with mirth.

'Don't you?' asked Miss Marple.

'No,' said Miss Temple.

This time the understanding was definitely established between them. They sat there companionably in silence. Presently Elizabeth Temple began to talk about gardens, and this garden in particular. 'It was designed by Holman,' she said, 'somewhere about 1800 or 1798. He died young. A pity. He had great genius.'

'It is so sad when anyone dies young,' said Miss Marple.

'I wonder,' said Elizabeth Temple.

She said it in a curious, meditative way.

'But they miss so much,' said Miss Marple. 'So many things.'

'Or escape so much,' said Miss Temple.

'Being as old as I am now,' said Miss Marple, 'I suppose I can't help feeling that early death means missing such a lot of things.'

'And I,' said Elizabeth Temple, 'having spent nearly all my life amongst the young, look at life as a period in time complete in itself. What did T. S. Eliot say: *The moment of the rose and the moment of the yew tree are of equal duration.*'

Miss Marple said, 'I see what you mean. . . . A life of whatever length is a complete experience. But don't you—' she hesitated, '—ever feel that a life could be incomplete because it has been cut unduly short?'

'Yes, that *is* so.'

Miss Marple said, looking at the flowers near her, 'How beautiful peonies are. That long border of them—so proud and yet so beautifully fragile.'

Elizabeth Temple turned her head towards her.

'Did you come on this trip to see the houses or to see gardens?' she asked.

'I suppose really to see the houses,' said Miss Marple. 'I shall enjoy the gardens most, though, but the houses—they will be a new experience for me. Their variety and their history, and the beautiful old furniture and the pictures.' She added: 'A kind friend gave me this trip as a gift. I am very grateful. I have not seen very many big and famous houses in my life.'

'A kind thought,' said Miss Temple.

'Do you often go on these sightseeing tours?' asked Miss Marple.

'No. This is not for me exactly a sightseeing tour.'

Miss Marple looked at her with interest. She half

opened her lips to speak but refrained from putting a question. Miss Temple smiled at her.

'You wonder why I am here, what my motive is, my reason. Well, why don't you make a guess?'

'Oh, I wouldn't like to do that,' said Miss Marple.

'Yes, do do so.' Elizabeth Temple was urgent. 'It would interest me. Yes, really interest me. Make a guess.'

Miss Marple was silent for quite a few moments. Her eyes looked at Elizabeth Temple steadily, ranging over her thoughtfully in her appraisement. She said,

'This is not from what I know about you or what I have been told about you. I know that you are quite a famous person and that your school is a very famous one. No. I am only making my guess from what you look like. I should—write you down as a pilgrim. You have the look of one who is on a pilgrimage.'

There was a silence and then Elizabeth said:

'That describes it very well. Yes. I am on a pilgrimage.'

Miss Marple said after a moment or two:

'The friend who sent me on this tour and paid all my expenses is now dead. He was a Mr Rafiel, a very rich man. Did you by any chance know him?'

'Jason Rafiel? I know him by name, of course. I never knew him personally, or met him. He gave a large endowment once to an educational project in which I was interested. I was very grateful. As you say, he was a very wealthy man. I saw the notice of his death in the papers a few weeks ago. So he was an old friend of yours?'

'No,' said Miss Marple. 'I had met him just over a year ago abroad. In the West Indies. I never knew much about him. His life or his family or any personal friends that he had. He was a great financier but otherwise, or so people always said, he was a man who was very reserved about himself. Did you know his family or anyone . . . ?' Miss Marple paused. 'I often wondered, but one does not like to ask questions and seem inquisitive.'

71

Elizabeth was silent for a minute—then she said:

'I knew a girl once. . . . A girl who had been a pupil of mine at Fallowfield, my school. She was no actual relation to Mr Rafiel, but she *was* at one time engaged to marry Mr Rafiel's son.'

'But she didn't marry him?' Miss Marple asked.

'No.'

'Why not?'

Miss Temple said:

'One might hope to say—like to say—because she had too much sense. He was not the type of a young man one would want anyone one was fond of to marry. She was a very lovely girl and a very sweet girl. I don't know why she didn't marry him. Nobody has ever told me.' She sighed and then said, 'Anyway, she died . . .'

'Why did she die?' said Miss Marple.

Elizabeth Temple stared at the peonies for some minutes. When she spoke she uttered one word. It echoed like the tone of a deep bell—so much so that it was startling.

'Love!' she said.

Miss Marple queried the word sharply. 'Love?'

'One of the most frightening words there is in the world,' said Elizabeth Temple.

Again her voice was bitter and tragic.

'Love. . . .'

7. An Invitation

MISS MARPLE decided to miss out on the afternoon's sightseeing. She admitted to being somewhat tired and would perhaps give a miss to an ancient church and its 14th-century glass. She would rest for a while and join them at the tea-room which had been pointed out to her in the main street. Mrs Sandbourne agreed that she was being very sensible.

Miss Marple, resting on a comfortable bench outside the tea-room, reflected on what she planned to do next and whether it would be wise to do it or not.

When the others joined her at tea-time it was easy for her to attach herself unobtrusively to Miss Cooke and Miss Barrow and sit with them at a table for four. The fourth chair was occupied by Mr Caspar whom Miss Marple considered as not sufficiently conversant with the English language to matter.

Leaning across the table, as she nibbled a slice of Swiss roll, Miss Marple said to Miss Cooke:

'You know, I am *quite* sure we have met before. I have been wondering and wondering about it—I'm not as good as I was at remembering faces, but I'm sure I have met you somewhere.'

Miss Cooke looked kindly but doubtful. Her eyes went to her friend, Miss Barrow. So did Miss Marple's. Miss Barrow showed no signs of helping to probe the mystery.

'I don't know if you've ever stayed in my part of the world,' went on Miss Marple, 'I live in St Mary Mead. Quite a small village, you know. At least, not so small nowadays, there is so much building going on everywhere. Not very far from Much Benham and only twelve miles from the coast at Loomouth.'

'Oh,' said Miss Cooke, 'let me see. Well, I know Loomouth quite well and perhaps——'

Suddenly Miss Marple made a pleased exclamation.

'Why, of *course*! I was in my garden one day at St Mary Mead and you spoke to me as you were passing by on the footpath. You said you were staying down there, I remember, with a friend——'

'Of course,' said Miss Cooke. 'How stupid of me. I do remember you now. We spoke of how difficult it was nowadays to get anyone—to do job gardening, I mean—anyone who was any use.'

'Yes, You were not living there, I think? You were staying with someone.'

'Yes, I was staying with . . . with . . .' for a moment Miss Cooke hesitated, with the air of one who hardly knows or remembers a name.

'With a Mrs Sutherland, was it?' suggested Miss Marple.

'No, no, it was . . . er . . . Mrs——'

'Hastings,' said Miss Barrow firmly as she took a piece of chocolate cake.

'Oh yes, in one of the new houses,' said Miss Marple.

'Hastings,' said Mr Caspar unexpectedly. He beamed. 'I have been to Hastings—I have been to Eastbourne, too.' He beamed again. 'Very nice—by the sea.'

'Such a coincidence,' said Miss Marple, 'meeting again so soon—such a small world, isn't it?'

'Oh, well, we are all so fond of gardens,' said Miss Cooke vaguely.

'Flowers very pretty,' said Mr Caspar. 'I like very much——' He beamed again.

'So many rare and beautiful shrubs,' said Miss Cooke.

Miss Marple went full speed ahead with a gardening conversation of some technicality—Miss Cooke responded. Miss Barrow put in an occasional remark.

Mr Caspar relapsed into smiling silence.

Later, as Miss Marple took her usual rest before dinner,

she conned over what she had collected. Miss Cooke *had* admitted being in St Mary Mead. She *had* admitted walking past Miss Marple's house. Had agreed it was quite a coincidence. Coincidence? thought Miss Marple meditatively, turning the word over in her mouth rather as a child might do to a certain lollipop to decide its flavour. Was it a coincidence? Or had she had some reason to come there? Had she been *sent* there? Sent there—for what reason? Was that a ridiculous thing to imagine?

'Any coincidence,' said Miss Marple to herself, 'is *always* worth noticing. You can throw it away later if it *is* only a coincidence.'

Miss Cooke and Miss Barrow appeared to be a perfectly normal pair of friends doing the kind of tour which, according to them, they did every year. They had been on an Hellenic cruise last year and a tour of bulbs in Holland the year before, and Northern Ireland the year before that. They seemed perfectly pleasant and ordinary people. But Miss Cooke, she thought, had for a moment looked as though she were about to disclaim her visit to St Mary Mead. She had looked at her friend, Miss Barrow, rather as though she were seeking instruction as to what to say. Miss Barrow, was presumably the senior partner——

'Of course, really, I may have been imagining all these things,' thought Miss Marple. 'They may have no significance whatever.'

The word danger came unexpectedly into her mind. Used by Mr Rafiel in his first letter—and there had been some reference to her needing a guardian angel in his second letter.

Was she going into danger in this business?—and why? From whom?

Surely not from Miss Cooke and Miss Barrow. Such an ordinary-looking couple.

All the same Miss Cooke *had* dyed her hair and altered her style of hairdressing. Disguised her appearance as much as she could, in fact. Which was odd, to say the least of it!

She considered once more her fellow travellers.

Mr Caspar, now, it would have been much easier to imagine that *he* might be dangerous. Did he understand more English than he pretended to do? She began to wonder about Mr Caspar.

Miss Marple had never quite succeeded in abandoning her Victorian view of foreigners. One never *knew* with foreigners. Quite absurd, of course, to feel like that—she had many friends from various foreign countries. All the same . . . ? Miss Cooke, Miss Barrow, Mr Caspar, that young man with the wild hair—Emlyn Something—a revolutionary—a practising anarchist? Mr and Mrs Butler —such nice Americans—but perhaps—too good to be true?

'Really,' said Miss Marple, 'I *must* pull myself together.'

She turned her attention to the itinerary of their trip. Tomorrow, she thought, was going to be rather strenuous. A morning's sightseeing drive, starting rather early: a long, rather athletic walk on a coastal path in the afternoon. Certain interesting marine flowering plants—it would be tiring. A tactful suggestion was appended. Anyone who felt like a rest could stay behind in their hotel, the Golden Boar, which had a very pleasant garden, or could do a short excursion which would only take an hour, to a beauty spot nearby. She thought perhaps that she would do that.

But though she did not know it then, her plans were to be suddenly altered.

As Miss Marple came down from her room in the Golden Boar the next day after washing her hands before luncheon, a woman in a tweed coat and skirt came forward rather nervously and spoke to her.

'Excuse me, are you Miss Marple—Miss Jane Marple?'

'Yes, that is my name,' said Miss Marple, slightly surprised.

'My name is Mrs Glynne. Lavinia Glynne. I and my two sisters live near here and—well, we heard you were coming, you see——'

'You heard I was coming?' said Miss Marple with some slight surprise.

'Yes. A very old friend of ours wrote to us—oh, quite some time ago, it must have been three weeks ago, but he asked us to make a note of this date. The date of the Famous Houses and Gardens Tour. He said that a great friend of his—or a relation, I'm not quite sure which—would be on that tour.'

Miss Marple continued to look surprised.

'I'm speaking of a Mr Rafiel,' said Mrs Glynne.

'Oh! Mr Rafiel,' said Miss Marple. 'You—you know that——'

'That he died? Yes. So sad. Just after his letter came. I think it must have been certainly very soon after he wrote to us. But we felt a special *urgency* to try to do what he had asked. He suggested, you know, that perhaps you would like to come and stay with us for a couple of nights. This part of the tour is rather strenuous. I mean, it's all right for the young people, but it is very trying for anyone older. It involves several miles of walking and a certain amount of climbing up difficult cliff paths and places. My sisters and I would be so very pleased if you could come and stay in our house here. It is only ten minutes' walk from the hotel and I'm sure we could show you many interesting things locally.'

Miss Marple hesitated a minute. She liked the look of Mrs Glynne, plump, good-natured, and friendly though a little shy. Besides—here again must be Mr Rafiel's instructions—the next step for her to take? Yes, it must be so.

She wondered why she felt nervous. Perhaps because she was now at home with the people in the tour, felt part of the group although as yet she had only known them for three days.

She turned to where Mrs Glynne was standing, looking up at her anxiously.

'Thank you—it is most kind of you. I shall be very pleased to come.'

8. The Three Sisters

MISS MARPLE stood looking out of a window. Behind her, on the bed, was her suitcase. She looked out over the garden with unseeing eyes. It was not often that she failed to see a garden she was looking at, in either a mood of admiration or a mood of criticism. In this case it would presumably have been criticism. It was a neglected garden, a garden on which little money had been spent possibly for some years, and on which very little work had been done. The house, too, had been neglected. It was well proportioned, the furniture in it had been good furniture once, but had had little in late years of polishing or attention. It was not a house, she thought, that had been, at any rate of late years, loved in any way. It lived up to its name: The Old Manor House. A house, built with grace and a certain amount of beauty, lived in once, cherished. The daughters and sons had married and left and now it was lived in by Mrs Glynne who, from a word she had let fall when she showed Miss Marple up to the bedroom appointed to her, had inherited it with her sisters from an uncle and had come here to live with her sisters after her husband had died. They had all grown older, their incomes had dwindled, labour had been more difficult to get.

The other sisters, presumably, had remained un-married, one older, one younger than Mrs Glynne, two Miss Bradbury-Scotts.

There was no sign of anything which belonged to a child in the house. No discarded ball, no old perambulator, no little chair or a table. This was just a house with three sisters.

'Sounds very Russian,' murmured Miss Marple to herself. She did mean The Three Sisters, didn't she? Chekhov, was it? or Dostoievsky? Really, she couldn't remember. Three sisters. But these would certainly not be the kind of three sisters who were yearning to go to Moscow. These three sisters were presumably, she was almost sure they were, content to remain where they were. She had been introduced to the other two who had come, one out of the kitchen and one down a flight of stairs, to welcome her. Their manners were well bred and gracious. They were what Miss Marple would have called in her youth by the now obsolete term 'ladies'—and what she once recalled calling: 'decayed ladies'. Her father had said to her:

'No, dear Jane, *not decayed*. Distressed gentlewomen.'

Gentlewomen nowadays were not so liable to be distressed. They were aided by Government or by Societies or by a rich relation. Or, perhaps—by someone like Mr Rafiel. Because, after all, that was the whole point, the whole reason for her being here, wasn't it? Mr Rafiel had arranged all this. He had taken, Miss Marple thought, a good deal of trouble about it. He had known presumably, some four or five weeks before his death, just when that death was likely to be, give and take a little, since doctors were usually moderately optimistic, knowing from experience that patients who ought to die within a certain period very often took an unexpected lease of life and lingered on, still doomed, but obstinately declining to take the final step. On the other hand, hospital nurses when in charge of patients, had, Miss Marple thought from her experience, always expected the patients to be dead the next day, and were much surprised when they were not. But in voicing their gloomy views to Doctor, when he came, they were apt to receive in reply as the doctor went out of the hall door, a private aside of, 'Linger a few weeks yet, I shouldn't wonder.' Very nice of Doctor to be so optimistic, Nurse would think, but surely Doctor was wrong. Doctor very often wasn't wrong. He knew that people who were in pain, helpless, crippled, even unhappy, still liked living and wanted to live. They would take one of Doctor's pills to help them pass the night, but they had no intention of taking a few more than necessary of Doctor's pills, just in order to pass the threshold to a world that they did not as yet know anything about!

Mr Rafiel. That was the person Miss Marple was thinking about as she looked across the garden with unseeing eyes. Mr Rafiel? She felt now that she was getting a little closer to understanding the task laid upon her, the project suggested to her. Mr Rafiel was a man who made plans. Made them in the same way that he planned financial deals and take-overs. In the words of her servant, Cherry, he had had a problem. When Cherry had a problem, she often came and consulted Miss Marple about it.

This was a problem that Mr Rafiel could not deal with himself, which must have annoyed him very much, Miss Marple thought, because he could usually deal with any problem himself and insisted on doing so. But he was bed-ridden and dying. He could arrange his financial affairs, communicate with his lawyers, with his employees and with such friends and relations as he had, but there was something or someone that he had not arranged for. A problem he had not solved, a problem he still wanted to solve, a project he still wanted to bring about. And apparently it was not one that could be settled by financial aid, by business dealings, by the services of a lawyer.

'So he thought of me,' said Miss Marple.

It still surprised her very much. Very much indeed. However, in the sense she was now thinking of it, his letter had been quite explicit. He had thought she had certain qualifications for doing something. It had to do, she thought once again, with something in the nature of crime or affected by crime. The only other thing he knew about Miss Marple was that she was devoted to gardens. Well it could hardly be a gardening problem that he wanted her to solve. But he might think of her in connection with crime. Crime in the West Indies and crimes in her own neighbourhood at home.

A crime—where?

Mr Rafiel had made arrangements. Arrangements, to begin with, with his lawyers. They had done their part. At the right interval of time they had forwarded to her his letter. It had been, she thought, a well considered and well thought out letter. It would have been simpler, certainly, to tell her exactly what he wanted her to do and why he wanted it. She was surprised in a way that he had not, before his death, sent for her, probably in a somewhat peremptory way and more or less lying on what he would have assured her was his death-bed, and would then have bullied her until she consented to do what he was asking her. But no, that would not really have been Mr Rafiel's way, she thought. He *could* bully people, none better, but this was not a case for bullying, and he did not wish either, she was sure, to appeal to her, to beg her to do him a favour, to urge her to redress a wrong. No. That again would not have been Mr Rafiel's way. He wanted, she thought, as he had probably wanted all his life, to pay for what he required. He wanted to pay her and therefore he wanted to interest her enough to enjoy doing certain work. The pay was offered to intrigue her, not really to tempt her. It was to arouse her interest. She did not think that he had said to himself, 'Offer enough money and she'll leap at it' because, as she knew very well herself, the money sounded very agreeable but she was not in urgent need of money. She had her dear and affectionate nephew who, if she was in straits for money of any kind, if she needed repairs to her house or visits to a specialist or special treats, dear Raymond would always provide them. No. The sum he offered was to be exciting. It was to be exciting in the same way as it was exciting when you had a ticket for the Irish Sweep. It was a fine big sum of money that you could never achieve by any other means except luck.

But all the same, Miss Marple thought to herself, she would need some luck as well as hard work, she would require a lot of thought and pondering and possibly what she was doing might involve a certain amount of danger. But she'd got to find out herself what it was all about, he wasn't going to tell her, partly perhaps because he did not want to influence her? It is hard to tell anyone about something without letting slip your own point of view about it. It could be that Mr Rafiel had thought that his own point of view might be wrong. It was not very like him to think such a thing, but it could be possible. He might suspect that his judgment, impaired by illness, was not quite as good as it used to be. So she, Miss Marple, his agent, his employee, was to make her own guesses, come to her own conclusions. Well, it was time she came to a few conclusions now. In other words, back to the old question, *what was all this about?*

She had been directed. Let her take that first. She had been directed by a man who was now dead. She had been directed away from St Mary Mead. Therefore, the task whatever it must be, could not be attacked from there. It was not a neighbourhood problem, it was not a problem that you could solve just by looking through newspaper cuttings or making inquiries, not, that is, until you found what you had to make inquiries about. She had been directed, first to the lawyer's office, then to read a letter— two letters—in her home, then to be sent on a pleasant and well run tour round some of the Famous Houses and Gardens of Great Britain. From that she had come to the next stepping stone. The house she was in at this moment. The Old Manor House, Jocelyn St Mary, where lived Miss Clotilde Bradbury-Scott, Mrs Glynne and Miss Anthea Bradbury-Scott. Mr Rafiel had arranged that, arranged it beforehand. Some weeks before he died. Probably it was the next thing he had done after instructing his lawyers and after booking a seat on the tour in her name. Therefore, she was in this house for a purpose. It might be for only two nights, it might be for longer. There might be certain things arranged which would lead her to stay longer or she would be asked to stay longer. That brought her back to where she stood now.

Mrs Glynne and her two sisters. They must be concerned, implicated in whatever this was. She would have to find out what it was. The time was short. That was the only trouble. Miss Marple had no doubt for one moment that she had the capacity to find out things. She was one of those chatty, fluffy old ladies whom other people expect to talk, to ask questions that were, on the face of it, merely gossipy questions. She would talk about her childhood and that would lead to one of the sisters talking about theirs. She'd talk about food she had eaten, servants she had had, daughters and cousins and relations, travel, marriages, births and—yes—deaths. There must be no show of special interest in her eyes when she heard about a death. Not at all. Almost automatically she was sure she could come up with the right response such as, 'Oh dear me, how *very* sad!' She would have to find out relationships, incidents, life stories, see if any suggestive incidents would pop up, so to speak. It might be some incidents in the neighbourhood, not directly concerned with these three people. Something they could know about, talk about, or were pretty sure to talk about. Anyway, there would be *something* here, some clue, some pointer. The second day from now she would rejoin the tour unless she had by that time some indication that she was *not* to rejoin the tour. Her mind swept from the house to the coach and the people who had sat in it. It might be that what she was seeking had been there in the coach, and would be there again when she rejoined it. One person, several people, some innocent (some not so innocent), some long-past story. She frowned a little, trying to remember something. Something that had flashed in her mind that she had thought: Really I am sure—of what had she been sure?

Her mind went back to the three sisters. She must not be too long up here. She must unpack a few modest needs for two nights, something to change into this evening, night clothes, sponge bag, and then go down and rejoin her hostesses and make pleasant talk. A main point had to be decided. Were the three sisters to be her allies or were the three sisters enemies? They might fall into either category. She must think about that carefully.

There was a tap on the door and Mrs Glynne entered.

'I do hope you will be quite comfortable here. Can I help you to unpack? We have a very nice woman who comes in but she is only here in the morning. But she'll help you with anything.'

'Oh no, thank you,' said Miss Marple. 'I only took out just a few necessities.'

'I thought I'd show you the way downstairs again. It's rather a rambling house, you know. There are two staircases and it does make it a little difficult. Sometimes people lose their way.'

'Oh, it's very kind of you,' said Miss Marple.

'I hope, then, you will come downstairs and we will have a glass of sherry before lunch.'

Miss Marple accepted gratefully and followed her guide down the stairs. Mrs Glynne, she judged, was a good many years younger than she herself was. Fifty, perhaps. Not much more. Miss Marple negotiated the stairs carefully, her left knee was always a little uncertain. There was, however, a banister at one side of the stairs. Very beautiful stairs they were, and she remarked on them.

'It is really a very lovely house,' she said. 'Built I suppose in the 1700's. Am I right?'

'1780,' said Mrs Glynne.

She seemed pleased with Miss Marple's appreciation.

She took Miss Marple into the drawing-room. A large graceful room. There were one or two rather beautiful pieces of furniture. A Queen Anne desk and a William and Mary oyster-shell bureau. There were also some rather cumbrous Victorian settees and cabinets. The curtains were of chintz, faded and somewhat worn, the carpet was, Miss Marple thought, Irish. Possibly a Limerick Aubusson type. The sofa was ponderous and the velvet of it much worn. The other two sisters were already sitting there. They rose as Miss Marple came in and approached her, one with a glass of sherry, the other directing her to a chair.

'I don't know whether you like sitting rather high? So many people do.'

'I do,' said Miss Marple. 'It's so much easier. One's back, you know.'

The sisters appeared to know about the difficulties of backs. The eldest of the sisters was a tall handsome woman, dark with a black coil of hair. The other one might have been a good deal younger. She was thin with grey hair that had once been fair hanging untidily on her shoulders and a faintly wraith-like appearance. She could be cast successfully as a mature Ophelia, Miss Marple thought.

Clotilde, Miss Marple thought, was certainly no Ophelia, but she would have made a magnificent Clytemnestra—she could have stabbed a husband in his bath with exultation. But since she had never had a husband, that solution wouldn't do. Miss Marple could not see her murdering anyone else but a husband—and there had been no Agamemnon in this house.

Clotilde Bradbury-Scott, Anthea Bradbury-Scott, Lavinia Glynne. Clotilde was handsome, Lavinia was plain but pleasant-looking, Anthea had one eyelid which twitched from time to time. Her eyes were large and grey and she had an odd way of glancing round to right and then to left, and then suddenly, in a rather strange

86

manner, behind her over her shoulder. It was as though she felt someone was watching her all the time. Odd, thought Miss Marple.

She wondered a little about Anthea.

They sat down and conversation ensued. Mrs Glynne left the room, apparently for the kitchen. She was, it seemed, the active domestic one of the three. The conversation took a usual course. Clotilde Bradbury-Scott explained that the house was a family one. It had belonged to her great-uncle and then to her uncle and when he had died it was left to her and her two sisters who had joined her there.

'He only had one son, you see,' explained Miss Bradbury-Scott, 'and he was killed in the war. We are really the last of the family, except for some very distant cousins.'

'A beautifully proportioned house,' said Miss Marple. 'Your sister tells me it was built about 1780.'

'Yes, I believe so. One could wish, you know, it was not quite so large and rambling.'

'Repairs too,' said Miss Marple, 'come very heavy nowadays.'

'Oh yes, indeed,' Clotilde sighed. 'And in many ways we have had to let a lot of it just fall down. Sad, but there it is. A lot of the outhouses, for instance, and a greenhouse. We had a very beautiful big greenhouse.'

'Lovely muscat grapevine in it,' said Anthea. 'And Cherry Pie used to grow all along the walls inside. Yes, I really regret that very much. Of course, during the war one could not get any gardeners. We had a very young gardener and then he was called up. One does not of course grudge that, but all the same it was impossible to get things repaired and so the whole greenhouse fell down.'

'So did the little conservatory near the house.'

Both sisters sighed, with the sighing of those who have noted time passing, and times changing—but not for the better.

87

There was a melancholy here in this house, thought Miss Marple. It was impregnated somehow with sorrow —a sorrow that could not be dispersed or removed since it had penetrated too deep. It had sunk in. . . . She shivered suddenly.

9. Polygonum Baldschuanicum

THE MEAL was conventional. A small joint of mutton, roast potatoes, followed by a plum tart with a small jug of cream and rather indifferent pastry. There were a few pictures round the dining-room wall, family pictures, Miss Marple presumed, Victorian portraits without any particular merit, the sideboard was large and heavy, a handsome piece of plum-coloured mahogany. The curtains were of dark crimson damask and at the big mahogany table ten people could easily have been seated.

Miss Marple chatted about the incidents of the tour in so far as she had been on it. As this, however, had only been three days, there was not very much to say.

'Mr Rafiel, I suppose, was an old friend of yours?' said the eldest Miss Bradbury-Scott.

'Not really,' said Miss Marple. 'I met him first when I was on a cruise to the West Indies. He was out there for his health, I imagine.'

'Yes, he had been very crippled for some years,' said Anthea.

'Very sad,' said Miss Marple. 'Very sad indeed. I really admired his fortitude. He seemed to manage to do so much work. Every day, you know, he dictated to his secretary and was continually sending off cables. He did not seem to give in at all kindly to being an invalid.'

'Oh no, he wouldn't,' said Anthea.

'We have not seen much of him of late years,' said Mrs Glynne. 'He was a busy man, of course. He always remembered us at Christmas very kindly.'

'Do you live in London, Miss Marple?' asked Anthea.

'Oh no,' said Miss Marple. 'I live in the country. A very small place half way between Loomouth and Market

Basing. About twenty-five miles from London. It used to be a very pretty old-world village but of course like everything else, it is becoming what they call developed nowadays.'

She added, 'Mr Rafiel, I suppose, lived in London? At least I noticed that in the St Honoré hotel register his address was somewhere in Eaton Square, I think, or was it Belgrave Square?'

'He had a country house in Kent,' said Clotilde. 'He used to entertain there, I think, sometimes. Business friends, mostly you know, or people from abroad. I don't think any of us ever visited him there. He nearly always entertained us in London on the rare occasions when we happened to meet.'

'It was very kind of him,' said Miss Marple, 'to suggest to you that you should invite me here during the course of this tour. Very thoughtful. One wouldn't really have expected a busy man such as he must have been to have had such kindly thoughts.'

'We have invited before friends of his who have been on these tours. On the whole they are very considerate the way they arrange these things. It is impossible, of course, to suit everybody's taste. The young ones naturally wish to walk, to make long excursions, to ascend hills for a view, and all that sort of thing. And the older ones who are not up to it, remain in the hotels, but hotels round here are not really at all luxurious. I am sure you would have found today's trip and the one to St Bonaventure tomorrow also, very fatiguing. Tomorrow I believe there is a visit to an island, you know, in a boat and sometimes it can be very rough.'

'Even going round houses can be very tiring,' said Mrs Glynne.

'Oh, I know,' said Miss Marple. 'So much walking and standing about. One's feet get very tired. I suppose really I ought not to take these expeditions, but it is such a temptation to see beautiful buildings and fine rooms and furniture. All these things. And of course some splendid pictures.'

'And the gardens,' said Anthea. 'You like gardens, don't you?'

'Oh yes,' said Miss Marple, 'specially the gardens. From the description in the prospectus I am really looking forward very much to seeing some of the really finely kept gardens of the historic houses we have still to visit.' She beamed round the table.

It was all very pleasant, very natural, and yet she wondered why for some reason she had a feeling of strain. A feeling that there was something unnatural here. But what did she mean by unnatural? The conversation was ordinary enough consisting mainly of platitudes. She herself was making conventional remarks and so were the three sisters.

The Three Sisters, thought Miss Marple once again considering that phrase. Why did anything thought of in threes somehow seem to suggest a sinister atmosphere? The Three Sisters. The Three Witches of Macbeth. Well, one could hardly compare these three sisters to the three witches. Although Miss Marple had always thought at the back of her mind that the theatrical producers made a mistake in the way in which they produced the three witches. One production which she had seen, indeed, seemed to her quite absurd. The witches had looked more like pantomime creatures with flapping wings and ridiculously spectacular steeple hats. They had danced and slithered about. Miss Marple remembered saying to her nephew, who was standing her this Shakespearean treat, 'You know, Raymond, my dear, if *I* were ever producing this splendid play I would make the three witches *quite* different. I would have them three ordinary, normal old women. Old Scottish women. They wouldn't dance or caper. They would look at each other rather slyly and you would feel a sort of menace just behind the ordinariness of them.'

Miss Marple helped herself to the last mouthful of plum tart and looked across the table at Anthea. Ordinary, untidy, very vague-looking, a bit scatty. Why should she feel that Anthea was sinister?

'I am imagining things,' said Miss Marple to herself. 'I mustn't do that.'

After luncheon she was taken on a tour of the garden. It was Anthea who was deputed to accompany her. It was, Miss Marple thought, rather a sad progress. Here, there had once been a well kept, though certainly not in any way an outstanding or remarkable, garden. It had had the elements of an ordinary Victorian garden. A shrubbery, a drive of speckled laurels, no doubt there had once been a well kept lawn and paths, a kitchen garden of about an acre and a half, too big evidently for the three sisters who lived here now. Part of it was unplanted and had gone largely to weeds. Ground elder had taken over most of the flower beds and Miss Marple's hands could hardly restrain themselves from pulling up the vagrant bindweed asserting its superiority.

Miss Anthea's long hair flapped in the wind, shedding from time to time a vague hairpin on the path or the grass. She talked rather jerkily.

'*You* have a very nice garden, I expect,' she said.

'Oh, it's a very small one,' said Miss Marple.

They had come along a grass path and were pausing in front of a kind of hillock that rested against the wall at the end of it.

'Our greenhouse,' said Miss Anthea, mournfully.

'Oh yes, where you had such a delightful grapevine.'

'Three vines,' said Anthea. 'A Black Hamburg and one of those small white grapes, very sweet, you know. And a third one of beautiful muscats.'

'And a heliotrope, you said.'

'Cherry Pie,' said Anthea.

'Ah yes, Cherry Pie. Such a lovely smell. Was there any bomb trouble round here? Did that—er—knock the greenhouse down?'

'Oh no, we never suffered from anything of that kind. This neighbourhood was quite free of bombs. No, I'm afraid it just fell down from decay. We hadn't been here so very long and we had no money to repair it, or to build it up again. And in fact, it wouldn't have been worth it really because we couldn't have kept it up even if we did. I'm afraid we just let it fall down. There was nothing else we could do. And now you see, it's all grown over.'

'Ah that, completely covered by—what is that flowering creeper just coming into bloom?'

'Oh yes. It's quite a common one,' said Anthea. 'It begins with a P. Now what is the name of it,' she said doubtfully. 'Poly something, something like that.'

'Oh yes. I think I do know the name. Polygonum Baldschuanicum. Very quick growing, I think, isn't it? Very useful really if one wants to hide any tumbledown building or anything ugly of that kind.'

The mound in front of her was certainly thickly covered with the all-enveloping green and white flowering plant. It was, as Miss Marple well knew, a kind of menace to anything else that wanted to grow. Polygonum covered everything, and covered it in a remarkably short time.

'The greenhouse must have been quite a big one,' she said.

'Oh yes—we had peaches in it, too—and nectarines.' Anthea looked miserable.

'It looks really very pretty now,' said Miss Marple in a consoling tone. 'Very pretty little white flowers, aren't they?'

'We have a very nice magnolia tree down this path to the left,' said Anthea. 'Once I believe there used to be a

93

very fine border here—a herbaceous border. But that again one cannot keep up. It is too difficult. Everything is too difficult. Nothing is like it used to be—it's all spoilt —everywhere.'

She led the way quickly down a path at right-angles which ran along a side wall. Her pace had increased. Miss Marple could hardly keep up with her. It was, thought Miss Marple, as though she were deliberately being steered away from the Polygonum mound by her hostess. Steered away as from some ugly or displeasing spot. Was she ashamed perhaps that the past glories no longer remained? The Polygonum certainly was growing with extraordinary abandonment. It was not even being clipped or kept to reasonable proportions. It made a kind of flowery wilderness of that bit of the garden.

She almost looks as though she was running away from it, thought Miss Marple, as she followed her hostess. Presently her attention was diverted to a broken down pig-sty which had a few rose tendrils round it.

'My great-uncle used to keep a few pigs,' explained Anthea, 'but of course one would never dream of doing anything of that kind nowadays, would one? Rather too noisome, I am afraid. We have a few floribunda roses near the house. I really think floribundas are such a great answer to difficulties.'

'Oh, I know,' said Miss Marple.

She mentioned the names of a few recent productions in the rose line. All the names, she thought, were entirely strange to Miss Anthea.

'Do you often come on these tours?'

The question came suddenly.

'You mean the tours of houses and of gardens?'

'Yes. Some people do it every year.'

'Oh I couldn't hope to do that. They're rather expensive, you see. A friend very kindly gave me a present of this to celebrate my next birthday. So kind.'

'Oh. I wondered. I wondered *why* you came. I mean—it's bound to be rather tiring, isn't it? Still, if you usually go to the West Indies, and places like that . . .'

'Oh, the West Indies was the result of kindness, too. On the part of a nephew, that time. A dear boy. So very thoughtful for his old aunt.'

'Oh, I see. Yes, I see.'

'I don't know what one would do without the younger generation,' said Miss Marple. 'They are so kind, are they not?'

'I—I suppose so. I don't really know. I—we haven't—any young relations.'

'Does your sister, Mrs Glynne, have any children? She did not mention any. One never likes to ask.'

'No. She and her husband never had any children. It's as well, perhaps.'

'And what do you mean by that?' Miss Marple wondered as they returned to the house.

10. 'Oh! Fond, Oh! Fair, the Days that Were'

AT HALF PAST EIGHT the next morning there was a smart tap on the door, and in answer to Miss Marple's 'Come in' the door was opened and an elderly woman entered, bearing a tray with a teapot, a cup and a milk jug and a small plate of bread and butter.

'Early morning tea, ma'am,' she said cheerfully. 'It's a nice day, it is. I see you've got your curtains drawn back already. You've slept well then?'

'Very well indeed,' said Miss Marple, laying aside a small devotional book which she had been reading.

'Well, it's a lovely day, it is. They'll have it nice for going to the Bonaventure Rocks. It's just as well you're not doing it. It's cruel hard on the legs, it is.'

'I'm really very happy to be here,' said Miss Marple. 'So kind of Miss Bradbury-Scott and Mrs Glynne to issue this invitation.'

'Ah well, it's nice for them too. It cheers them up to have a bit of company come to the house. Ah, it's a sad place nowadays, so it is.' She pulled the curtains at the window rather more fully, pushed back a chair and deposited a can of hot water in the china basin.

'There's a bathroom on the next floor,' she said, 'but we think it's better always for someone elderly to have hot water here, so they don't have to climb the stairs.'

'It's very kind of you—you know this house well?'

'I was here as a girl—I was the housemaid then. Three servants they had—a cook, a housemaid—a parlour-maid —kitchen maid too at one time. That was in the old Colonel's time. Horses he kept too, and a groom. Ah, those were the days. Sad it is when things happen the way they do. He lost his wife young, the Colonel did. His son was killed in the war and his only daughter went away to live on the other side of the world. Married a New Zealander she did. Died having a baby and the baby died too. He was a sad man living alone here, and he let the house go—it wasn't kept up as it should have been. When he died he left the place to his niece Miss Clotilde and her two sisters, and she and Miss Anthea came here to live—and later Miss Lavinia lost her husband and came to join them—' she sighed and shook her head. 'They never did much to the house—couldn't afford it—and they let the garden go as well——'

'It all seems a great pity,' said Miss Marple.

'And such nice ladies as they all are, too—Miss Anthea is the scatty one, but Miss Clotilde went to university and is very brainy—she talks three languages—and Mrs Glynne, she's a very nice lady indeed. I thought when she came to join them as things might go better. But you never know, do you, what the future holds? I feel sometimes, as though there was a doom on this house.'

Miss Marple looked inquiring.

'First one thing and then another. The dreadful plane accident—in Spain it was—and everybody killed. Nasty things, aeroplanes—I'd never go in one of them. Miss Clotilde's friends were both killed, they were husband and wife—the daughter was still at school, luckily, and escaped, but Miss Clotilde brought her here to live and did everything for her. Took her abroad for trips—to Italy and France, treated her like a daughter. She was such a happy girl—and a very sweet nature. You'd never dream that such an awful thing could happen.'

'An awful thing. What was it? Did it happen here?'

'No, not here, thank God. Though in a way you might say it *did* happen here. It was here that she met him. He was in the neighbourhood—and the ladies knew his father, who was a very rich man, so he came here to visit—that was the beginning——'

'They fell in love?'

'Yes, she fell in love with him right away. He was an attractive-looking boy, with a nice way of talking and passing the time of day. You'd never think—you'd never think for one moment——' she broke off.

'There was a love affair? And it went wrong? And the girl committed suicide?'

'Suicide?' The old woman stared at Miss Marple with startled eyes.

'Whoever now told you *that*? Murder it was, barefaced murder. Strangled and her head beaten to pulp. Miss Clotilde had to go and identify her—she's never been quite the same since. They found her body a good thirty miles from here—in the scrub of a disused quarry. And it's believed that it wasn't the first murder he'd done. There had been other girls. Six months she'd been missing. And the police searching far and wide. Oh! A wicked devil he was—a bad lot from the day he was born or so it seems. They say nowadays as there are those as can't help what they do—not right in the head, and they can't be held responsible. I don't believe a word of it! Killers are killers. And they won't even hang them nowadays. I know as there's often madness as runs in old families— there was the Derwents over to Brassington—every second generation one or other of them died in the loony bin— and there was old Mrs Paulett; walked about the lanes in her diamond tiara saying she was Marie Antoinette until they shut her up. But there wasn't anything really wrong with her—just silly like. But this boy. Yes, he was a devil right enough.'

'What did they do to him?'

'They'd abolished hanging by then—or else he was too young. I can't remember it all now. They found him guilty. It may have been Bostol or Broadsand—one of those places beginning with "B" as they sent him to.'

'What was the name of the boy?'

'Michael—can't remember his last name. It's ten years ago that it happened—one forgets. Italian sort of name—like a picture. Someone who paints pictures—Raffle, that's it——'

'Michael Rafiel?'

'That's right! There was a rumour as went about that his father being so rich got him wangled out of prison. An escape like the Bank Robbers. But I think as that was just talk——'

So it had not been suicide. It had been murder. 'Love!' Elizabeth Temple had named as the cause of a girl's death. In a way she was right. A young girl had fallen in love with a killer—and for love of him had gone unsuspecting to an ugly death.

Miss Marple gave a little shudder. On her way along the village street yesterday she had passed a newspaper placard: EPSOM DOWNS MURDER, SECOND GIRL'S BODY DISCOVERED, YOUTH ASKED TO ASSIST POLICE.

So history repeated itself. An old pattern—an ugly pattern. Some lines of verse came into her brain:

> *Rose white youth, passionate, pale,*
> *A singing stream in a silent vale,*
> *A fairy prince in a prosy tale,*
> *Oh there's nothing in life so finely frail*
> *As Rose White Youth.*

Who was there to guard Youth from Pain and Death? Youth who could not, who had never been able to, guard itself. Did they know too little? Or was it that they knew too much? And therefore thought they knew it all.

2

Miss Marple, coming down the stairs that morning, probably rather earlier than she had been expected, found no immediate sign of her hostesses. She let herself out at

99

the front door and wandered once round the garden. It was not because she'd really enjoyed this particular garden. It was some vague feeling that there was something here that she ought to notice, something that would give her some idea, or that had given her some idea only she had not—well, frankly, she had not been bright enough to realize just what the bright idea had been. Something she ought to take note of, something that had a bearing.

She was not at the moment anxious to see any of the three sisters. She wanted to turn a few things over in her mind. The new facts that had come to her through Janet's early tea chat.

A side gate stood open and she went through it to the village street and along a line of small shops to where a steeple poked up announcing the site of the church and its churchyard. She pushed open the lych-gate and wandered about among the graves, some dating from quite a while back, some by the far wall later ones, and one or two beyond the wall in what was obviously a new enclosure. There was nothing of great interest among the older tombs. Certain names recurred as they do in villages. A good many Princes of village origin had been buried. Jasper Prince, deeply regretted, Margery Prince, Edgar and Walter Prince, Melanie Prince, 4 years old. A family record. Hiram Broad—Ellen Jane Broad, Eliza Broad, 91 years.

She was turning away from the latter when she observed an elderly man moving in slow motion among the graves, tidying up as he walked. He gave her a salute and a 'good morning'.

'Good morning,' said Miss Marple. 'A very pleasant day.'

'It'll turn to rain later,' said the old man.

He spoke with the utmost certainty.

'There seem to be a lot of Princes and Broads buried here,' said Miss Marple.

'Ah yes, there've always been Princes here. Used to own quite a bit of land once. There have been Broads a good many years, too.'

'I see a child is buried here. Very sad when one sees a child's grave.'

'Ah, that'll be little Melanie that was. Mellie, we called her. Yes, it was a sad death. Run over, she was. Ran out into the street, went to get sweets at the sweet shop. Happens a lot nowadays with cars going through at the pace they do.'

'It is sad to think,' said Miss Marple, 'that there are so many deaths all the time. And one doesn't really notice it until one looks at the inscriptions in the churchyard. Sickness, old age, children run over, sometimes even more dreadful things. Young girls killed. Crimes, I mean.'

'Ah, yes, there's a lot of that about. Silly girls, I call most of 'em. And their mums haven't got time to look after them properly nowadays—what with going out to work so much.'

Miss Marple appreciated his criticism, but had no wish to waste time in agreement on the trend of the day.

'Staying at The Old Manor House, aren't you?' the old man asked. 'Come here on the coach tour I saw. But it got too much for you, I suppose. Some of those that are gettin' on can't always take it.'

'I *did* find it a little exhausting,' confessed Miss Marple, 'and a very kind friend of mine, a Mr Rafiel, wrote to some friends of his here and they invited me to stay for a couple of nights.'

The name, Rafiel, clearly meant nothing to the elderly gardener. 'Mrs Glynne, and her two sisters have been very kind,' said Miss Marple. 'I suppose they've lived here a long time?'

'Not so long as that. Twenty years maybe. Belonged to old Colonel Bradbury-Scott, The Old Manor House did. Close on seventy he was when he died.'

'Did he have any children?'

'A son what was killed in the war. That's why he left the place to his nieces. Nobody else to leave it to.'

He went back to his work amongst the graves.

Miss Marple went into the church. It had felt the hand of a Victorian restorer, and had bright Victorian glass in the windows. One or two brasses and some tablets on the walls was all that was left of the past.

Miss Marple sat down in an uncomfortable pew and wondered about things.

Was she on the right track now? Things were connecting up—but the connections were far from clear.

A girl had been murdered—(actually several girls had been murdered)—suspected young men (or 'youths' as they were usually called nowadays) had been rounded up by the police, to 'assist them in their inquiries'. A common pattern. But this was all old history, dating back ten or twelve years. There was nothing to find out—now, no problems to solve. A tragedy labelled Finis.

What could be done by her? What could Mr Rafiel possibly want her to do?

Elizabeth Temple. . . . She must get Elizabeth Temple to tell her more. Elizabeth had spoken of a girl who had been engaged to be married to Michael Rafiel. But was that really so? That fact did not seem to be known to those in The Old Manor House.

A more familiar version came into Miss Marple's mind —the kind of story that had been reasonably frequent in her own village. Starting as always, 'Boy meets girl'. Developing in the usual way——

'And then the girl finds she is pregnant,' said Miss Marple to herself, 'and she tells the boy and she wants him to marry her. But he, perhaps, doesn't want to marry her—he has never had any idea of marrying her. But things may be made difficult for him in this case. His father, perhaps, won't hear of such a thing. Her relations will insist that he "does the right thing". And by now he is tired of the girl—he's got another girl perhaps. And so he takes a quick brutal way out—strangles her, beats her head to a pulp to avoid identification. It fits with his record—a brutal sordid crime—*but* forgotten and done with.'

She looked round the church in which she was still sitting. It looked so peaceful. The reality of Evil was hard to believe in. A *flair* for Evil—that was what Mr Rafiel had attributed to her. She rose and walked out of the church and stood looking round the churchyard again. Here, amongst the gravestones and their worn inscriptions no sense of Evil moved in her.

Was it Evil she had sensed yesterday at The Old Manor House? That deep depression of despair, that dark desperate grief. Anthea Bradbury-Scott, her eyes gazing fearfully back over *one* shoulder, as though fearing some presence that stood there—always stood there—behind her. They knew something, those Three Sisters, but what was it that they knew?

Elizabeth Temple, she thought again. She pictured Elizabeth Temple with the rest of the coach party, striding across the downs at this moment, climbing up a steep path and gazing over the cliffs out to sea.

Tomorrow, when she rejoined the tour, she would get Elizabeth Temple to tell her more.

Miss Marple retraced her steps to The Old Manor House, walking rather slowly because she was by now tired. She could not really feel that her morning had been productive in any way. So far The Old Manor House had given her no distinctive ideas of any kind, a tale of a past tragedy told by Janet, but there were always past tragedies treasured in the memories of domestic workers and which were remembered quite as clearly as all the happy events such as spectacular weddings, big entertainments and successful operations or accidents from which people had recovered in a miraculous manner.

As she drew near the gate she saw two female figures standing there. One of them detached itself and came to meet her. It was Mrs Glynne.

'Oh, there you are,' she said. 'We wondered, you know. I thought you must have gone out for a walk somewhere and I did so hope you wouldn't overtire yourself. If I had known you had come downstairs and gone out, I would have come with you to show anything there is to show. Not that there is very much.'

'Oh, I just wandered around,' said Miss Marple. 'The churchyard, you know, and the church. I'm always very interested in churches. Sometimes there are very curious epitaphs. Things like that. I make quite a collection of them. I suppose the church here was restored in Victorian times?'

'Yes, they did put in some rather ugly pews, I think. You know, good quality wood, and strong and all that, but not very artistic.'

'I hope they didn't take away anything of particular interest.'

'No, I don't think so. It's not really a very old church.'

'There did not seem to be many tablets or brasses or anything of that kind,' agreed Miss Marple.

'You are quite interested in ecclesiastical architecture?'

'Oh, I don't make a study of it or anything like that, but of course in my own village, St Mary Mead, things do rather revolve round the church. I mean, they always have. In my young days, that was so. Nowadays of course it's rather different. Were you brought up in this neighbourhood?'

'Oh, not really. We lived not very far away, about thirty miles or so. At Little Herdsley. My father was a retired serviceman—a Major in the Artillery. We came over here occasionally to see my uncle—indeed to see my great-uncle before him. No. I've not even been here very much of late years. My other two sisters moved in after my uncle's death, but at that time I was still abroad with my husband. He only died about four or five years ago.'

'Oh, I see.'

'They were anxious I should come and join them here and really, it seemed the best thing to do. We had lived in India for some years. My husband was still stationed there at the time of his death. It is very difficult nowadays to know where one would wish to—should I say, put one's roots down.'

'Yes, indeed. I can quite see that. And you felt, of course, that you had roots here since your family had been here for a long time.'

'Yes. Yes, one did feel that. Of course, I'd always kept up with my sisters, had been to visit them. But things are always very different from what one thinks they will be. I have bought a small cottage near London, near Hampton Court, where I spend a good deal of my time, and I do a little occasional work for one or two charities in London.'

'So your time is fully occupied. How wise of you.'

'I have felt of late that I should spend more time here, perhaps. I've been a little worried about my sisters.'

'Their health?' suggested Miss Marple. 'One *is* rather worried nowadays, especially as there is not really anyone competent whom one can employ to look after people as they become rather feebler or have certain ailments. So much rheumatism and arthritis about. One is always so afraid of people falling down in the bath or an accident coming down stairs. Something of that kind.'

'Clotilde has always been very strong,' said Mrs Glynne. 'Tough, I should describe her. But I am rather worried sometimes about Anthea. She is vague, you know, very vague indeed. And she wanders off sometimes—and doesn't seem to know where she is.'

'Yes, it is sad when people worry. There is so much to worry one.'

'I don't really think there is much to worry Anthea.'

'She worries about income tax, perhaps, money affairs,' suggested Miss Marple.

'No, no, not that so much but—oh, she worries so much about the garden. She remembers the garden as it used to be, and she's very anxious, you know, to—well, to spend money in putting things right again. Clotilde has had to tell her that really one can't afford that nowadays. But she keeps talking of the hot-houses, the peaches that used to be there. The grapes—and all that.'

'And the Cherry Pie on the walls?' suggested Miss Marple, remembering a remark.

'Fancy your remembering that. Yes, Yes, it's one of the things one does remember. Such a charming smell, heliotrope. And such a nice name for it, Cherry Pie. One always remembers that. And the grapevine. The little, small, early sweet grapes. Ah well, one must not remember the past too much.'

'And the flower borders too, I suppose,' said Miss Marple.

'Yes. Yes, Anthea would like to have a big well kept herbaceous border again. Really *not* feasible now. It is as much as one can do to get local people who will come and mow the lawns every fortnight. Every year one seems to employ a different firm. And Anthea would like pampas grass planted again. And the Mrs Simpkin pinks. White, you know. All along the stone edge border. And a fig tree that grew just outside the greenhouse. She remembers all these and talks about them.'

'It must be difficult for you.'

'Well, yes. Arguments, you see, hardly appeal in any way. Clotilde, of course, is very downright about things. She just refuses point-blank and says she doesn't want to hear another word about it.'

'It is difficult,' said Miss Marple, 'to know how to take things. Whether one should be firm. Rather authoritative. Perhaps, even, well, just a little—a little *fierce*, you know, or whether one should be sympathetic. Listen to things and perhaps hold out hopes which one knows are not justified. Yes, it's difficult.'

'But it's easier for me because you see I go away again, and then come back now and then to stay. So it's easy for me to pretend things may be easier soon and that something may be done. But really, the other day when I came home and I found that Anthea had tried to engage a most expensive firm of landscape gardeners to renovate the garden, to build up the greenhouses again—which is *quite* absurd because even if you put vines in they would not bear for another two or three years. Clotilde knew nothing about it and she was extremely angry when she discovered the estimate for this work on Anthea's desk. She was really quite unkind.'

'So many things are difficult,' said Miss Marple.

It was a useful phrase which she used often.

'I shall have to go rather early tomorrow morning, I think,' said Miss Marple. 'I was making inquiries at the Golden Boar where I understand the coach party assembles tomorrow morning. They are making quite an early start. Nine o'clock, I understand.'

'Oh dear. I hope you will not find it too fatiguing.'

'Oh, I don't think so. I gather we are going to a place called—now wait a minute, what was it called?—Stirling St Mary. Something like that. And it does not seem to be very far away. There's an interesting church to see on the way and a castle. In the afternoon there is a quite pleasant garden, not too many acres, but some special flowers. I feel sure that after this very nice rest that I have had here, I shall be quite all right. I understand now that I would have been very tired if I had had these two days of climbing cliffs and all the rest of it.'

'Well, you must rest this afternoon, so as to be fresh for tomorrow,' said Mrs Glynne, as they went into the house. 'Miss Marple has been to visit the church,' said Mrs Glynne to Clotilde.

'I'm afraid there is not very much to see,' said Clotilde. 'Victorian glass of a most hideous kind, I think myself. No expense spared. I'm afraid my uncle was partly to blame. He was very pleased with those rather crude reds and blues.'

'Very crude. Very vulgar, I always think,' said Lavinia Glynne.

Miss Marple settled down after lunch to have a nap, and she did not join her hostesses until nearly dinner time. After dinner a good deal of chat went on until it was bedtime. Miss Marple set the tone in remembrances. . . . Remembrances of her own youth, her early days, places she had visited, travels or tours she had made, occasional people she had known.

She went to bed tired, with a sense of failure. She had learned nothing more, possibly because there was nothing more to learn. A fishing expedition where the fish did not rise—possibly because there were no fish there. Or it could be that she did not know the right bait to use?

11. Accident

MISS MARPLE'S TEA was brought at seven-thirty the following morning so as to allow her plenty of time to get up and pack her few belongings. She was just closing her small suitcase when there was a rather hurried tap on the door and Clotilde came in, looking upset.

'Oh dear, Miss Marple, there is a young man downstairs who has called to see you. Emlyn Price. He is on the tour with you and they sent him here.'

'Of course, I remember him. Yes. Quite young?'

'Oh yes. Very modern-looking, and a lot of hair and all that, but he has really come to—well, to break some bad news to you. There has been, I am sorry to say, an accident.'

'An accident?' Miss Marple stared. 'You mean—to the coach? There has been an accident on the road? Someone has been hurt?'

'No. No, it was not the coach. There was no trouble there. It was in the course of the expedition yesterday afternoon. There was a great deal of wind you may remember, though I don't think that had anything to do with it. People strayed about a bit, I think. There is a regular path, but you can also climb up and go across the downs. Both ways lead to the Memorial Tower on the top of Bonaventure—where they were all making for. People got separated a bit and I suppose, really, there was no one actually guiding them or looking after them which, perhaps, there ought to have been. People aren't very sure-footed always and the slope overhanging the gorge is very steep. There was a bad fall of stones or rocks which came crashing down the hillside and knocked someone out on the path below.'

'Oh dear,' said Miss Marple, 'I am sorry. I am most terribly sorry. Who was it who was hurt?'

'A Miss Temple or Tenderdon, I understand.'

'Elizabeth Temple,' said Miss Marple. 'Oh dear, I am sorry. I talked to her a good deal. I sat in the next seat to her on the coach. She is, I believe, a retired schoolmistress, a very well known one.'

'Of course,' said Clotilde, 'I know her quite well. She was Headmistress of Fallowfield, quite a famous school. I'd no idea she was on this tour. She retired as Headmistress, I think a year or two ago, and there is a new, rather young Headmistress there now with rather advanced progressive ideas. But Miss Temple is not very old, really, she's about sixty, I should think, and very active, fond of climbing and walking and all the rest of it. This really seems *most* unfortunate. I hope she's not badly hurt. I haven't heard any details yet.'

'This is quite ready now,' said Miss Marple, snapping down the lid of her suitcase. 'I will come down at once and see Mr Price.'

Clotilde seized the suitcase.

'Let me. I can carry this perfectly. Come down with me, and be careful of the stairs.'

Miss Marple came down. Emlyn Price was waiting for her. His hair was looking even wilder than usual and he was wearing a splendid array of fancy boots and a leather jerkin and brilliant emerald green trousers.

'Such an unfortunate business,' he said, seizing Miss Marple's hand. 'I thought I'd come along myself and—well, break it to you about the accident. I expect Miss Bradbury-Scott has told you. It's Miss Temple. You know. The school dame. I don't know quite what she was doing or what happened, but some stones, or rather boulders, rolled down from above. It's rather a precipitous slope and it knocked her out and they had to take her off to hospital with concussion last night. I gather she's rather bad. Anyway, the tour for today is cancelled and we are stopping on here tonight.'

'Oh dear,' said Miss Marple, 'I am sorry. I'm very sorry.'

'I think they've decided not to go on today because they really have to wait and see what the medical report is, so we are proposing to spend one more night here at the Golden Boar and to rearrange the tour a little, so that perhaps we shall miss out altogether going to Grangmering which we were going to do tomorrow, and which is not very interesting really, or so they say. Mrs Sandbourne has gone off early to the hospital to see how things are this morning. She's going to join us at the Golden Boar for coffee at eleven o'clock. I thought perhaps you'd like to come along and hear the latest news.'

'I'll certainly come along with you,' said Miss Marple. 'Of course. At once.'

She turned to say goodbye to Clotilde and Mrs Glynne who had joined her.

'I must thank you so much,' she said. 'You have been so kind and it has been so delightful to have these two nights here. I feel so rested and everything. Most unfortunate this has occurred.'

'If you would like to spend another night,' said Mrs Glynne, 'I am sure——' She looked at Clotilde.

It occurred to Miss Marple, who had as sharp a sideways glance as anyone could desire, that Clotilde had a slightly disapproving look. She almost shook her head, though it was such a small movement that it was hardly noticeable. But she was, Miss Marple thought, hushing down the suggestion that Mrs Glynne was making.

'. . . although of course I expect it would be nicer for you to be with the others and to——'

'Oh yes, I think it would be better,' said Miss Marple. 'I shall know then what the plans are and what to do about things, and perhaps I could be of help in some way.

One never knows. So thank you again very much. It will not be difficult, I expect, to get a room at the Golden Boar.' She looked at Emlyn, who said reassuringly:

'That'll be all right. Several rooms have been vacated today. They won't be full at all. Mrs Sandbourne, I think, has booked for all the party to stay there tonight, and tomorrow we shall see—well, we shall see how this all goes on.'

Goodbyes were said again and thanks. Emlyn Price took Miss Marple's belongings and started out at a good striding pace.

'It's really only just round the corner, and then the first street to the left,' he said.

'Yes, I passed it yesterday, I think. Poor Miss Temple. I do hope she's not badly hurt.'

'I think she is rather,' said Emlyn Price. 'Of course, you know what doctors are, and hospital people. They say the same thing always: "as well as can be expected". There's no local hospital—they had to take her to Carristown which is about eight miles away. Anyway, Mrs Sandbourne will be back with the news by the time we've fixed you up at the hotel.'

They got there to find the tour assembled in the coffee room and coffee and morning buns and pastries were being served. Mr and Mrs Butler were talking at the moment.

'Oh, it's just too, too tragic this happening,' said Mrs Butler. 'Just too upsetting, isn't it? Just when we were all so happy and enjoying everything so much. Poor Miss Temple. And I always thought she was very sure-footed. But there, you know, you never can tell, can you, Henry?'

'No, indeed,' said Henry. 'No, indeed. I am wondering really—yes, our time's very short you know—whether we hadn't better—well, give up this tour at this point here. Not continue with it. It seems to me that there's bound to be a bit of difficulty resuming things until we know definitely. If this was—well—I mean, if this should be so serious that it could prove fatal, there might—well—I mean there might have to be an inquest or something of that kind.'

'Oh Henry, don't say dreadful things like that!'

'I'm sure,' said Miss Cooke, 'that you are being a little too pessimistic, Mr Butler. I am sure that things couldn't be as serious as that.'

In his foreign voice Mr Caspar said: 'But yes, they are serious. I hear yesterday. When Mrs Sandbourne talk on telephone to doctor. It is very, very serious. They say she has concussion bad—very bad. A special doctor he is coming to look at her and see if he can operate or if impossible. Yes—it is all very bad.'

'Oh dear,' said Miss Lumley. 'If there's any doubt, perhaps we ought to go home, Mildred. I must look up the trains, I think.' She turned to Mrs Butler. 'You see, I have made arrangements about my cats with the neighbours, and if I was delayed a day or two it might make great difficulties for *everyone*.'

'Well, it's no good our working ourselves up too much,' said Mrs Riseley-Porter, in her deep, authoritative voice. 'Joanna, put this bun in the waste-paper basket, will you? It is really quite uneatable. Most unpleasant jam. But I don't want to leave it on my plate. It might make for bad feeling.'

Joanna got rid of the bun. She said:

'Do you think it would be all right if Emlyn and I went out for a walk? I mean, just saw something of the town. It's not much good our sitting about here, making gloomy remarks, is it? We can't *do* anything.'

'I think you'd be very wise to go out,' said Miss Cooke.

'Yes, you go along,' said Miss Barrow before Mrs Riseley-Porter could speak.

Miss Cooke and Miss Barrow looked at each other and sighed, shaking their heads.

'The grass was very slippery,' said Miss Barrow. 'I slid

113

once or twice myself, you know, on that very short turf.'

'And the stones, too,' said Miss Cooke. 'Quite a shower of small stones fell down just as I was turning a corner on the path. Yes, one struck me on the shoulder quite sharply.'

Tea, coffee, biscuits and cakes despatched, everyone seemed somewhat dissociated and ill at ease. When a catastrophe has occurred, it is very difficult to know what is the proper way to meet it. Everyone had given their view, had expressed surprise and distress. They were now awaiting news and at the same time had a slight hankering after some form of sightseeing, some interest to carry them through the morning. Lunch would not be served until one o'clock and they really felt that to sit around and repeat their same remarks would be rather a gloomy business.

Miss Cooke and Miss Barrow rose as one woman and explained that it was necessary for them to do a little shopping. One or two things they needed, and they also wished to go to the post office and buy stamps.

'I want to send off one or two postcards. And I want to inquire about postal dues on a letter to China,' said Miss Barrow.

'And I want to match some wools,' said Miss Cooke. 'And also it seemed to me there was rather an interesting building on the other side of the Market Square.'

'I think it would do us all good to get out,' said Miss Barrow.

Colonel and Mrs Walker also rose, and suggested to Mr and Mrs Butler that they too might go out and see what there was to see. Mrs Butler expressed hopes of an antique shop.

'Only I don't really mean a real antique shop. More what you would call a junk shop. Sometimes you can pick up some really interesting things there.'

They all trooped out. Emlyn Price had already sidled

to the door and disappeared in pursuit of Joanna without troubling to use conversation to explain his departure. Mrs Riseley-Porter, having made a belated attempt to call her niece back, said she thought that at least the lounge would be rather more pleasant to sit in. Miss Lumley agreed—Mr Caspar escorted the ladies with the air of a foreign equerry.

Professor Wanstead and Miss Marple remained.

'I think myself,' said Professor Wanstead, addressing Miss Marple, 'that it would be pleasant to sit outside the hotel. There is a small terrace giving on the street. If I might persuade you?'

Miss Marple thanked him and rose to her feet. She had hardly exchanged a word so far with Professor Wanstead. He had several learned-looking books with him, one of which he was usually perusing; even in the coach he continued to try and read.

'But perhaps you too want to shop,' he said. 'For myself, I would prefer to wait somewhere peacefully for the return of Mrs Sandbourne. It is important, I think, that we should know exactly what we are in for.'

'I quite agree with you, as to that,' said Miss Marple. 'I did a certain amount of walking round the town yesterday and I don't feel any necessity to do so again today. I'd rather wait here in case there is anything I can do to help. Not that I suppose there is, but then, one never knows.'

They moved together through the hotel door and round the corner to where there was a little square of garden with a raised stone walk close to the wall of the hotel and on which there were various forms of basket chairs. There was no one there at the moment so they sat down. Miss Marple looked thoughtfully at her vis-à-vis. At his corrugated and wrinkled face, his bushy brows, his luxuriant head of grey hair. He walked with a slight stoop. He had an interesting face, Miss Marple decided. His voice was dry and caustic, a professional man of some kind, she thought.

'I am not wrong, am I,' said Professor Wanstead. 'You *are* Miss Jane Marple?'

'Yes, I am Jane Marple.'

She was slightly surprised, though for no particular reason.

Their party had not been long enough together for people to be identified by the other travellers. The last two nights she had not been with the rest of the party. It was quite natural.

'I thought so,' said Professor Wanstead, 'from a description I have had of you.'

'A description of me?' Miss Marple was again slightly surprised.

'Yes, I had a description of you——' he paused for a moment. His voice was not exactly lowered, but it lost volume, although she could still hear it quite easily. '——from Mr Rafiel.'

'Oh,' said Miss Marple, startled. 'From Mr Rafiel.'

'You are surprised?'

'Well, yes, I am rather.'

'I don't know that you should be.'

'I didn't expect——' began Miss Marple and then stopped.

Professor Wanstead did not speak. He was merely sitting, looking at her intently. In a minute or two, thought Miss Marple to herself, he will say to me, 'What symptoms exactly, dear lady? Any discomfort in swallowing? Any lack of sleep? Digestion in good order?' She was almost sure now that he was a doctor.

'When did he describe me to you? That must have been——'

'You were going to say some time ago—some weeks ago. Before his death—that is so. He told me that you would be on this tour.'

116

'And he knew that you would be on it too—that you were going on it.'

'You can put it that way,' said Professor Wanstead. 'He said,' he continued, 'that you would be travelling on this tour, that he had in fact arranged for you to be travelling on this tour.'

'It was very kind of him,' said Miss Marple. 'Very kind indeed. I was most surprised when I found he'd booked me. Such a treat. Which I could not have afforded for myself.'

'Yes,' said Professor Wanstead. 'Very well put.' He nodded his head as one who applauds a good performance by a pupil.

'It is sad that it has been interrupted in this fashion,' said Miss Marple. 'Very sad indeed. When I am sure we were all enjoying ourselves so much.'

'Yes,' said Professor Wanstead. 'Yes, very sad. And unexpected, do you think, or not unexpected?'

'Now what do you mean by that, Professor Wanstead?'

His lips curled in a slight smile as he met her challenging look.

'Mr Rafiel,' he said, 'spoke to me about you at some length, Miss Marple. He suggested that I should be on this tour with you. I should in due course almost certainly make your acquaintance, since members in a tour inevitably do make each other's acquaintance, though it usually takes a day or two for them to split up, as it were, into possible groupings led by similar tastes or interests. And he further suggested to me that I should, shall we say, keep an eye on you.'

'Keep an eye on me?' said Miss Marple, showing some slight displeasure. 'And for what reason?'

'I think reasons of protection. He wanted to be quite sure that nothing should happen to you.'

'Happen to me? What should happen to me, I should like to know?'

'Possibly what happened to Miss Elizabeth Temple,' said Professor Wanstead.

Joanna Crawford came round the corner of the hotel. She was carrying a shopping basket. She passed them, nodding a little, she looked towards them with slight curiosity and went on down the street. Professor Wanstead did not speak until she had gone out of sight.

'A nice girl,' he said, 'at least I think so. Content at present to be a beast of burden to an autocratic aunt, but I have no doubt will reach the age of rebellion fairly soon.'

'What did you mean by what you said just now?' said Miss Marple, uninterested for the moment in Joanna's possible rebellion.

'That is a question which, perhaps, owing to what has happened we shall have to discuss.'

'You mean because of the accident?'

'Yes. If it was an accident.'

'Do you think it *wasn't* an accident?'

'Well, I think it's just possible. That's all.'

'I don't of course know anything about it,' said Miss Marple, hesitating.

'No. You were absent from the scene. You were—shall I put it this way—were you just possibly on duty elsewhere?'

Miss Marple was silent for a moment. She looked at Professor Wanstead once or twice and then she said:

'I don't think I know exactly what you mean.'

'You are being careful. You are quite right to be careful.'

'I have made it a habit,' said Miss Marple.

'To be careful?'

'I should not put it exactly like that, but I have made a point of being always ready to disbelieve as well as believe anything that is told to me.'

'Yes, and you are quite right too. You don't know anything about me. You know my name from the

118

passenger list of a very agreeable tour visiting castles and historic houses and splendid gardens. Possibly the gardens are what will interest you most.'

'Possibly.'

'There are other people here too who are interested in gardens.'

'Or profess to be interested in gardens.'

'Ah,' said Professor Wanstead. 'You, also, have noticed that.'

He went on, 'Well, it was my part, or at any rate to begin with, to observe you, to watch what you were doing, to be near at hand in case there was any possibility of— well, we might call it roughly—dirty work of any kind. But things are slightly altered now. You must make up your mind if I am your enemy or your ally.'

'Perhaps you are right,' said Miss Marple. 'You put it very clearly but you have not given me any information about yourself yet on which to judge. You were a friend, I presume, of the late Mr Rafiel?'

'No,' said Professor Wanstead, 'I was not a friend of Mr Rafiel. I had met him once or twice. Once on a committee of a hospital, once at some other public event. I knew about him. He, I gather, also knew about me. If I say to you, Miss Marple, that I am a man of some eminence in my own profession, you may think me a man of bounding conceit.'

'I don't think so,' said Miss Marple. 'I should say, if you say that about yourself, that you are probably speaking the truth. You are, perhaps, a medical man.'

'Ah. You are perceptive, Miss Marple. Yes, you are quite perceptive. I have a medical degree, but I have a speciality too. I am a pathologist and psychologist. I don't carry credentials about with me. You will probably have to take my word up to a certain point, though I can show you letters addressed to me, and possibly official documents that might convince you. I undertake mainly

119

specialist work in connection with medical jurisprudence. To put it in perfectly plain everyday language, I am interested in the different types of criminal brain. That has been a study of mine for many years. I have written books on the subject, some of them violently disputed, some of them which have attracted adherence to my ideas. I do not do very arduous work nowadays, I spend my time mainly writing up my subject, stressing certain points that have appealed to me. From time to time I come across things that strike me as interesting. Things that I want to study more closely. This I am afraid must seem rather tedious to you.'

'Not at all,' said Miss Marple. 'I am hoping perhaps, from what you are saying now, that you will be able to explain to me certain things which Mr Rafiel did not see fit to explain to me. He asked me to embark upon a certain project but he gave me no useful information on which to work. He left me to accept it and to proceed, as it were, completely in the dark. It seemed to me extremely foolish of him to treat the matter in that way.'

'But you accepted it?'

'I accepted it. I will be quite honest with you. I had a financial incentive.'

'Did that weigh with you?'

Miss Marple was silent for a moment and then she said slowly,

'You may not believe it, but my answer to that is, "Not really".'

'I am not surprised. But your interest was aroused. That is what you are trying to tell me.'

'Yes. My interest was aroused. I had known Mr Rafiel not well, casually, but for a certain period of time—some weeks in fact—in the West Indies. I see you know about it, more or less.'

'I know that that was where Mr Rafiel met you and where—shall I say—you two collaborated.'

Miss Marple looked at him rather doubtfully. 'Oh,' she said, 'he said that, did he?' She shook her head.

'Yes, he did,' said Professor Wanstead. 'He said you had a remarkable flair for criminal matters.'

Miss Marple raised her eyebrows as she looked at him.

'And I suppose that seems to you most unlikely,' she said. 'It surprises you.'

'I seldom allow myself to be surprised at what happens,' said Professor Wanstead. 'Mr Rafiel was a very shrewd and astute man, a good judge of people. He thought that you, too, were a good judge of people.'

'I would not set myself up as a good judge of people,' said Miss Marple. 'I would only say that certain people remind me of certain other people that I have known, and that therefore I can presuppose a certain likeness between the way they would act. If you think I know all about what I am supposed to be doing here, you are wrong.'

'By accident more than design,' said Professor Wanstead, 'we seem to have settled here in a particularly suitable spot for discussion of certain matters. We do not appear to be overlooked, we cannot easily be overheard, we are not near a window or a door and there is no balcony or window overhead. In fact, we can talk.'

'I should appreciate that,' said Miss Marple. 'I am stressing the fact that I am myself completely in the dark as to what I am doing or supposed to be doing. I don't know why Mr Rafiel wanted it that way.'

'I think I can guess that. He wanted you to approach a certain set of facts, of happenings, unbiased by what anyone would tell you first.'

'So you are not going to tell me anything, either?' Miss Marple sounded irritated. 'Really!' she said, 'there are limits.'

'Yes,' said Professor Wanstead. He smiled suddenly. 'I agree with you. We must do away with some of these limits. I am going to tell you certain facts that will make certain things fairly clear to you. You in turn may be able to tell me certain facts.'

'I rather doubt it,' said Miss Marple. 'One or two rather peculiar indications perhaps, but indications are not facts.'

'Therefore——' said Professor Wanstead, and paused.

'For goodness' sake, tell me something,' said Miss Marple.

12. A Consultation

'I'M NOT GOING to make a long story of things. I'll explain quite simply how I came into this matter. I act as confidential adviser from time to time for the Home Office. I am also in touch with certain institutions. There are certain establishments which, in the event of crime, provide board and lodging for certain types of criminal who have been found guilty of certain acts. They remain there at what is termed Her Majesty's pleasure, sometimes for a definite length of time and in direct association with their age. If they are below a certain age they have to be received in some place of detention specially indicated. You understand that, no doubt.'

'Yes, I understand quite well what you mean.'

'Usually I am consulted fairly soon after whatever the —shall we call it—crime has happened, to judge such matters as treatment, possibilities in the case, prognosis favourable or unfavourable, all the various words. They do not mean much and I will not go into them. But occasionally also I am consulted by a responsible Head of such an institution for a particular reason. In this matter I received a communication from a certain Department which was passed to me through the Home Office. I went to visit the Head of this institution. In fact, the Governor responsible for the prisoners or patients or whatever you like to call them. He was by way of being a friend of mine. A friend of fairly long standing though not one with whom I was on terms of great intimacy. I went down to the institution in question and the Governor laid his troubles before me. They referred to one particular inmate. He was not satisfied about this inmate. He had certain doubts. This was the case of a young man or one who had been a young man, in fact little more than a boy, when he came there. That was now several years ago. As time went on, and after the present Governor had taken up his own residence there (he had not been there at the original arrival of this prisoner), he became worried. Not because he himself was a professional man, but because he was a man of experience of criminal patients and prisoners. To put it quite simply, this had been a boy who from his early youth had been completely unsatisfactory. You can call it by what term you like. A young delinquent, a young thug, a bad lot, a person of diminished responsibility. There are many terms. Some of them fit, some of them don't fit, some of them are merely puzzling. He was a criminal type. That was certain. He had joined gangs, he had beaten up people, he was a thief, he had stolen, he had embezzled, he had taken part in swindles, he had initiated certain frauds. In fact, he was a son who would be any father's despair.'

'Oh, I see,' said Miss Marple.

'And what do you see, Miss Marple?'

'Well, what I think I see is that you are talking of Mr Rafiel's son.'

'You are quite right. I am talking of Mr Rafiel's son. What do you know about him?'

'Nothing,' said Miss Marple. 'I only heard—and that was yesterday—that Mr Rafiel had a delinquent, or unsatisfactory, if we like to put it mildly, son. A son with a criminal record. I know very little about him. Was he Mr Rafiel's only son?'

'Yes, he was Mr Rafiel's only son. But Mr Rafiel also had two daughters. One of them died when she was fourteen, the elder daughter married quite happily but had no children.'

'Very sad for him.'

'Possibly,' said Professor Wanstead. 'One never knows. His wife died young and I think it possible that *her* death saddened him very much, though he was never willing to show it. How much he cared for his son and daughters I don't know. He provided for them. He did his best for them. He did his best for this son, but what his feelings were one cannot say. He was not an easy man to read that way. I think his whole life and interest lay in his profession of making money. It was the making of it, like all great financiers, that interested him. Not the actual money which he secured by it. That, as you might say, was sent out like a good servant to earn more money in more interesting and unexpected ways. He enjoyed finance. He loved finance. He thought of very little else.

'I think he did all that was possible for his son. He got him out of scrapes at school, he employed good lawyers to get him released from Court proceedings whenever possible, but the final blow came, perhaps presaged by some earlier happenings. The boy was taken to Court on a charge of assault against a young girl. It was said to be assault and rape and he suffered a term of imprisonment for it, with some leniency shown because of his youth. But later, a second and really serious charge was brought against him.'

'He killed a girl,' said Miss Marple. 'Is that right? That's what I heard.'

'He lured a girl away from her home. It was some time before her body was found. She had been strangled. And afterwards her face and head had been disfigured by some heavy stones or rocks, presumably to prevent her identity being made known.'

'Not a very nice business,' said Miss Marple, in her most old-ladylike tone.

Professor Wanstead looked at her for a moment or two.

'You describe it that way?'

'It is how it seems to me,' said Miss Marple. 'I don't like that sort of thing. I never have. If you expect me to feel sympathy, regret, urge an unhappy childhood. blame bad environment; if you expect me in fact to weep over him, this young murderer of yours, I do not feel inclined so to do. I do not like evil beings who do evil things.'

'I am delighted to hear it,' said Professor Wanstead. 'What I suffer in the course of my profession from people weeping and gnashing their teeth, and blaming everything on some happening in the past, you would hardly believe. If people knew the bad environments that people have had, the unkindness, the difficulties of their lives and the fact that nevertheless they can come through unscathed, I don't think they would so often take the opposite point of view. The misfits are to be pitied, yes, they are to be pitied if I may say so for the genes with which they are born and over which they have no control themselves. I pity epileptics in the same way. If you know what genes are——'

'I know, more or less,' said Miss Marple. 'It's common knowledge nowadays, though naturally I have no exact chemical or technical knowledge.'

'The Governor, a man of experience, told me exactly why he was so anxious to have my verdict. He had felt increasingly in his experience of this particular inmate that, in plain words, the boy was *not* a killer. He didn't think he was the type of a killer, he was like no killer he had ever seen before, he was of the opinion that the boy was the kind of criminal type who would never go straight no matter what treatment was given to him, would never reform himself; and for whom nothing in one sense of the word could be done, but at the same time he felt increasingly certain that the verdict upon him had been a wrong one.

'He did not believe that the boy had killed a girl, first strangled her and then disfigured her after rolling her body into a ditch. He just couldn't bring himself to believe it. He'd looked over the facts of the case, which seemed to be fully proved. This boy had known the girl, he had been seen with her on several different occasions before the crime. They had presumably slept together and there were other points. His car had been seen in the neighbourhood. He himself had been recognized and all the rest of it. A perfectly fair case. But my friend was unhappy about it, he said. He was a man who had a very strong feeling for justice. He wanted a different opinion. He wanted, in fact, not the police side which he knew, he wanted a professional medical view. That was my field, he said. My line of country entirely. He wanted me to see this young man and talk with him, visit him, make a professional appraisal of him and give him my opinion.'

'Very interesting,' said Miss Marple. 'Yes, I call that very interesting. After all, your friend—I mean your Governor—was a man of experience, a man who loved justice. He was a man whom you'd be willing to listen to. Presumably then, you did listen to him.'

'Yes,' said Professor Wanstead, 'I was deeply interested. I saw the subject, as I will call him, I approached him from several different attitudes. I talked to him, I discussed various changes likely to occur in the law. I told him it might be possible to bring down a lawyer, a Queen's Counsel, to see what points there might be in his favour, and other things. I approached him as a friend but also as an enemy so that I could see how he responded to different approaches, and I also made a good many physical tests, such as we use very frequently nowadays. I will not go into those with you because they are wholly technical.'

'Then what did you think in the end?'

'I thought,' said Professor Wanstead, 'I thought my friend was likely to be right. I did not think that Michael Rafiel was a murderer.'

'What about the earlier case you mentioned?'

'That told against him, of course. Not in the jury's mind, because of course they did not hear about that until after the judge's summing up, but certainly in the judge's mind. It told against him, but I made a few inquiries myself afterwards. He had assaulted a girl. He had conceivably raped her, but he had not attempted to strangle her and in my opinion—I have seen a great many cases which come before the Assizes—it seemed to me highly unlikely that there was a very definite case of rape. Girls, you must remember, are far more ready to be raped nowadays than they used to be. Their mothers insist, very often, that they should call it rape. The girl in question had had several boy-friends who had gone further than friendship. I did not think it counted very greatly as evidence against him. The actual murder case—yes, that was undoubtedly murder—but I continued to feel by all tests, physical tests, mental tests, psychological tests, none of them accorded with this particular crime.'

'Then what did you do?'

'I communicated with Mr Rafiel. I told him that I would like an interview with him on a certain matter concerning his son. I went to him. I told him what I thought, what the Governor thought, that we had no evidence, that there were no grounds of appeal, at present, but that we both believed that a miscarriage of justice had been committed. I said I thought possibly an inquiry might be held, it might be an expensive business, it might bring out certain facts that could be laid before the Home Office, it might be successful, it might not. There might be something there, some evidence if you looked for it. I said it would be expensive to look for it but I presumed that would make no difference to anyone in his position. I had realized by that time that he was a sick man, a very ill man. He told me so himself. He told me that he had been in expectation of an early death, that he'd been warned two years ago that death could not be delayed for what they first thought was about a year, but later they realized that he would last rather longer because of his unusual physical strength. I asked him what he felt about his son.'

'And what did he feel about his son?' inquired Miss Marple.

'Ah, you want to know that. So did I. He was, I think, extremely honest with me even if——'

'——even if rather ruthless?' said Miss Marple.

'Yes, Miss Marple. You are using the right word. He was a ruthless man, but he was a just man and an honest man. He said, "I've known what my son was like for many years. I have not tried to change him because I don't believe that anyone could change him. He is made a certain way. He is crooked. He's a bad lot. He'll always be in trouble. He's dishonest. Nobody, nothing could make him go straight. I am well assured of that. I have in a sense washed my hands of him. Though not legally or outwardly; he has always had money if he required it. Help legal or otherwise if he gets into trouble. I have done always what I could do. Well, let us say if I had a son who was a spastic, who was sick, who was epileptic, I would do what I could for him. If you have a son who is sick morally, shall we say, and for whom there is no cure, I have done what I could also. No more and no less. What can I do for him now?" I told him that it depended what he wanted to do. "There's no difficulty about that," he said. "I am handicapped but I can see quite clearly what I want to do. I want to get him vindicated. I want to get him released from confinement. I want to get him free to continue to lead his own life as best he can lead it. If he must lead it in further dishonesties, then he must lead it that way. I will leave provision for him, to do for him everything that can be done. I don't want him suffering, imprisoned, cut off from his life because of a perfectly natural and unfortunate mistake. If somebody else, some other man killed that girl, I want the fact brought to light and recognized. I want justice for Michael. But I am handicapped. I am a very ill man. My time is measured now not in years or months but in weeks."

'Lawyers, I suggested—I know a firm—— He cut me short. "Your lawyers will be useless. You can employ them but they will be useless. I must arrange what I can arrange in such a limited time." He offered me a large fee to undertake the search for the truth and to undertake everything possible with no expense spared. "I can do next to nothing myself. Death may come at any moment. I empower you as my chief help, and to assist you at my request I will try to find a certain person." He wrote down a name for me. Miss Jane Marple. He said "I don't want to give you her address. I want you to meet her in surroundings of my own choosing," and he then told me of this tour, this charming, harmless, innocent tour of historic houses, castles and gardens. He would provide me with a reservation on it ahead for a certain date. "Miss Jane Marple," he said, "will also be on that tour. You will meet her there, you will encounter her casually, and thus it will be seen clearly to be a casual meeting."

'I was to choose my own time and moment to make myself known to you, if I thought it advisable; or not to make myself known to you if I thought that that would be the better way. You have already asked me if I or my friend, the Governor, had any reason to suspect or know of any other person who might have been guilty of the murder. My friend the Governor certainly suggested nothing of the kind, and he had already taken up the matter with the police officer who had been in charge of the case. A most reliable detective-superintendent with very good experience in these matters.'

'No other man was suggested? No other friend of the girl's? No other former friend who might have been supplanted?'

'There was nothing of that kind to find. I asked him to tell me a little about you. He did not however consent to do so. He told me you were elderly. He told me that you were a person who knew about people. He told me one other thing.' He paused.

'What's the other thing?' said Miss Marple. 'I have some natural curiosity, you know. I really can't think of any other advantage I conceivably could have. I am slightly deaf. My eyesight is not quite as good as it used to be. I cannot really think that I have any advantages beyond the fact that I may, I suppose, seem rather foolish and simple, and am in fact, what used to be called in rather earlier days an "old pussy". I *am* an old pussy. Is that the sort of thing he said?'

'No,' said Professor Wanstead. 'What he said was he thought you had a very fine sense of evil.'

'Oh,' said Miss Marple. She was taken aback.

Professor Wanstead was watching her.

'Would you say that was true?' he said.

Miss Marple was quiet for quite a long time. At last she said,

'Perhaps it is. Yes, perhaps. I have at several different times in my life been apprehensive, have recognized that there was evil in the neighbourhood, the surroundings, that the environment of someone who was evil was near me, connected with what was happening.'

She looked at him suddenly and smiled.

'It's rather, you know,' she said, 'like being born with a very keen sense of smell. You can smell a leak of gas when other people can't do so. You can distinguish one perfume from another very easily. I had an aunt once,' continued Miss Marple thoughtfully, 'who said she could smell when people told a lie. She said there was quite a distinctive odour came to her. Their noses twitched, she said, and then the smell came. I don't know if it was true or not, but—well, on several occasions she was quite remarkable. She said to my uncle once, "Don't, Jack, engage that young man you were talking to this morning.

He was telling you lies the whole time he was talking." That turned out to be quite true.'

'A sense of evil,' said Professor Wanstead. 'Well, if you do sense evil, tell me. I shall be glad to know. I don't think I have a particular sense of evil myself. Ill-health, yes, but not—not evil up here.' He tapped his forehead.

'I'd better tell you briefly how I came into things now,' said Miss Marple. 'Mr Rafiel, as you know, died. His lawyers asked me to come and see them, apprised me of his proposition. I received a letter from him which explained nothing. After that I heard nothing more for some little time. Then I got a letter from the company who run these tours saying that Mr Rafiel before his death had made a reservation for me knowing that I should enjoy a trip very much, and wanting to give it me as a surprise present. I was very astonished but took it as an indication of the first step that I was to undertake. I was to go on this tour and presumably in the course of the tour some other indication or hint or clue or direction would come to me. I think it did. Yesterday, no, the day before, I was received on my arrival here by three ladies who live at an old manor house here and who very kindly extended an invitation to me. They had heard from Mr Rafiel, they said, who had written some time before his death, saying that a very old friend of his would be coming on this tour and would they be kind enough to put her up for two or three days as he thought she was not fit to attempt the particular ascent of this rather difficult climb up the head-land to where there was a memorial tower which was the principal event of yesterday's tour.'

'And you took that also as an indication of what you were to do?'

'Of course,' said Miss Marple. 'There can be no other reason for it. He was not a man to shower benefits for nothing, out of compassion for an old lady who wasn't good at walking up hills. No. He *wanted* me to go there.'

'And you went there? And what then?'

'Nothing,' said Miss Marple. 'Three sisters.'

'Three weird sisters?'

'They ought to have been,' said Miss Marple, 'but I don't think they were. They didn't seem to be, anyway. I don't know yet. I suppose they may have been—they may be, I mean. They seem ordinary enough. They didn't belong to this house. It had belonged to an uncle of theirs and they'd come here to live some years ago. They are in rather poor circumstances, they are amiable, not particularly interesting. All slightly different in type. They do not appear to have been well acquainted with Mr Rafiel. Any conversation I have had with them appears to yield nothing.'

'So you learnt nothing during your stay?'

'I learnt the facts of the case you've just told me. Not from them. From an elderly servant, who started her reminiscences dating back to the time of the uncle. She knew of Mr Rafiel only as a name. But she was eloquent on the theme of the murder, it had all started with the visit here of a son of Mr Rafiel's who was a bad lot, of how the girl had fallen in love with him and that he'd strangled the girl, and how sad and tragic and terrible it all was. "With bells on," as you might say,' said Miss Marple, using a phrase of her youth. 'Plenty of exaggeration, but it was a nasty story, and she seemed to believe that the police view was that this hadn't been his only murder.'

'It didn't seem to you to connect up with the three weird sisters?'

'No, only that they'd been the guardians of the girl— and had loved her dearly. No more than that.'

'They might know something—something about another man?'

'Yes—that's what we want, isn't it? The other man— a man of brutality, who wouldn't hesitate to bash in a girl's head after he'd killed her. The kind of man who could be driven frantic with jealousy. There are men like that.'

'No other curious things happened at The Old Manor?'

'Not really. One of the sisters, the youngest I think, kept talking about the garden. She sounded as though she was a very keen gardener, but she couldn't be because she didn't know the names of half the things. I laid a trap or two for her, mentioning special rare shrubs and saying did she know it? and yes, she said, wasn't it a wonderful plant? I said it was not very hardy and she agreed. But she didn't know anything about plants. That reminds me——'

'Reminds you of what?'

'Well, you'll think I'm just silly about gardens and plants, but I mean one does *know* things about them. I mean, I know a few things about birds and I know some things about gardens.'

'And I gather that it's not birds but gardens that are troubling you.'

'Yes. Have you noticed two middle-aged women on this tour? Miss Barrow and Miss Cooke.'

'Yes. I've noticed them. Pair of middle-aged spinsters travelling together.'

'That's right. Well, I've found out something odd about Miss Cooke. That is her name, isn't it? I mean it's her name on the tour.'

'Why—has she got another name?'

'I think so. She's the same person who visited me—I won't say visited me exactly, but she was outside my garden fence in St Mary Mead, the village where I live. She expressed pleasure at my garden and talked about gardening with me. Told me she was living in the village and working in somebody's garden, who'd moved into a new house there. I rather think,' said Miss Marple, 'yes, I rather think that the whole thing was lies. There again, she knew nothing about gardening. She pretended to but it wasn't true.'

'Why do you think she came there?'

'I'd no idea at the time. She said her name was Bartlett —and the name of the woman she said she was living with began with "H", though I can't remember it for the moment. Her hair was not only differently done but it was a different colour and her clothes were of a different style. I didn't recognize her at first on this trip. Just wondered why her face was vaguely familiar. And then suddenly it came to me. Because of the dyed hair. I said where I had seen her before. She admitted that she'd been there—but pretended that she, too, hadn't recognized *me*. All lies.'

'And what's your opinion about all that?'

'Well, one thing certainly—Miss Cooke (to give her her present name) came to St Mary Mead just to have a look at me—so that she'd be quite sure to be able to recognize me when we met again——'

'And why was that felt to be necessary?'

'I don't know. There are two possibilities. I'm not sure that I like one of them very much.'

'I don't know,' said Professor Wanstead, 'that I like it very much either.'

They were both silent for a minute or two, and then Professor Wanstead said:

'I don't like what happened to Elizabeth Temple. You've talked to her during this trip?'

'Yes, I have. When she's better I'd like to talk to her again—she could tell me—us—things about the girl who was murdered. She spoke to me of this girl—who had been at her school, who had been going to marry Mr Rafiel's son—but didn't marry him. Instead she died. I asked how or why she died—and she answered with the word "Love". I took it as meaning a suicide—but it was murder. Murder through jealousy would fit. Another man. Some other man we've got to find. Miss Temple may be able to tell us who he was.'

'No other sinister possibilities?'

'I think, really, it is casual information we need. I see no reason to believe that there is any sinister suggestion in any of the coach passengers—or any sinister suggestion about the people living in The Old Manor House. But one of those three sisters may have known or remembered something that the girl or Michael once said. Clotilde used to take the girl abroad. Therefore, she may know of something that occurred on some foreign trip perhaps. Something that the girl said or mentioned or did on some trip. Some man that the girl met. Something which has nothing to do with The Old Manor House here. It is difficult because only by talking, by casual information, can you get any clue. The second sister, Mrs Glynne, married fairly early, has spent time, I gather, in India and in Africa. She may have heard of something through her husband, or through her husband's relations, through various things that are unconnected with The Old Manor House here although she has visited it from time to time. She knew the murdered girl presumably, but I should think she knew her much less well than the other two. But that does not mean that she may not know some significant *facts* about the girl. The third sister is more scatty, more localized, does not seem to have known the girl as well. But still, she too *may* have information about possible lovers—or boy-friends—or may have seen the girl with an unknown man. That's her, by the way, passing the hotel now.'

Miss Marple, however occupied by her tête-à-tête, had not relinquished the habits of a lifetime. A public thoroughfare was always to her an observation post. All the passers-by, either loitering or hurrying, had been noticed automatically.

'Anthea Bradbury-Scott—the one with the big parcel.

She's going to the post office, I suppose. It's just round the corner, isn't it?'

'Looks a bit daft to me,' said Professor Wanstead, 'all that floating hair—grey hair too—a kind of Ophelia of fifty.'

'I thought of Ophelia too, when I first saw her. Oh dear, I wish I knew what I ought to do next. Stay here at the Golden Boar for a day or two, or go on with the coach tour. It's like looking for a needle in a haystack. If you stick your fingers in it long enough, you ought to come up with something—even if one does get pricked in the process.'

13. Black and Red Check

MRS SANDBOURNE returned just as the party was sitting down to lunch. Her news was not good. Miss Temple was still unconscious. She certainly could not be moved for several days.

Having given the bulletin, Mrs Sandbourne turned the conversation to practical matters. She produced suitable time-tables of trains for those who wished to return to London and proposed suitable plans for the resumption of the tour on the morrow or the next day. She had a list of suitable short expeditions in the near neighbourhood for this afternoon—small groups in hired cars.

Professor Wanstead drew Miss Marple aside as they went out of the dining-room.

'You may want to rest this afternoon. If not, I will call for you here in an hour's time. There is an interesting church you might care to see——?'

'That would be very nice,' said Miss Marple.

2

Miss Marple sat quite still in the car that had come to fetch her. Professor Wanstead had called for her at the time he had said.

'I thought you might enjoy seeing this particular church. And a very pretty village, too,' he explained. 'There's no reason really why one should not enjoy the local sights when one can.'

'It's very kind of you, I'm sure,' Miss Marple had said. She had looked at him with that slightly fluttery gaze of hers.

'*Very* kind,' she said. 'It just seems—well, I don't want

to say it seems heartless, but well, you know what I mean.'

'My dear lady, Miss Temple is not an old friend of yours or anything like that. Sad as this accident has been.'

'Well,' said Miss Marple again, 'this is very kind of you.'

Professor Wanstead had opened the door of the car and Miss Marple got into it. It was, she presumed, a hired car. A kindly thought to take an elderly lady to see one of the sights of the neighbourhood. He might have taken somebody younger, more interesting and certainly better looking. Miss Marple looked at him thoughtfully once or twice as they drove through the village. He was not looking at her. He was gazing out of his own window.

When they had left the village behind and were on a second class country road twisting round the hillside, he turned his head and said to her,

'We are not going to a church, I am afraid.'

'No,' said Miss Marple, 'I thought perhaps we weren't.'

'Yes, the idea would have come to you.'

'Where are we going, may I ask?'

'We are going to a hospital, in Carristown.'

'Ah yes, that was where Miss Temple was taken?'

It was a question, though it hardly needed to be one.

'Yes,' he said. 'Mrs Sandbourne saw her and brought me back a letter from the Hospital Authorities. I have just finished talking to them on the telephone.'

'Is she going on well?'

'No. Not going on very well.'

'I see. At least—I hope I don't see,' said Miss Marple.

'Her recovery is very problematical but there is nothing that can be done. She may not recover consciousness again. On the other hand, she may have a few lucid intervals.'

'And you are taking *me* there? Why? I am not a friend of hers, you know. I only just met her for the first time on this trip.'

'Yes, I realize that. I'm taking you there because in one of the lucid intervals she has had, she asked for **you.**'

'I see,' said Miss Marple. 'I wonder why she should ask for *me*, why she should have thought that I—that I could be useful in any way to her, or do anything. She is a woman of perception. In her way, you know, a great woman. As Headmistress of Fallowfield she occupied a prominent position in the educational world.'

'The best girls' school there is, I suppose?'

'Yes. She was a great personality. She was herself a woman of considerable scholarship. Mathematics were her speciality, but she was an "all round"—what I should call an educator. Was interested in education, what girls were fitted for, how to encourage them. Oh, many other things. It is sad and very cruel if she dies,' said Miss Marple. 'It will seem such a waste of a life. Although she had retired from her Headmistress-ship she still exercised a lot of power. This accident——' She stopped. 'Perhaps you do not want us to discuss the accident?'

'I think it is better that we should do so. A big boulder crashed down the hillside. It has been known to happen before though only at very long divided intervals of time. However, somebody came and spoke to me about it,' said Professor Wanstead.

'Came and spoke to you about the accident? Who was it?'

'The two young people. Joanna Crawford and Emlyn Price.'

'What did they say?'

'Joanna told me that she had the impression there was someone on the hillside. Rather high up. She and Emlyn were climbing up from the lower main path, following a rough track that wound round the curve of the hill. As they turned a corner she definitely saw, outlined against the skyline, a man or a woman who was trying to roll a big boulder forward along the ground. The boulder was rocking—and finally it started to roll, at first slowly and then gathering speed down the hillside. Miss Temple was walking along the main path below, and had come to a point just underneath it when the boulder hit her. If it was done deliberately it might not, of course, have succeeded; it might have missed her—but it did succeed. If what was being attempted was a deliberate attack on the woman walking below it succeeded only too well.'

'Was it a man or a woman they saw?' asked Miss Marple.

'Unfortunately, Joanna Crawford could not say. Whoever it was, was wearing jeans or trousers, and had on a lurid polo-neck pullover in red and black checks. The figure turned and moved out of sight almost immediately. She is inclined to think it was a man but cannot be certain.'

'And she thinks, or you think, that it was a deliberate attempt on Miss Temple's life?'

'The more she mulls it over, the more she thinks that that was exactly what it was. The boy agrees.'

'You have no idea who it might have been?'

'No idea whatever. No more have they. It might be one of our fellow travellers, someone who went for a stroll that afternoon. It might be someone completely unknown who knew that the coach was making a halt here and chose this place to make an attack on one of the passengers. Some youthful lover of violence for violence's sake. Or it might have been an enemy.'

'It seems very melodramatic if one says "a secret enemy",' said Miss Marple.

'Yes, it does. Who would want to kill a retired and respected Headmistress? That is a question we want answered. It is possible, faintly possible that Miss Temple herself might be able to tell us. She might have recognized the figure above her or she might more likely have known of someone who bore her ill-will for some special reason.'

'It still seems unlikely.'

'I agree with you,' said Professor Wanstead. 'She seems

a totally unlikely person to be a fit victim of attack, but yet when one reflects, a Headmistress knows a great many people. A great many people, shall we put it this way, have passed through her hands.'

'A lot of girls you mean have passed through her hands.'

'Yes. Yes, that is what I meant. Girls and their families. A Headmistress must have knowledge of many things. Romances, for instance, that girls might indulge in, unknown to their parents. It happens, you know. It happens very often. Especially in the last ten or twenty years. Girls are said to mature earlier. That is physically true, though in a deeper sense of the word, they mature late. They remain childish longer. Childish in the clothes they like to wear, childish with their floating hair. Even their mini skirts represent a worship of childishness. Their Baby Doll nightdresses, their gym-slips and shorts—all children's fashions. They wish *not* to become adult—*not* to have to accept our kind of responsibility. And yet like all children, they want to be *thought* grown up, and free to do what they think are grown up things. And that leads sometimes to tragedy and sometimes to the aftermath of tragedy.'

'Are you thinking of some particular case?'

'No. No, not really. I'm only thinking—well, shall we say letting possibilities pass through my mind. I cannot believe that Elizabeth Temple had a *personal* enemy. An enemy ruthless enough to wish to take an opportunity of killing her. What I do think—' he looked at Miss Marple, '—would you like to make a suggestion?'

'Of a possibility? Well, I think I know or guess what you *are* suggesting. You are suggesting that Miss Temple knew something, knew some fact or had some knowledge that would be inconvenient or even dangerous to somebody if it was known.'

'Yes, I do feel exactly that.'

'In that case,' said Miss Marple, 'it seems indicated that there is someone on our coach tour who recognized Miss

Temple or knew who she was, but who perhaps after the passage of some years was not remembered or might even not have been recognized by Miss Temple. It seems to throw it back on our passengers, does it not?' She paused. 'That pullover you mentioned—red and black checks, you said?'

'Oh yes? The pullover——' He looked at her curiously. 'What was it that struck you about that?'

'It was very noticeable,' said Miss Marple. 'That is what your words led me to infer. It was very mentionable. So much so that the girl Joanna mentioned it specifically.'

'Yes. And what does that suggest to you?'

'The trailing of flags,' said Miss Marple thoughtfully. 'Something that will be seen, remembered, observed, recognized.'

'Yes.' Professor Wanstead looked at her with encouragement.

'When you describe a person you have seen, seen not close at hand but from a distance, the first thing you will describe will be their clothes. Not their faces, not their walk, not their hands, not their feet. A scarlet tam-o'-shanter, a purple cloak, a bizarre leather jacket, a pullover of brilliant reds and blacks. Something very recognizable, very noticeable. The object of it being that when that person removes that garment, gets rid of it, sends it by post in a parcel to some address, say, about a hundred miles away, or thrusts it in a rubbish bin in a city or burns it or tears it up or destroys it, she or he will be the one person modestly and rather drably attired who will not be suspected or looked at or thought of. It must have been *meant*, that scarlet and black check jersey. Meant so that it will be recognized again though actually it will never again be seen on that particular person.'

'A very sound idea,' said Professor Wanstead. 'As I have told you,' continued the Professor, 'Fallowfield is situated not very far from here. Sixteen miles, I think. So this is

Elizabeth Temple's part of the world, a part she knows well with people in it that she also might know well.'

'Yes. It widens the possibilities,' said Miss Marple. 'I agree with you,' she said presently, 'that the attacker is more likely to have been a man than a woman. That boulder, if it was done with intent, was sent on its course very accurately. Accuracy is more a male quality than a female one. On the other hand there might easily have been someone on our coach, or possibly in the neighbourhood, who saw Miss Temple in the street, a former pupil of hers in past years. Someone whom she herself might not recognize after a period of time. But the girl or woman would have recognized her, because a Headmaster or Headmistress of over sixty is not unlike the same Headmaster or Headmistress at the age of fifty. She is recognizable. Some woman who recognized her former mistress and also knew that her mistress knew something damaging about her. Someone who might in some way prove a danger to her.' She sighed. 'I myself do not know this part of the world at all. Have you any particular knowledge of it?'

'No,' said Professor Wanstead. 'I could not claim a personal knowledge of this part of the country. I know something, however, of various things that have happened in this part of the world entirely because of what you have told me. If it had not been for my acquaintanceship with you and the things you have told me I should have been more at sea than I am.

'What are you yourself actually doing here? You do not know. Yet you were sent here. It was deliberately arranged by Rafiel that you should come here, that you should take this coach tour, that you and I should meet. There have been other places where we have stopped or through which we have passed, but special arrangements here were made so that you should actually stay for a couple of nights here. You were put up with former friends of his who would not

144

have refused any request he made. Was there a reason for that?'

'So that I could learn certain facts that I had to know,' said Miss Marple.

'A series of murders that took place a good many years ago?' Professor Wanstead looked doubtful. 'There is nothing unusual in that. You can say the same of many places in England and Wales. These things seem always to go in a series. First a girl found assaulted and murdered. Then another girl not very far away. Then something of the same kind perhaps twenty miles away. The same pattern of death.

'Two girls were reported missing from Jocelyn St Mary itself, the one that we have been discussing whose body was found six months later, many miles away and who was last seen in the company of Michael Rafiel——'

'And the other?'

'A girl called Nora Broad. *Not* a "quiet girl with no boy-friends". Possibly with one boy-friend too many. Her body was never found. It will be—one day. There have been cases when twenty years have passed,' said Wanstead. He slowed down: 'We have arrived. This is Carristown, and here is the hospital.'

Shepherded by Professor Wanstead, Miss Marple entered. The Professor was obviously expected. He was ushered into a small room where a woman rose from a desk. 'Oh yes,' she said, 'Professor Wanstead. And—er— this is—er——' She hesitated slightly.

'Miss Jane Marple,' said Professor Wanstead. 'I talked to Sister Barker on the telephone.'

'Oh yes. Sister Barker said that she would be accompanying you.'

'How is Miss Temple?'

'Much the same, I think. I am afraid there is not much improvement to report.' She rose. 'I will take you to Sister Barker.'

Sister Barker was a tall, thin woman. She had a low, decisive voice and dark grey eyes that had a habit of looking at you and looking away almost immediately, leaving you with the feeling that you had been inspected in a very short space of time, and judgment pronounced upon you.

'I don't know what arrangements you have in mind,' said Professor Wanstead.

'Well, I had better tell Miss Marple just what we have arranged. First I must make it clear to you that the patient, Miss Temple, is still in a coma with very rare intervals. She appears to come to occasionally, to recognize her surroundings and to be able to say a few words. But there is nothing one can do to stimulate her. It has to be left to the utmost patience. I expect Professor Wanstead has already told you that in one of her intervals of consciousness she uttered quite distinctly the words "Miss Jane Marple". And then: "*I want to speak to her. Miss Jane Marple.*" After that she relapsed into unconsciousness. Doctor thought it advisable to get in touch with the other occupants of the coach. Professor Wanstead came to see us and explained various matters and said he would bring you over. I am afraid that all we can ask you to do is to sit in the private ward where Miss Temple is, and perhaps be ready to make a note of any words she should say, if she does regain consciousness. I am afraid the prognosis is not very helpful. To be quite frank, which is better I think, since you are not a near relative and are unlikely to be disturbed by this information, Doctor thinks that she is sinking fast, that she may die without recovering consciousness. There is nothing one can do to relieve the concussion. It is important that someone should hear what she says and Doctor thinks it advisable that she should not see too many people round her if she regains consciousness. If Miss Marple is not worried at the thought of sitting there alone, there will be a nurse in the room, though not obviously so. That is, she will not be noticed from the bed, and will not move unless she's asked for. She will sit in a corner of the room shielded by a screen.' She added, 'We have a police official there also, ready to take down anything. The Doctor thinks it advisable that he also should not be noticed by Miss Temple. One person alone, and that possibly a person she *expects* to see, will not alarm her or make her lose knowledge of what she wants to say to you. I hope this will not be too difficult a thing to ask you?'

'Oh no,' said Miss Marple, 'I'm quite prepared to do that. I have a small notebook with me and a Biro pen that will not be in evidence. I can remember things by heart for a very short time, so I need not appear to be obviously taking notes of what she says. You can trust my memory and I am not deaf—not deaf in the real sense of the word. I don't think my hearing is quite as good as it used to be, but if I am sitting near a bedside, I ought to be able to hear anything she says quite easily even if it is whispered. I am used to sick people. I have had a good deal to do with them in my time.'

Again the lightning glance of Sister Barker went over Miss Marple. This time a faint inclination of the head showed satisfaction.

'It is kind of you,' she said, 'and I am sure that if there is any help you can give, we can rely on you to give it. If Professor Wanstead likes to sit in the waiting-room downstairs, we can call him at any moment if it should be necessary. Now, Miss Marple, perhaps you will accompany me.'

Miss Marple followed Sister along a passage and into a small well appointed single room. In the bed there, in a dimly-lighted room since the blinds were half drawn, lay Elizabeth Temple. She lay there like a statue, yet she did not give the impression of being asleep. Her breath came uncertainly in slight gasps. Sister Barker bent to examine her patient, motioned Miss Marple into a chair beside the bed. She then crossed the room to the door again. A young man with a notebook in his hand came from behind the screen there.

'Doctor's orders, Mr Reckitt,' said Sister Barker.

A nurse also appeared. She had been sitting in the opposite corner of the room.

'Call me if necessary, Nurse Edmonds,' said Sister Barker, 'and get Miss Marple anything she may need.'

Miss Marple loosened her coat. The room was warm. The nurse approached and took it from her. Then she retired to her former position, Miss Marple sat down in the chair. She looked at Elizabeth Temple thinking, as she had thought before when looking at her in the coach, what a fine shaped head she had. Her grey hair drawn back from it, fitted her face in a perfect cap-like effect. A handsome woman, and a woman of personality. Yes, a thousand pities, Miss Marple thought, a thousand pities if the world was going to lose Elizabeth Temple.

Miss Marple eased the cushion at her back, moved the chair a fraction of an inch and sat quietly to wait. Whether to wait in vain or to some point, she had no idea. Time passed. Ten minutes, twenty minutes, half an hour, thirty-five minutes. Then suddenly, quite unexpectedly as it were, a voice came. Low, but distinct, slightly husky. None of the resonance it had once held.

'Miss Marple.'

Elizabeth Temple's eyes were open now. They were looking at Miss Marple. They looked competent, perfectly sensible. She was studying the face of the woman who was sitting by her bed, studying her without any sign of emotion, of surprise. Only, one would say, of scrutiny. Fully conscious scrutiny. And the voice spoke again.

'Miss Marple. You are Jane Marple?'

'That is right. Yes,' said Miss Marple, 'Jane Marple.'

'Henry often spoke of you. He said things about you.'

The voice stopped. Miss Marple said with a slight query in her voice, 'Henry?'

'Henry Clithering, an old friend of mine—very old friend.'

'An old friend of mine too,' said Miss Marple. 'Henry Clithering.'

Her mind went back to the many years she had known him, Sir Henry Clithering, the things he had said to her, the assistance he had asked from her sometimes, and the assistance that she had asked from him. A very old friend.

'I remembered your name. On the passenger list. I thought it must be you. You could help. That's what he—Henry, yes—would say if he were here. You might be able to help. To find out. It's important. Very important although—it's a long time ago now—a—long time—ago.'

Her voice faltered a little, her eyes half closed. Nurse got up, came across the room, picked up a small glass and held it to Elizabeth Temple's lips. Miss Temple took a sip, nodded her head dismissively. Nurse put down the glass and went back to her chair.

'If I can help, I will,' said Miss Marple. She asked no further questions.

Miss Temple said, 'Good,' and after a minute or two, again, 'Good.'

For two or three minutes she lay with her eyes closed. She might have been asleep or unconscious. Then her eyes opened again suddenly.

'Which,' she said, 'which of them? That's what one has got to know. Do you know what I am talking about?'

'I think so. A girl who died—Nora Broad?' A frown came quickly to Elizabeth Temple's forehead.

'No, no, no. The other girl. Verity Hunt.'

There was a pause and then, 'Jane Marple. You're old—older than when he talked about you. You're older, but you can still find out things, can't you?'

Her voice became slightly higher, more insistent.

'You can, can't you? Say you can. I've not much time. I know that. I know it quite well. One of them, but which? Find out. Henry would have said you can. It may be dangerous for you—but you'll find out, won't you?'

'With God's help, I will,' said Miss Marple. It was a vow.

'Ah.' The eyes closed, then opened again. Something like a smile seemed to try and twitch the lips.

'The big stone from above. The Stone of Death.'

'Who rolled that stone down?'

'Don't know. No matter—only—Verity. Find out about Verity. Truth. Another name for truth, Verity.'

Miss Marple saw the faint relaxation of the body on the bed. There was a faintly whispered: 'Goodbye. Do your best . . .'

Her body relaxed, the eyes closed. The nurse came again to the bedside. This time she took up the pulse, felt it, and beckoned to Miss Marple. Miss Marple rose obediently and followed her out of the room.

'That's been a big effort for her,' said the nurse. 'She won't regain consciousness again for some time. Perhaps not at all. I hope you learnt something?'

'I don't think I did,' said Miss Marple, 'but one never knows, does one?'

'Did you get anything?' asked Professor Wanstead, as they went out to the car.

'A name,' said Miss Marple. 'Verity. Was that the girl's name?'

'Yes. Verity Hunt.'

Elizabeth Temple died an hour and a half later. She died without regaining consciousness.

14. Mr Broadribb Wonders

'SEEN *The Times* this morning?' said Mr Broadribb to his partner, Mr Schuster.

Mr Schuster said he couldn't afford *The Times*, he took the *Telegraph*.

'Well, it may be in that, too,' said Mr Broadribb. 'In the deaths. Miss Elizabeth Temple, D.Sc.'

Mr Schuster looked faintly puzzled.

'Headmistress of Fallowfield. You've heard of Fallowfield, haven't you?'

'Of course,' said Schuster. 'Girls' school. Been going for fifty years or so. First class, fantastically expensive. So she was the headmistress of it, was she? I thought the headmistress had resigned some time ago. Six months at least. I'm sure I read about it in the paper. That is to say there was a bit about the new headmistress. Married woman. Youngish. Thirty-five to forty. Modern ideas. Give the girls lessons in cosmetics, let 'em wear trouser suits. Something of that kind.'

'Hum,' said Mr Broadribb, making the noise that solicitors of his age are likely to make when they hear something which elicits criticism based on long experience. 'Don't think she'll ever make the name that Elizabeth Temple did. Quite someone, she was. Been there a long time, too.'

'Yes,' said Mr Schuster, somewhat uninterested. He wondered why Broadribb was so interested in defunct schoolmistresses.

Schools were not really of particular interest to either of the two gentlemen. Their own offspring were now more or less disposed of. Mr Broadribb's two sons were respectively in the Civil Service and in an oil firm, and Mr Schuster's rather younger progeny were at different universities where both of them respectively were making as much trouble for those in authority as they possibly could do. He said:

'What about her?'

'She was on a coach tour,' said Mr Broadribb.

'Those coaches,' said Mr Schuster. 'I wouldn't let any of my relations go on one of those. One went off a precipice in Switzerland last week and two months ago one had a crash and twenty were killed. Don't know who drives these things nowadays.'

'It was one of those Country Houses and Gardens and Objects of Interest in Britain—or whatever they call it—tours,' said Mr Broadribb. 'That's not quite the right name, but you know what I mean.'

'Oh yes, I know. Oh the—er—yes, that's the one we sent Miss What's-a-name on. The one old Rafiel booked.'

'Miss Jane Marple was on it.'

'She didn't get killed too, did she?' asked Mr Schuster.

'Not so far as I know,' said Mr Broadribb. 'I just wondered a bit, though.'

'Was it a road accident?'

'No. It was at one of the beauty spot places. They were walking on a path up a hill. It was a stiff walk. Up a rather steep hill with boulders and things on it. Some of the boulders got loose and came rushing down the mountainside. Miss Temple was knocked out and taken to hospital with concussion and died——'

'Bad luck,' said Mr Schuster, and waited for more.

'I only wondered,' said Mr Broadribb, 'because I happened to remember that—well, that Fallowfield was the school where the girl was at.'

'What girl? I don't really know what you're talking about, Broadribb.'

'The girl who was done in by young Michael Rafiel. I was just recalling a few things which might seem to have

152

some slight connection with this curious Jane Marple business that old Rafiel was so keen on. Wish he'd told us more.'

'What's the connection?' said Mr Schuster.

He looked more interested now. His legal wits were in process of being sharpened, to give a sound opinion on whatever it was that Mr Broadribb was about to confide to him.

'That girl. Can't remember her last name now. Christian name was Hope or Faith or something like that. Verity, that was her name. Verity Hunter, I think it was. She was one of that series of murdered girls. Found her body in a ditch about thirty miles away from where she'd gone missing. Been dead six months. Strangled apparently, and her head and face had been bashed in—to delay recognition, they thought, but she *was* recognized all right. Clothes, handbag, jewellery nearby—some mole or scar. Oh yes, she was identified quite easily——'

'Actually, she was the one the trial was all about, wasn't she?'

'Yes. Suspected of having done away with perhaps three other girls during the past year, Michael was. But evidence wasn't so good in the other deaths—so the police went all out on this one—plenty of evidence—bad record. Earlier cases of assault and rape. Well, we all know what rape is nowadays. Mum tells the girl she's got to accuse the young man of rape even if the young man hasn't had much chance, with the girl at him all the time to come to the house while mum's away at work, or dad's gone on holiday. Doesn't stop badgering him until she's forced him to sleep with her. Then, as I say, mum tells the girl to call it rape. However, that's not the point,' said Mr Broadribb. 'I wondered if things mightn't tie up a bit, you know. I thought this Jane Marple business with Rafiel might have something to do with Michael.'

'Found guilty, wasn't he? And given a life sentence?'

'I can't remember now—it's so long ago. Or did they get away with a verdict of diminished responsibility?'

'And Verity Hunter or Hunt was educated at that school. Miss Temple's school? She wasn't still a schoolgirl though, was she, when she was killed? Not that I can remember.'

'Oh no. She was eighteen or nineteen, living with relations or friends of her parents, or something like that. Nice house, nice people, nice girl by all accounts. The sort of girl whose relations always say "she was a very quiet girl, rather shy, didn't go about with strange people and had no boy-friends." Relations never know what boy-friends a girl has. The girls take mighty good care of that. And young Rafiel was said to be very attractive to girls.'

'Never been any doubt that he did it?' asked Mr Schuster.

'Not a scrap. Told a lot of lies in the witness box, anyway. His Counsel would have done better not to have let him give evidence. A lot of his friends gave him an alibi that didn't stand up, if you know what I mean. All his friends seemed to be fluent liars.'

'What's your feeling about it, Broadribb?'

'Oh, I haven't got any feelings,' said Mr Broadribb, 'I was just wondering if this woman's death might tie up.'

'In what way?'

'Well, you know—about these boulders that fall down cliff sides and drop on top of someone. It's not always in the course of nature. Boulders usually stay where they are, in my experience.'

15. Verity

'VERITY,' said Miss Marple.

Elizabeth Margaret Temple had died the evening before. It had been a peaceful death. Miss Marple, sitting once more amidst the faded chintz of the drawing-room in The Old Manor House, had laid aside the baby's pink coat which she had previously been engaged in knitting and had substituted a crocheted purple scarf. This half-mourning touch went with Miss Marple's early Victorian ideas of tactfulness in face of tragedy.

An inquest was to be held on the following day. The vicar had been approached and had agreed to hold a brief memorial service in the church as soon as arrangements could be made. Undertakers suitably attired, with proper mourning faces, took general charge of things in liaison with the police. The inquest was to take place on the following morning at 11 o'clock. Members of the coach tour had agreed to attend the inquest. And several of them had chosen to remain on so as to attend the church service also.

Mrs Glynne had come to the Golden Boar and urged Miss Marple to return to The Old Manor House until she finally returned to the tour.

'You will get away from all the reporters.'

Miss Marple had thanked all three sisters warmly and had accepted.

The coach tour would be resumed after the memorial service, driving first to South Bedestone, thirty-five miles away, where there was a good class hotel which had been originally chosen for a stopping place. After that the tour would go on as usual.

There were, however, as Miss Marple had considered

likely, certain persons who were disengaging themselves and returning home, or were going in other directions and not continuing on the tour. There was something to be said in favour of either decision. To leave what would become a journey of painful memories, or to continue with the sightseeing that had already been paid for and which had been interrupted only by one of those painful accidents that may happen on any sightseeing expedition. A lot would depend, Miss Marple thought, on the outcome of the inquest.

Miss Marple, after exchanging various conventional remarks proper to the occasion with her three hostesses, had devoted herself to her purple wool and had sat considering her next line of investigation. And so it was that with her fingers still busy, she had uttered the one word, 'Verity'. Throwing it as one throws a pebble into a stream, solely to observe what the result—if any—would be. Would it mean something to her hostesses? It might or it might not. Otherwise, when she joined the members of the tour at their hotel meal this evening, which had been arranged, she would try the effect of it there. It had been, she thought to herself, the last word or almost the last word that Elizabeth Temple had spoken. So therefore, thought Miss Marple (her fingers still busy because she did not need to look at her crocheting, she could read a book or conduct a conversation while her fingers, though slightly crippled with rheumatism, would proceed correctly through their appointed movements). So therefore, 'Verity'.

Like a stone into a pool, causing ripples, a splash, something? Or nothing. Surely there would be a reaction of one sort or another. Yes, she had not been mistaken. Although her face registered nothing, the keen eyes behind her glasses had watched three people in a simultaneous manner as she had trained herself to do for many years now, when wishing to observe her neighbours either in church, mother's meetings, or at other public functions in St Mary Mead when she had been on the track of some interesting piece of news or gossip.

Mrs Glynne had dropped the book she was holding and had looked across towards Miss Marple with slight surprise. Surprise, it seemed, at the particular word coming from Miss Marple, but not surprised really to hear it.

Clotilde reacted differently. Her head shot up, she leant forward a little, then she looked not at Miss Marple but across the room in the direction of the window. Her hands clenched themselves, she kept very still. Miss Marple, although dropping her head slightly as though she was not looking any more, noted that her eyes were filling with tears. Clotilde sat quite still and let the tears roll down her cheeks. She made no attempt to take out a handkerchief, she uttered no word. Miss Marple was impressed by the aura of grief that came from her.

Anthea's reaction was different. It was quick, excited, almost pleasurable.

'Verity? Verity, did you say? Did you know her? I'd no idea. It is Verity Hunt you mean?'

Lavinia Glynne said, 'It's a Christian name?'

'*I* never knew anyone of that name,' said Miss Marple, 'but I *did* mean a Christian name. Yes. It is rather unusual, I think. Verity.' She repeated it thoughtfully.

She let her purple wool ball fall and looked round with the slightly apologetic and embarrassed look of one who realizes she has made a serious *faux pas*, but not sure why.

'I—I am so sorry. Have I said something I shouldn't? It was only because . . .'

'No, of course not,' said Mrs Glynne. 'It was just that it is—it is a name we know, a name with which we have—associations.'

'It just came into my mind,' said Miss Marple, still apologetic, 'because, you know, it was poor Miss Temple who said it. I went to see her, you know, yesterday afternoon. Professor Wanstead took me. He seemed to think that I might be able to—to—I don't know if it's the proper word—to *rouse* her, in some way. She was in a coma and they thought—not that I was a friend of hers at any time, but we had chatted together on the tour and we often sat beside each other, as you know, on some of the days and we had talked. And he thought perhaps I might be of some use. I'm afraid I wasn't though. Not at all. I just sat there and waited and then she did say one or two words, but they didn't seem to mean anything. But finally, just when it was time for me to go, she did open her eyes and looked at me—I don't know if she was mistaking me for someone—but she did say that word. Verity! And, well of course it stuck in my mind, especially with her passing away yesterday evening. It must have been some-one or something that she had in her mind. But of course it might just mean—well, of course it might just mean Truth. That's what verity means, doesn't it?'

She looked from Clotilde to Lavinia to Anthea.

'It was the Christian name of a girl we knew,' said Lavinia Glynne. 'That is why it startled us.'

'Especially because of the awful way she died,' said Anthea.

Clotilde said in her deep voice, 'Anthea! there's no need to go into these details.'

'But after all, everyone knows quite well about her,' said Anthea. She looked towards Miss Marple. 'I thought perhaps you might have known about her because you knew Mr Rafiel, didn't you? Well, I mean, he wrote to us about you so you must have known him. And I thought perhaps—well, he'd mentioned the whole thing to you.'

'I'm so sorry,' said Miss Marple, 'I'm afraid I don't quite understand what you're talking about.'

'They found her body in a ditch,' said Anthea.

There was never any holding Anthea, Miss Marple thought, not once she got going. But she thought that

Anthea's vociferous talk was putting additional strain on Clotilde. She had taken out a handkerchief now in a quiet, non-committal way. She brushed tears from her eyes and then sat upright, her back very straight, her eyes deep and tragic.

'Verity,' she said, 'was a girl we cared for very much. She lived here for a while. I was very fond of her——'

'And she was very fond of you,' said Lavinia.

'Her parents were friends of mine,' said Clotilde. 'They were killed in a plane accident.'

'She was at school at Fallowfield,' explained Lavinia. 'I suppose that was how Miss Temple came to remember her.'

'Oh I see,' said Miss Marple. 'Where Miss Temple was headmistress, is that it? I have heard of Fallowfield often, of course. It's a very fine school, isn't it?'

'Yes,' said Clotilde. 'Verity was a pupil there. After her parents died she came to stay with us for a time while she could decide what she wanted to do with her future. She was eighteen or nineteen. A very sweet girl and a very affectionate and loving one. She thought perhaps of training for nursing, but she had very good brains and Miss Temple was very insistent that she ought to go to university. So she was studying and having coaching for that when—when this terrible thing happened.'

She turned her face away.

'I—do you mind if we don't talk about it any more just now.'

'Oh, of course not,' said Miss Marple. 'I'm so sorry to have impinged on some tragedy. I didn't know. I—I haven't heard . . . I thought—well, I mean . . .' She became more and more incoherent.

That evening she heard a little more. Mrs Glynne came to her bedroom when she was changing her dress to go out and join the others at the hotel.

'I thought I ought to come and explain a little to you,' said Mrs Glynne, 'about—about the girl Verity Hunt. Of course you couldn't know that our sister Clotilde was particularly fond of her and that her really horrible death was a terrible shock. We never mention her if we can help it, but—I think it would be easier if I told you the facts completely and you will understand. Apparently Verity had, without our knowledge, made friends with an undesirable—a more than undesirable—it turned out to be a dangerous—young man who already had a criminal record. He came here to visit us when he was passing through once. We knew his father very well.' She paused. 'I think I'd better tell you the whole truth if you don't know, and you don't seem to. He was actually Mr Rafiel's son, Michael——'

'Oh dear,' said Miss Marple, 'not—not—I can't remember his name but I do remember hearing that there was a son—and, that he hadn't been very satisfactory.'

'A little more than that,' said Mrs Glynne. 'He'd always given trouble. He'd been had up in court once or twice for various things. Once assaulting a teenager—other things of that type. Of course I consider myself that the magistrates are too lenient with that kind of thing. They don't want to upset a young man's university career. And so they let them off with a—I forget what they call it—a suspended sentence, something of that kind. If these boys were sent to gaol at once it would perhaps warn them off that type of life. He was a thief, too. He had forged cheques, he pinched things. He was a thoroughly bad lot. We were friends of his mother's. It was lucky for her, I think, that she died young before she had time to be upset by the way her son was turning out. Mr Rafiel did all he could, I think. Tried to find suitable jobs for the boy, paid fines for him and things like that. But I think it was a great blow to him, though he pretended to be more or less indifferent and to write it off as one of those things that happen. We had, as probably people here in the village will tell you, we had a bad outbreak of murders and violence in this district. Not only here. They were in different parts of the country, twenty miles away, sometimes fifty miles away. One or two, it's suspected by the police, were nearly a hundred miles away. But they seemed to centre more or less on this part of the world. Anyway, Verity one day went out to visit a friend and—well, she didn't come back. We went to the police about it, the police sought for her, searched the whole countryside but they couldn't find any trace of her. We advertised, they advertised, and they suggested that she'd gone off with a boy-friend. Then word began to get round that she had been seen with Michael Rafiel. By now the police had their eye on Michael as a possibility for certain crimes that had occurred, although they couldn't find any direct evidence. Verity was said to have been seen, described by her clothing and other things, with a young man of Michael's appearance and in a car that corresponded to a description of his car. But there was no further evidence until her body was discovered six months later, thirty miles from here in a rather wild part of wooded country, in a ditch covered with stones and piled earth. Clotilde had to go to identify it—it was Verity all right. She'd been strangled and her head beaten in. Clotilde has never quite got over the shock. There were certain marks, a mole and an old scar and of course her clothes and the contents of her handbag. Miss Temple was very fond of Verity. She must have thought of her just before she died.'

'I'm sorry,' said Miss Marple. 'I'm really very, very sorry. Please tell your sister that I didn't know. I had no idea.'

16. The Inquest

MISS MARPLE walked slowly along the village street on her way towards the market place where the inquest was to take place in the old-fashioned Georgian building which had been known for a hundred years as the Curfew Arms. She glanced at her watch. There was still a good twenty minutes before she need be there. She looked into the shops. She paused before the shop that sold wool and babies' jackets, and peered inside for a few moments. A girl in the shop was serving. Small woolly coats were being tried on two children. Further along the counter there was an elderly woman.

Miss Marple went into the shop, went along the counter to a seat opposite the elderly woman, and produced a sample of pink wool. She had run out, she explained, of this particular brand of wool and had a little jacket she needed to finish. The match was soon made, some more samples of wool that Miss Marple had admired, were brought out for her to look at, and soon she was in conversation. Starting with the sadness of the accident which had just taken place. Mrs Merrypit, if her name was identical with that which was written up outside the shop, was full of the importance of the accident, and the general difficulties of getting local governments to do anything about the dangers of footpaths and public rights of way.

'After the rain, you see, you get all the soil washed off and then the boulders get loose and then down they comes. I remember one year they had three falls—three accidents there was. One boy was nearly killed, he was, and then later that year, oh six months later, I think, there was a man got his arm broken, and the third time it was poor old Mrs Walker. Blind she was and pretty well deaf too. She never heard nothing or she could have got out of the way they say. Somebody saw it and they called out to her, but they was too far away to reach her or to run to get her. And so she was killed.'

'Oh how sad,' said Miss Marple, 'how tragic. The sort of thing that's not easily forgotten, is it?'

'No indeed. I expect the Coroner'll mention it today.'

'I expect he will,' said Miss Marple. 'In a terrible way it seems quite a natural thing to happen, doesn't it, though of course there are accidents sometimes by pushing things about, you know. Just pushing, making stones rock. That sort of thing.'

'Ah well, there's boys as be up to anything. But I don't think I've ever seen them up that way, fooling about.'

Miss Marple went on to the subject of pullovers. Bright coloured pullovers.

'It's not for myself,' she said, 'it's for one of my great-nephews. You know, he wants a polo-necked pullover and very bright colours he'd like.'

'Yes, they do like bright colours nowadays, don't they?' agreed Mrs Merrypit. 'Not in jeans. Black jeans they like. Black or dark blue. But they like a bit of brightness up above.'

Miss Marple described a pullover of check design in bright colours. There appeared to be quite a good stock of pullovers and jerseys, but anything in red and black did not seem to be on display, nor even was anything like it mentioned as having been lately in stock. After looking at a few samples Miss Marple prepared to take her departure, chatting first about the former murders she had heard about which had been committed in this part of the country.

'They got the fellow in the end,' said Mrs Merrypit. 'Nice-looking boy, hardly have thought it of him. He'd been well brought up, you know. Been to university and all that. Father was very rich, they say. Touched in the head, I suppose. Not that they sent him to Broadway, or whatever the place is. No, they didn't do that, but I think myself he must have been a mental case—there was five or six other girls, so they said. The police had one after another of the young men round hereabouts to help them. Geoffrey Grant they had up. They were pretty sure it was him to begin with. He was always a bit queer, ever since he was a boy. Interfered with little girls going to school, you know. He used to offer them sweets and get them to come down the lanes with him and see the primroses, or something like that. Yes, they had very strong suspicions about him. But it wasn't him. And then there was another one. Bert Williams, but he'd been far away on two occasions, at least—what they call an alibi, so it couldn't be him. And then at last it came to this—what's-'is-name, I can't remember him now. Luke I think his name was— no, Mike something. Very nice-looking, as I say, but he had a bad record. Yes, stealing, forging cheques, all sorts of things like that. And two what-you-call 'em paternity cases, no, I don't mean that, but you know what I mean. When a girl's going to have a baby. You know and they make an order and make the fellow pay. He'd got two girls in the family way before this.'

'Was this girl in the family way?'

'Oh yes, she was. At first we thought when the body was found it might have been Nora Broad. That was Mrs Broad's niece, down at the mill shop. Great one for going with the boys, she was. She'd gone away missing from home in the same way. Nobody knew where she was. So when this body turned up six months later they thought at first it was her.'

'But it wasn't?'

'No—someone quite different.'

'Did her body ever turn up?'

'No. I suppose it might some day, but they think on the whole it was pushed into the river. Ah well, you never know, do you? You never know what you may dig up off a ploughed field or something like that. I was taken once to see all that treasure. Luton Loo was it—some name like that? Somewhere in the East Counties. Under a ploughed field it was. Beautiful. Gold ships and Viking ships and gold plate, enormous great platters. Well, you never know. Any day you may turn up a dead body or you may turn up a gold platter. And it may be hundreds of years old like that gold plate was, or it may be a three- or four-years-old body, like Mary Lucas who'd been missing for four years, they say. Somewhere near Reigate she was found. Ah well, all these things! It's a sad life. Yes, it's a very sad life. You never know what's coming.'

'There was another girl who'd lived here, wasn't there?' said Miss Marple, 'Who was killed.'

'You mean the body they thought was Nora Broad's but it wasn't? Yes. I've forgotten her name now. Hope, it was, I think. Hope or Charity. One of those sort of names, if you know what I mean. Used to be used a lot in Victorian times but you don't hear them so much nowadays. Lived at the Manor House, she did. She'd been there for some time after her parents were killed.'

'Her parents died in an accident, didn't they?'

'That's right. In a plane going to Spain or Italy, one of those places.'

'And you say she came to live here? Were they relations of hers?'

'I don't know if they were relations, but Mrs Glynne as she is now, was I think a great friend of her mother's or something that way. Mrs Glynne, of course, was married and gone abroad but Miss Clotilde—that's the eldest one, the dark one—she was very fond of the girl. She took her abroad, to Italy and France and all sorts of places, and she had her trained, a bit of typewriting and shorthand and that sort of thing, and art classes too. She's very arty, Miss Clotilde is. Oh, she was mighty fond of the girl. Brokenhearted she was when she disappeared. Quite different to Miss Anthea——'

'Miss Anthea is the youngest one, isn't she?'

'Yes. Not quite all there, some people say. Scatty like, you know, in her mind. Sometimes you see her walking along, talking to herself, you know, and tossing her head in a very queer way. Children get frightened of her sometimes. They say she's a bit queer about things. I don't know. You hear everything in a village, don't you? The great-uncle who lived here before, he was a bit peculiar too. Used to practise revolver shooting in the garden. For no reason at all so far as anyone could see. Proud of his marksmanship, he said he was, whatever marksmanship is.'

'But Miss Clotilde is not peculiar?'

'Oh no, she's clever, she is. Knows Latin and Greek, I believe. Would have liked to go to university but she had to look after her mother who was an invalid for a long time. But she was very fond of Miss—now, what was her name?—Faith perhaps. She was very fond of her and treated her like a daughter. And then along comes this young what's-his-name, Michael I think it was—and then one day the girl just goes off without saying a word to anyone. I don't know if Miss Clotilde knew as she was in the family way.'

'But you knew,' said Miss Marple.

'Ah well, I've got a lot of experience. I usually know when a girl's that way. It's plain enough to the eye. It's not only the shape, as you might say, you can tell by the look in their eyes and the way they walk and sit, and the sort of giddy fits they get and sick turns now and again. Oh yes, I thought to myself, here's another one of them. Miss Clotilde had to go and identify the body. Nearly broke her up, it did. She was like a different woman for weeks afterwards. Fairly loved that girl, she did.'

'And the other one—Miss Anthea?'

'Funnily enough, you know, I thought she had a kind of pleased look as though she was—yes, just pleased. Not nice, eh? Farmer Plummer's daughter used to look like that. Always used to go and see pigs killed. Enjoyed it. Funny things goes on in families.'

Miss Marple said goodbye, saw she had another ten minutes to go and passed on to the post office. The post office and general store of Jocelyn St Mary was just off the Market Square.

Miss Marple went into the post office, bought some stamps, looked at some of the postcards and then turned her attention to various paperback books. A middle-aged woman with rather a vinegary face presided behind the postal counter. She assisted Miss Marple to free a book from the wire support in which the books were.

'Stick a bit sometimes, they do. People don't put them back straight, you see.'

There was by now no one else in the shop. Miss Marple looked with distaste at the jacket of the book, a naked girl with blood-stained markings on her face and a sinister-looking killer bending over her with a blood-stained knife in his hand.

'Really,' she said, 'I don't like these horrors nowadays.'

'Gone a bit too far with some of their jackets, haven't they,' said Mrs Vinegar. 'Not everyone as likes them. Too fond of violence in every way, I'd say nowadays.'

Miss Marple detached a second book. '*Whatever Happened to Baby Jane*,' she read. 'Oh dear, it's a sad world one lives in.'

'Oh yes, I know. Saw in yesterday's paper, I did, some woman left her baby outside a supermarket and then someone else comes along and wheels it away. And all for no reason as far as one can see. The police found her all right. They all seem to say the same things, whether they steal from a supermarket or take away a baby. Don't know what came over them, they say.'

'Perhaps they really don't,' suggested Miss Marple.

Mrs Vinegar looked even more like vinegar.

'Take me a lot to believe that, it would.'

Miss Marple looked round—the post office was still empty. She advanced to the window.

'If you are not too busy, I wonder if you could answer a question of mine,' said Miss Marple. 'I have done something extremely stupid. Of late years I make so many mistakes. This was a parcel addressed to a charity. I send them clothes—pullovers and children's woollies, and I did it up and addressed it and it was sent off—and only this morning it came to me suddenly that I'd made a mistake and written the wrong address. I *don't* suppose any list is kept of the addresses of parcels—but I thought someone might have just happened to remember it. The address I meant to put was The Dockyard and Thames Side Welfare Association.'

Mrs Vinegar was looking quite kindly now, touched by Miss Marple's patent incapacity and general state of senility and dither.

'Did you bring it yourself?'

'No, I didn't—I'm staying at The Old Manor House—and one of them, Mrs Glynne, I think—said she or her sister would post it. Very kind of her——'

'Let me see now. It would have been on Tuesday, would it? It wasn't Mrs Glynne who brought it in, it was the youngest one, Miss Anthea.'

'Yes, yes, I think that was the day——'

'I remember it quite well. In a good sized dress box—and moderately heavy, I think. But not what you said, Dockyard Association—I can't recall anything like that. It was the Reverend Mathews—The East Ham Women and Children's Woollen Clothing Appeal.'

'Oh yes.' Miss Marple clasped her hands in an ecstasy of relief. 'How clever of you—I see now how I came to do it. At Christmas I *did* send things to the East Ham

Society in answer to a special appeal for knitted things, so I must have copied down the wrong address. Can you just repeat it?' She entered it carefully in a small notebook.

'I'm afraid the parcel's gone off, though——'

'Oh yes, but I can write, explaining the mistake and ask them to forward the parcel to the Dockyard Association instead. Thank you *so* much.'

Miss Marple trotted out.

Mrs Vinegar produced stamps for her next customer, remarking in an aside to a colleague—'Scatty as they make them, poor old creature. Expect she's always doing that sort of thing.'

Miss Marple went out of the post office and ran into Emlyn Price and Joanna Crawford.

Joanna, she noticed, was very pale and looked upset.

'I've got to give evidence,' she said. 'I don't know—what will they ask me? I'm so afraid. I—I don't like it. I told the police sergeant, I told him what I thought we saw.'

'Don't you worry, Joanna,' said Emlyn Price. 'This is just a coroner's inquest, you know. He's a nice man, a doctor, I believe. He'll just ask you a few questions and you'll say what you saw.'

'You saw it too,' said Joanna.

'Yes, I did,' said Emlyn. 'At least I saw there was someone up there. Near the boulders and things. Now come on, Joanna.'

'They came and searched our rooms in the hotel,' said Joanna. 'They asked our permission but they had a search warrant. They looked in our rooms and among the things in our luggage.'

'I think they wanted to find that check pullover you described. Anyway, there's nothing for you to worry about. If you'd had a black and scarlet pullover yourself you wouldn't have talked about it, would you. It was black and scarlet, wasn't it?'

'I don't know,' said Emlyn Price. 'I don't really know the colours of things very well. I think it was a sort of bright colour. That's all I know.'

'They didn't find one,' said Joanna. 'After all, none of us have very many things with us. You don't when you go on a coach travel. There wasn't anything like that among anybody's things. I've never seen anyone—of our lot, I mean, wearing anything like that. Not so far. Have you?'

'No, I haven't, but I suppose—I don't know that I should know if I *had* seen it,' said Emlyn Price. 'I don't always know red from green.'

'No, you're a bit colour blind, aren't you,' said Joanna. 'I noticed that the other day.'

'What do you mean, you noticed it.'

'My red scarf. I asked if you'd seen it. You said you'd seen a green one somewhere and you brought me the red one. I'd left it in the dining-room. But you didn't really know it was red.'

'Well, don't go about saying I'm colour blind. I don't like it. Puts people off in some way.'

'Men are more often colour blind than women,' said Joanna. 'It's one of those sex-link things,' she added, with an air of erudition. 'You know, it passes through the female and comes out in the male.'

'You make it sound as though it was measles,' said Emlyn Price. 'Well, here we are.'

'You don't seem to mind,' said Joanna, as they walked up the steps.

'Well, I don't really. I've never been to an inquest. Things are rather interesting when you do them for the first time.'

Dr Stokes was a middle-aged man with greying hair and spectacles. Police evidence was given first, then the medical evidence with technical details of the concussion injuries which had caused death. Mrs Sandbourne gave particulars of the coach tour, the expedition as arranged for that particular afternoon, and particulars of how the fatality had occurred. Miss Temple, she said, although not young, was a very brisk walker. The party were going along a well known footpath which led round the curve of a hill which slowly mounted to the old Moorland Church originally built in Elizabethan times, though repaired and added to later. On an adjoining crest was what was called the Bonaventure Memorial. It was a fairly steep ascent and people usually climbed it at different pace from each other. The younger ones very often ran or walked ahead and reached their destination much earlier than the others. The elderly ones took it slowly. She herself usually kept at the rear of the party so that she could, if necessary, suggest to people who were tired that they could, if they liked, go back.

Miss Temple, she recalled, had been talking to a Mr and Mrs Butler. Miss Temple, though she was over sixty, had been slightly impatient at their slow pace and had out-distanced them, had turned a corner and gone on ahead rather rapidly, which she had done often before. She was inclined to get impatient if waiting for people to catch up for too long, and preferred to make her own pace. They had heard a cry ahead, and she and the others had run on, turned a curve of the pathway and had found Miss Temple lying on the ground. A large boulder detached from the hillside above where there were several others of the same kind, must, they had thought, have rolled down the hillside and struck Miss Temple as she was going along the path below. A most unfortunate and tragic accident.

'You had no idea there was anything but an accident?'

'No, indeed. I can hardly see how it could have been anything but an accident.'

'You saw no one above you on the hillside?'

'No. This is the main path round the hill but of course

people do wander about over the top. I did not see anyone that particular afternoon.'

Then Joanna Crawford was called. After particulars of her name and age Dr Stokes asked, 'You were not walking with the remainder of the party?'

'No, we had left the path. We'd gone round the hill a little higher up the slope.'

'You were walking with a companion?'

'Yes. With Mr Emlyn Price.'

'There was no one else actually walking with you?'

'No. We were talking and we were looking at one or two of the flowers. They seemed of rather an uncommon kind. Emlyn's interested in botany.'

'Were you out of sight of the rest of the party?'

'Not all the time. They were walking along the main path—some way below us, that is.'

'Did you see Miss Temple?'

'I think so. She was walking ahead of the others, and I think I saw her turn a corner of the path ahead of them after which we didn't see her because the contour of the hill hid her.'

'Did you see someone walking above you on the hillside?'

'Yes. Up amongst a good many boulders. There's a sort of great patch of boulders on the side of the hill.'

'Yes,' said Dr Stokes, 'I know exactly the place you mean. Large granite boulders. People call them the Wethers, or the Grey Wethers sometimes.'

'I suppose they might look like sheep from a distance but we weren't so very far away from them.'

'And you saw someone up there?'

'Yes. Someone was more or less in the middle of the boulders, leaning over them.'

'Pushing them, do you think?'

'Yes. I thought so, and wondered why. He seemed to be pushing at one on the outside of the group near the edge.

They were so big and so heavy I would have thought it was impossible to push them. But the one he or she was pushing seemed to be balanced rather like a rocking stone.'

'You said first *he*, now you say *he* or *she*, Miss Crawford. Which do you think it was?'

'Well, I thought—I suppose—I suppose I thought it was a man, but I wasn't actually thinking at the time. It was— he or she was—wearing trousers and a pullover, a sort of man's pullover with a polo neck.'

'What colour was the pullover?'

'Rather a bright red and black in checks. And there was longish hair at the back of a kind of beret, rather like a woman's hair, but then it might just as well have been a man's.'

'It certainly might,' said Dr Stokes, rather dryly. 'Identifying a male or female figure by their hair is certainly not easy these days.' He went on, 'What happened next?'

'Well, the stone began to roll over. It sort of toppled over the edge and then it began to gain speed. I said to Emlyn, "Oh it's going to go right over down the hill." Then we heard a sort of crash as it fell. And I think I heard a cry from below but I might have imagined it.'

'And then?'

'Oh, we ran on up a bit and round the corner of the hill to see what had happened to the stone.'

'And what did you see?'

'We saw the boulder below on the path with a body underneath it—and people coming running round the corner.'

'Was it Miss Temple who uttered the cry?'

'I think it must have been. It might have been one of the others who was catching up and turned the corner. Oh! it was—it was horrible.'

'Yes, I'm sure it was. What had happened to the figure you'd seen above. The man or woman in the red and black pullover? Was that figure still there among the stones?'

'I don't know. I never looked up there. I was—I was busy looking at the accident, and running down the hill to see if one could do anything. I did just look up, I think, but there wasn't anyone in sight. Only the stones. There were a lot of contours and you could lose anyone quite easily from view.'

'Could it have been one of your party?'

'Oh, no. I'm sure it wasn't one of us. I would have known because, I mean, one would have known by their clothes. I'm sure nobody was wearing a scarlet and black pullover.'

'Thank you, Miss Crawford.'

Emlyn Price was called next. His story was practically a replica of Joanna's.

There was a little more evidence which did not amount to much.

The Coroner brought in that there was not sufficient evidence to show how Elizabeth Temple had come to her death, and adjourned the inquest for a fortnight.

17. Miss Marple Makes a Visit

AS THEY WALKED BACK from the inquest to the Golden Boar hardly anyone spoke. Professor Wanstead walked beside Miss Marple, and since she was not a very fast walker, they fell slightly behind the others.

'What will happen next?' Miss Marple asked at last.

'Do you mean legally or to us?'

'I suppose both,' said Miss Marple, 'because one will surely affect the other.'

'It will be presumably a case of the police making further inquiries, arising out of the evidence given by those two young people.'

'Yes.'

'Further inquiry will be necessary. The inquest was bound to be adjourned. One can hardly expect the Coroner to give a verdict of accidental death.'

'No, I understand that.' She said, 'What did you think of their evidence?'

Professor Wanstead directed a sharp glance from under his beetling eyebrows.

'Have you any ideas on the subject, Miss Marple?' His voice was suggestive. 'Of course,' said Professor Wanstead, 'we knew beforehand what they were going to say.'

'Yes.'

'What you mean is that you are asking what I thought about them themselves, their feelings about it.'

'It was interesting,' said Miss Marple. 'Very interesting. The red and black check pullover. Rather important, I think, don't you? Rather striking?'

'Yes, exactly that.'

He shot again that look at her under his eyebrows. 'What does it suggest to you exactly?'

'I think,' said Miss Marple. 'I think the description of that might give us a valuable clue.'

They came to the Golden Boar. It was only about half past twelve and Mrs Sandbourne suggested a little refreshment before going in to luncheon. As sherry and tomato juice and other liquors were being consumed, Mrs Sandbourne proceeded to make certain announcements.

'I have taken advice,' she said, 'both from the Coroner and Inspector Douglas. Since the medical evidence has been taken fully, there will be at the church a funeral memorial service tomorrow at eleven o'clock. I'm going to make arrangements with Mr Courtney, the local vicar, about it. On the following day it will be best, I think, to resume our tour. The programme will be slightly altered, since we have lost three days, but I think it can be re-organized on rather simpler lines. I have heard from one or two members of our party that they would prefer to return to London, presumably by rail. I can quite understand the feelings lying behind this, and would not like to try and influence you in any way. This death has been a very sad occurrence. I still cannot help but believe that Miss Temple's death *was* the result of an accident. Such a thing has happened before on that particular pathway, though there do not appear in this case to have been any geological or atmospherical conditions causing it. I think a good deal more investigation will have to be made. Of course, some hiker on a walking tour—that kind of thing—may have been pushing about boulders quite innocently, not realizing that there was a danger for someone walking below in what he or she was doing. If so, if that person comes forward, the whole thing may be cleared up quite quickly, but I agree one cannot take that for granted at present. It seems unlikely that the late Miss Temple could have had any enemy, or anyone who wished her harm of any kind. What I should suggest is, that we do not discuss the accident any further. Investigations will be made by the local authorities whose business it is. I think we will probably all like to attend the memorial service in the church tomorrow. And after that, on continuing the tour, I hope that it may distract our minds from the shock we have had. There are still some very interesting and famous houses to see and some very beautiful scenery also.'

Luncheon being announced shortly after that, the subject was not discussed any further. That is to say, not openly.

After lunch, as they took their coffee in the lounge, people were prone to get together in little groups, discussing their further arrangements.

'Are you continuing on the tour?' asked Professor Wanstead of Miss Marple.

'No,' said Miss Marple. She spoke thoughtfully. 'No. I think—I think that what has happened inclines me to remain here a little longer.'

'At the Golden Boar or at The Old Manor House?'

'That rather depends as to whether I receive any further invitation to go back to The Old Manor House. I would not like to suggest it myself because my original invitation was for the two nights that the tour was to have stayed here originally. I think possibly it would be better for me to remain at the Golden Boar.'

'You don't feel like returning to St Mary Mead?'

'Not yet,' said Miss Marple. 'There are one or two things I could do here, I think. One thing I have done already.' She met his inquiring gaze. 'If you are going on,' she said, 'with the rest of the party, I will tell you what I have put in hand, and suggest a small side-line of inquiry that might be helpful. The other reason that I wish to stay here I will tell you later. There are certain inquiries—local inquiries—that I want to make. They may not lead anywhere so I think it as well not to mention them now. And you?'

'I should like to return to London. I have work there

waiting to be done. Unless, that is, I can be helpful to you here?'

'No,' said Miss Marple, 'I do not think so at present. I expect you have various inquiries of your own that you wish to put in hand.'

'I came on the tour to meet you, Miss Marple.'

'And now you have met me and know what I know, or practically all that I know, you have other inquiries to put in hand. I understand that. But before you leave here, I think there are one or two things—well, that might be helpful, might give a result.'

'I see. You have ideas.'

'I am remembering what you said.'

'You have perhaps pinned down the smell of evil?'

'It is difficult,' said Miss Marple, 'to know exactly what something wrong in the atmosphere really means.'

'But you do feel that there is something wrong in the atmosphere?'

'Oh yes. Very clearly.'

'And especially since Miss Temple's death which, of course, was not an accident, no matter what Mrs Sandbourne hopes.'

'No,' said Miss Marple, 'it was not an accident. What I don't think I have told you is that Miss Temple said to me once that she was on a pilgrimage.'

'Interesting,' said the Professor. 'Yes, interesting. She didn't tell you what the pilgrimage was, to where or to whom?'

'No,' said Miss Marple, 'if she'd lived just a little longer and not been so weak, she might have told me. But unfortunately, death came a little too soon.'

'So that you have not any further ideas on that subject.'

'No. Only a feeling of assurance that her pilgrimage was put an end to by malign design. Someone wanted to stop her going wherever she was going, or stop her going to whomever she was going to. One can only hope that chance or Providence may throw light on that.'

'That's why you're staying here?'

'Not only that,' said Miss Marple. 'I want to find out something more about a girl called Nora Broad.'

'Nora Broad.' He looked faintly puzzled.

'The other girl who disappeared about the same time as Verity Hunt did. You remember you mentioned her to me. A girl who had boy-friends and was, I understand, very *ready* to *have* boy-friends. A foolish girl, but attractive apparently to the male sex. I think,' said Miss Marple, 'that to learn a little more about her might help me in my inquiries.'

'Have it your own way, Detective-Inspector Marple,' said Professor Wanstead.

The service took place on the following morning. All the members of the tour were there. Miss Marple looked round the church. Several of the locals were there also. Mrs Glynne was there and her sister Clotilde. The youngest one, Anthea, did not attend. There were one or two people from the village also, she thought. Probably not acquainted with Miss Temple but there out of a rather morbid curiosity in regard to what was now spoken of by the term 'foul play'. There was, too, an elderly clergyman; in gaiters, well over seventy, Miss Marple thought, a broad-shouldered old man with a noble mane of white hair. He was slightly crippled and found it difficult both to kneel and to stand. It was a fine face, Miss Marple thought, and she wondered who he was. Some old friend of Elizabeth Temple, she presumed, who might perhaps have come from quite a long distance to attend the service?

As they came out of the church Miss Marple exchanged a few words with her fellow travellers. She knew now pretty well who was doing what. The Butlers were returning to London.

'I told Henry I just couldn't go on with it,' said Mrs Butler. 'You know—I feel all the time that any minute just as we might be walking round a corner, someone, you know, might shoot us or throw a stone at us. Someone who has got a down perhaps on the Famous Houses of England.'

'Now then, Mamie, now then,' said Mr Butler, 'don't you let your imagination go as far as that!'

'Well, you just don't know nowadays. What with hijackers about and kidnapping and all the rest of it, I don't feel really protected anywhere.'

Old Miss Lumley and Miss Bentham were continuing with the tour, their anxieties allayed.

'We've paid very highly for this tour and it seems a pity to miss anything just because this very sad accident has happened. We rang up a very good neighbour of ours last night, and they are going to see to the cats, so we don't need to worry.'

It was going to remain an accident for Miss Lumley and Miss Bentham. They had decided it was more comfortable that way.

Mrs Riseley-Porter was also continuing on the tour. Colonel and Mrs Walker were resolved that nothing would make them miss seeing a particularly rare collection of fuchsias in the garden due to be visited the day after tomorrow. The architect, Jameson, was also guided by his wish to see various buildings of special interest for him. Mr Caspar, however, was departing by rail, he said. Miss Cooke and Miss Barrow seemed undecided.

'Pretty good walks round here,' said Miss Cooke. 'I think we'll stay at the Golden Boar for a little. That's what you're going to do, isn't it, Miss Marple?'

'I really think so,' said Miss Marple. 'I don't feel quite equal to going on travelling and all that. I think a day or two's rest would be helpful to me after what's happened.'

As the little crowd dispersed, Miss Marple took an unostentatious route of her own. From her handbag she took out a leaf torn from her notebook on which she had entered two addresses. The first, a Mrs Blackett, lived in a neat little house and garden just by the end of the road where it sloped down towards the valley. A small neat woman opened the door.

'Mrs Blackett?'

'Yes, yes, ma'am, that's my name.'

'I wonder if I might just come in and speak to you for a minute or two. I have just been to the service and I am feeling a little giddy. If I could just sit down for a minute or two?'

'Dear me, now, dear me. Oh, I'm sorry for that. Come right in, ma'am, come right in. That's right. You sit down here. Now I'll get you a glass of water—or maybe you'd like a pot of tea?'

'No, thank you,' said Miss Marple, 'a glass of water would put me right.'

Mrs Blackett returned with a glass of water and a pleasurable prospect of talking about ailments and giddiness and other things.

'You know, I've got a nephew like that. He oughtn't to be at his age, he's not much over fifty but now and then he'll come over giddy all of a sudden and unless he sits down at once—why you don't know, sometimes he'll pass out right on the floor. Terrible, it is. Terrible. And doctors, they don't seem able to do anything about it. Here's your glass of water.'

'Ah,' said Miss Marple, sipping, 'I feel much better.'

'Been to the service, have you, for the poor lady as got done in, as some say, or accident as others. I'd say it's accident every time. But these inquests and coroners, they always want to make things look criminal, they do.'

'Oh yes,' said Miss Marple. 'I've been so sorry to hear of a lot of things like that in the past. I was hearing a great deal about a girl called Nora. Nora Broad, I think.'

'Ah, Nora, yes. Well, she was my cousin's daughter.

Yes. A long while ago, that was. Went off and never come back. These girls, there's no holding them. I said often, I did, to Nancy Broad—that's my cousin—I said to her, "You're out working all day" and I said "What's Nora doing? You know she's the kind that likes the boys. Well," I said, "there'll be trouble. You see if there isn't." And sure enough, I was quite right.'

'You mean——?'

'Ah, the usual trouble. Yes, in the family way. Mind you, I don't think as my cousin Nancy knew about it yet. But of course, I'm sixty-five and I know what's what and I know the way a girl looks and I think I know who it was, but I'm not sure. I might have been wrong because he went on living in the place and he was real cut up when Nora was missing.'

'She went off, did she?'

'Well, she accepted a lift from someone—a stranger. That's the last time she was seen. I forget the make of the car now. Some funny name it had. An Audit or something like that. Anyway, she'd been seen once or twice in that car. And off she went in it. And it was said it was that same car that the poor girl what got herself murdered used to go riding in. But I don't think as that happened to Nora. If Nora'd been murdered, the body would have come to light by now. Don't you think so?'

'It certainly seems likely,' said Miss Marple. 'Was she a girl who did well at school and all that?'

'Ah no, she wasn't. She was idle and she wasn't too clever at her books either. No. She was all for the boys from the time she was twelve years old onwards. I think in the end she must have gone off with someone or other for good. But she never let anyone know. She never sent as much as a postcard. Went off, I think, with someone as promised her things. You know. Another girl I knew—but that was when I was young—went off with one of them Africans. He told her as his father was a Shake. Funny sort

182

of word, but a shake I think it was. Anyway it was somewhere in Africa or in Algiers. Yes, in Algiers it was. Somewhere there. And she was going to have all sorts of wonderful things. He had six camels, the boy's father, she said and a whole troop of horses and she was going to live in a wonderful house, she was, with carpets hanging up all over the walls, which seems a funny place to put carpets. And off she went. She come back again three years later. Yes. Terrible time, she'd had. Terrible. They lived in a nasty little house made of earth. Yes, it was. And nothing much to eat except what they call cos-cos which I always thought was lettuce, but it seems it isn't. Something more like semolina pudding. Oh terrible it was. And in the end he said she was no good to him and he'd divorce her. He said he'd only got to say "I divorce you" three times, and he did and walked out and somehow or other, some kind of Society out there took charge of her and paid her fare home to England. And there she was. Ah, but that was about thirty to forty years ago, that was. Now Nora, that was only about seven or eight years ago. But I expect she'll be back one of these days, having learnt her lesson and finding out that all these fine promises didn't come to much.'

'Had she anyone to go to here except her—her mother —your cousin, I mean? Anyone who——'

'Well, there's many as was kind to her. There was the people at The Old Manor House, you know. Mrs Glynne wasn't there then, but Miss Clotilde, she was always one to be good to the girls from school. Yes, many a nice present she's given Nora. She gave her a very nice scarf and a pretty dress once. Very nice, it was. A summer frock, a sort of foulard silk. Ah, she was very kind, Miss Clotilde was. Tried to make Nora take more interest in her schooling. Lots of things like that. Advised her against the way she was going on because, you see—well, I wouldn't like to say it, not when she's my cousin's child though, mark you, my cousin is only one who married my boy cousin, that is to say—but I mean it was something terrible the way she went on with all the boys. Anyone could pick her up. Real sad it is. I'd say she'll go on the streets in the end. I don't believe she has any future but that. I don't like to say these things, but there it is. Anyway, perhaps it's better than getting herself murdered like Miss Hunt did, what lived at The Old Manor House. Cruel, that was. They thought she'd gone off with someone and the police, they was busy. Always asking questions and having the young men who'd been with the girl, up to help them with their inquiries and all that. Geoffrey Grant there was, Billy Thompson, and the Langford's Harry. All unemployed—with plenty of jobs going if they'd wanted to take them. Things usedn't to be like that when I was young. Girls behaved proper. And the boys knew they'd got to work if they wanted to get anywhere.'

Miss Marple talked a little more, said that she was now quite restored, thanked Mrs Blackett, and went out.

Her next visit was to a girl who was planting out lettuces.

'Nora Broad? Oh, *she* hasn't been in the village for years. Went off with someone, she did. She was a great one for boys. I always wondered where she'd end up. Did you want to see her for any particular reason?'

'I had a letter from a friend abroad,' said Miss Marple, untruthfully. 'A very nice family and they were thinking of engaging a Miss Nora Broad. She'd been in some trouble, I think. Married someone who was rather a bad lot and had left her and gone off with another woman, and she wanted to get a job looking after children. My friend knew nothing about her, but I gathered she came from this village. So I wondered if there was anyone here who could—well, tell me something about her. You went to school with her, I understand?'

'Oh yes, we were in the same class, we were. Mind you,

I didn't approve of all Nora's goings-on. She was boy mad, she was. Well, I had a nice boy-friend myself that I was going steady with at the time, and I told her she'd do herself no good going off with every Tom, Dick and Harry that offered her a lift in a car or took her along to a pub where she told lies about her age, as likely as not. She was a good mature girl as looked a lot older than she was.'

'Dark or fair?'

'Oh, she had dark hair. Pretty hair it was. Always loose like, you know, as girls do.'

'Were the police worried about her when she disappeared?'

'Yes. You see, she didn't leave no word behind. She just went out one night and didn't come back. She was seen getting into a car and nobody saw the car again and nobody saw her. Just at that time there'd been a good many murders, you know. Not specially round here, but all over the country. The police, they were rounding up a lot of young men and boys. Thought as Nora might be a body at the time we did. But not she. She was all right. I'd say as likely as not she's making a bit of money still in London or one of these big towns doing a strip-tease, something of that kind. That's the kind she was.'

'I don't think,' said Miss Marple, 'that if it's the same person, that she'd be very suitable for my friend.'

'She'd have to change a bit if she was to be suitable,' said the girl.

18. Archdeacon Brabazon

WHEN MISS MARPLE, slightly out of breath and rather tired, got back to the Golden Boar, the receptionist came out from her pen and across to greet her.

'Oh, Miss Marple, there is someone here who wants to speak to you. Archdeacon Brabazon.'

'Archdeacon Brabazon?' Miss Marple looked puzzled.

'Yes. He's been trying to find you. He had heard you were with this tour and he wanted to talk to you before you might have left or gone to London. I told him that some of them were going back to London by the later train this afternoon, but he is very, very anxious to speak to you before you go. I have put him in the television lounge. It is quieter there. The other is very noisy just at this moment.'

Slightly surprised, Miss Marple went to the room indicated. Archdeacon Brabazon turned out to be the elderly cleric whom she had noticed at the memorial service. He rose and came towards her.

'Miss Marple. Miss Jane Marple?'

'Yes, that is my name. You wanted——'

'I am Archdeacon Brabazon. I came here this morning to attend the service for a very old friend of mine, Miss Elizabeth Temple.'

'Oh yes?' said Miss Marple. 'Do sit down.'

'Thank you, I will. I am not quite as strong as I was.' He lowered himself carefully into a chair.

'And you——'

Miss Marple sat down beside him.

'Yes,' she said, 'you wanted to see me?'

'Well, I must explain how that comes about. I'm quite aware that I am a complete stranger to you. As a matter of fact I made a short visit to the hospital at Carristown, talking to the matron before going on to the church here. It was she who told me that before she died Elizabeth had asked to see a fellow member of the tour. Miss Jane Marple. And that Miss Jane Marple had visited her and sat with her just a very, very short time before Elizabeth died.'

He looked at her anxiously.

'Yes,' said Miss Marple, 'that is so. It surprised me to be sent for.'

'You are an old friend of hers?'

'No,' said Miss Marple. 'I only met her on this tour. That's why I was surprised. We had expressed ideas to each other, occasionally sat next to each other in the coach, and had struck up quite an acquaintanceship. But I was surprised that she should have expressed a wish to see me when she was so ill.'

'Yes. Yes, I can quite imagine that. She was, as I have said, a very old friend of mine. In fact, she was coming to see me, to visit me. I live in Fillminster, which is where your coach tour will be stopping the day after tomorrow. And by arrangement she was coming to visit me there, she wanted to talk to me about various matters about which she thought I could help her.'

'I see,' said Miss Marple. 'May I ask you a question? I hope it is not too intimate a question.'

'Of course, Miss Marple. Please ask me anything you like.'

'One of the things Miss Temple said to me was that her presence on the tour was *not* merely because she wished to visit historic homes and gardens. She described it by a rather unusual word to use, as a pilgrimage.'

'Did she,' said Archdeacon Brabazon. 'Did she indeed now? Yes, that's interesting. Interesting and perhaps significant.'

'So what I am asking you is, do you think that the pilgrimage she spoke of was her visit to you?'

'I think it must have been,' said the Archdeacon. 'Yes, I think so.'

'We had been talking,' said Miss Marple, 'about a young girl. A girl called Verity.'

'Ah yes. Verity Hunt.'

'I did not know her surname. Miss Temple, I think, mentioned her only as Verity.'

'Verity Hunt is dead,' said the Archdeacon. 'She died quite a number of years ago. Did you know that?'

'Yes,' said Miss Marple. 'I knew it. Miss Temple and I were talking about her. Miss Temple told me something that I did not know. She said she had been engaged to be married to the son of a Mr Rafiel. Mr Rafiel is, or again I must say was, a friend of mine. Mr Rafiel has paid the expenses of this tour out of his kindness. I think, though that possibly he wanted—indeed, intended—me to meet Miss Temple on this tour. I think he thought she could give me certain information.'

'Certain information about Verity?'

'Yes.'

'That is why she was coming to me. She wanted to know certain facts.'

'She wanted to know,' said Miss Marple, 'why Verity broke off her engagement to marry Mr Rafiel's son.'

'Verity,' said Archdeacon Brabazon, 'did *not* break off her engagement. I am certain of that. As certain as one can be of anything.'

'Miss Temple did not know that, did she?'

'No. I think she was puzzled and unhappy about what happened and was coming to me to ask me why the marriage did not take place.'

'And why did it not take place?' asked Miss Marple. 'Please do not think that I am unduly curious. It's not idle curiosity that is driving me. I too am on—not a pilgrimage —but what I should call a mission. I too want to know why Michael Rafiel and Verity Hunt did not marry.'

The Archdeacon studied her for a moment or two.

'You are involved in some way,' he said. 'I see that.'

'I am involved,' said Miss Marple, 'by the dying wishes of Michael Rafiel's father. He asked me to do this for him.'

'I have no reason not to tell you all I know,' said the Archdeacon slowly. 'You are asking me what Elizabeth Temple would have been asking me, you are asking me something I do not know myself. Those two young people, Miss Marple, intended to marry. They had made arrangements to marry. I was going to marry them. It was a marriage, I gather, which was being kept secret. I knew both these young people. I knew that dear child Verity from a long way back. I prepared her for confirmation, I used to hold services in Lent, for Easter, on other occasions, in Elizabeth Temple's school. A very fine school it was, too. A very fine woman she was. A wonderful teacher with a great sense of each girl's capabilities—for what she was best fitted for in studies. She urged careers on girls she thought would relish careers, and did not force girls that she felt were not really suited to them. She was a great woman and a very dear friend. Verity was one of the most beautiful children—girls, rather—that I have come across. Beautiful in mind, in heart, as well as in appearance. She had the great misfortune to lose her parents before she was truly adult. They were both killed in a charter plane going on a holiday to Italy. Verity went to live when she left school with a Miss Clotilde Bradbury-Scott whom you know, probably, as living here. She had been a close friend of Verity's mother. There are three sisters, though the second one was married and living abroad, so there were only two of them living here. Clotilde, the eldest one, became extremely attached to Verity. She did everything possible to give her a happy life. She took her abroad once or twice, gave her art lessons in Italy and loved and cared for her dearly in every way. Verity, too, came to love her probably as much as she could have loved her own mother. She depended on Clotilde. Clotilde herself was an intellectual and well educated woman. She did not urge a university career on Verity, but this I gather was really because Verity did not really yearn after one. She preferred to study art and music and such subjects. She lived here at The Old Manor House and had, I think, a very happy life. She always seemed to be happy. Naturally, I did not see her after she came here since Fillminster where I was in the cathedral, is nearly sixty miles from here. I wrote to her at Christmas and other festivals, and she remembered me always with a Christmas card. But I saw nothing of her until the day came when she suddenly turned up, a very beautiful and fully grown young woman by then, with an attractive young man whom I also happened to know slightly, Mr Rafiel's son, Michael. They came to me because they were in love with each other and wanted to get married.'

'And you agreed to marry them?'

'Yes, I did. Perhaps, Miss Marple, you may think that I should not have done so. They had come to me in secret, it was obvious. Clotilde Bradbury-Scott, I should imagine, had tried to discourage the romance between them. She was well within her rights in doing so. Michael Rafiel, I will tell you frankly, was not the kind of husband you would want for any daughter or relation of yours. She was too young really, to make up her mind, and Michael had been a source of trouble ever since his very young days. He had been had up before junior courts, he had had unsuitable friends, he had been drawn into various gangster activities, he'd sabotaged buildings and telephone boxes. He had been on intimate terms with various girls, had maintenance claims which he had had to meet. Yes, he was a bad lot with the girls as well as in other ways, yet he was extremely attractive and they fell for him and behaved in an extremely silly fashion. He had served two short jail sentences. Frankly, he had a criminal record.

I was acquainted with his father, though I did not know him well, and I think that his father did all that he could—all that a man of his character could—to help his son. He came to his rescue, he got him jobs in which he might have succeeded. He paid up his debts, paid out damages. He did all this. I don't know——'

'But he could have done more, you think?'

'No,' said the Archdeacon, 'I've come to an age now when I know that one must accept one's fellow human beings as being the kind of people and having the kind of, shall we say in modern terms, genetic make-up which gives them the characters they have. I don't think that Mr Rafiel had affection for his son, a great affection at any time. To say he was reasonably fond of him would be the most you could say. He gave him no love. Whether it would have been better for Michael if he had had love from his father, I do not know. Perhaps it would have made no difference. As it was, it was sad. The boy was not stupid. He had a certain amount of intellect and talent. He could have done well if he had wished to do well, and had taken the trouble. But he was by nature—let us admit it frankly—a delinquent. He had certain qualities one appreciated. He had a sense of humour, he was in various ways generous and kindly. He would stand by a friend, help a friend out of a scrape. He treated his girl-friends badly, got them into trouble as the local saying is, and then more or less abandoned them and took up with somebody else. So there I was faced with those two and —yes—I agreed to marry them. I told Verity, I told her quite frankly, the kind of boy she wanted to marry. I found that he had not tried to deceive her in any way. He'd told her that he'd always been in trouble both with the police, and in every other way. He told her that he was going, when he married her, to turn over a new leaf. Everything would be changed. I warned her that that would not happen, he would not change. People do not change. He might *mean* to change. Verity, I think, knew that almost as well as I did. She admitted that she knew it. She said, "I know what Mike is like. I know he'll probably always be like it, but I love him. I may be able to help him and I may not. But I'll take that risk." And I will tell you this, Miss Marple. I know—none better, I have done a lot with young people, I have married a lot of young people and I have seen them come to grief, I have seen them unexpectedly turn out well—but I know this and recognize it. I know when a couple are really in love with each other. And by that I do not mean just sexually attracted. There is too much talk about sex, too much attention is paid to it. I do not mean that anything about sex is wrong. That is nonsense. But sex cannot take the place of love, it goes *with* love but it cannot succeed by itself. To love means the words of the marriage service. For better, for worse, for richer for poorer, in sickness and in health. That is what you take on if you love and wish to marry. Those two loved each other. To love and to cherish until death do us part. And that,' said the Archdeacon, 'is where my story ends. I cannot go on because *I do not know what happened*. I only know that I agreed to do as they asked, that I made the necessary arrangements; we settled a day, an hour, a time, a place. I think perhaps that I was to blame for agreeing to the secrecy.'

'They didn't want anyone to know?' said Miss Marple.

'No. Verity did not want anyone to know, and I should say most certainly Mike did not want anyone to know. They were afraid of being stopped. To Verity, I think, besides love, there was also a feeling of escape. Natural, I think, owing to the circumstances of her life. She had lost her real guardians, her parents, she had entered on her new life after their death, at an age when a schoolgirl arrives at having a "crush" on someone. An attractive mistress. Anything from the games mistress to the mathematics mistress, or a prefect or an older girl. A state that does not last for very long, is merely a natural part of life.

'Then from that you go on to the next stage when you realize that what you want in your life is what complements yourself. A relationship between a man and a woman. You start then to look about you for a mate. The mate you want in life. And if you are wise, you take your time, you have friends, but you are looking, as the old nurses used to say to children, for Mr Right to come along. Clotilde Bradbury-Scott was exceptionally good to Verity, and Verity, I think, gave her what I should call hero-worship. She was a personality as a woman. Handsome, accomplished, interesting. I think Verity adored her in an almost romantic way and I think Clotilde came to love Verity as though she were her own daughter. And so Verity grew to maturity in an atmosphere of adoration, lived an interesting life with interesting subjects to stimulate her intellect. It was a happy life, but I think little by little she was conscious—conscious without knowing she was conscious, shall we say—of a wish to escape. Escape from being loved. To escape, she didn't know into what or *where*. But she did know after she met Michael. She wanted to escape to a life where male and female come together to create the next stage of living in this world. But she knew that it was impossible to make Clotilde understand how she felt. She knew that Clotilde would be bitterly opposed to her taking her love for Michael seriously. And Clotilde, I fear, was right in her belief. . . . I know that now. He was not a husband that Verity ought to have taken or had. The road that she started out on led not to life, not to increased living and happiness. It led to shock, pain, death. You see, Miss Marple, that I have a grave feeling of guilt. My motives were good, but I didn't know what I ought to have known. I knew Verity, *but I didn't know Michael*. I understood Verity's wish for secrecy because I knew what a strong personality Clotilde Bradbury-Scott had. She might have had a strong enough influence over Verity to persuade her to give up the marriage.'

'You think then that that was what she did do? You think Clotilde told her enough about Michael to persuade her to give up the idea of marrying him?'

'No, I do *not* believe that. I still do not. Verity would have told me if so. She would have got word to me.'

'What did actually happen on that day?'

'I haven't told you that yet. The day was fixed. The time, the hour and the place, and I waited. Waited for a bride and bridegroom who didn't come, who sent no word, no excuse, *nothing*. I didn't know why! I never *have* known why. It still seems to me unbelievable. Unbelievable, I mean, not that they did not come, that could be explicable easily enough, but that they sent no word. Some scrawled line of writing. And that is why I wondered and hoped that Elizabeth Temple, before she died, might have told *you* something. Given you some message perhaps for me. If she knew or had any idea that she was dying, she might have wanted to get a message to me.'

'She wanted information *from* you,' said Miss Marple. 'That, I am sure, was the reason she was coming to you.'

'Yes. Yes, that is probably true. It seemed to me, you see, that Verity would have said nothing to the people who could have stopped her, Clotilde and Anthea Bradbury-Scott, but because she had always been very devoted to Elizabeth Temple—and Elizabeth Temple had had great influence over her—it seems to me that she would have written and given her information of some kind.'

'I think she did,' said Miss Marple.

'Information, you think?'

'The information she gave to Elizabeth Temple,' said Miss Marple, 'was this. That she was going to marry Michael Rafiel. Miss Temple knew that. It was one of the things she said to me. She said: "I knew a girl called

Verity who was going to marry Michael Rafiel" and the only person who could have told her that was Verity herself. Verity must have written to her or sent some word to her. And then when I said "Why didn't she marry him?" she said: "She died".'

'Then we come to a full stop,' said Archdeacon Brabazon. He sighed. 'Elizabeth and I know no more than those two facts. Elizabeth, that Verity was going to marry Michael. And I that those two were going to marry, that they had arranged it and that they were coming on a settled day and time. And I waited for them, but there was no marriage. No bride, no bridegroom, no word.'

'And you have no idea what happened?' said Miss Marple.

'I do not for one minute believe that Verity or Michael definitely parted, broke off.'

'But *something* must have happened between them? Something that opened Verity's eyes perhaps, to certain aspects of Michael's character and personality, that she had not realized or known before.'

'That is not a satisfying answer because still she would have let me know. She would not have left me waiting to join them together in holy matrimony. To put the most ridiculous side of it, she was a girl with beautiful manners, well brought up. She would have sent word. No. I'm afraid that only one thing could have happened.'

'Death?' said Miss Marple. She was remembering that one word that Elizabeth Temple had said which had sounded like the deep tone of a bell.

'Yes.' Archdeacon Brabazon sighed. 'Death.'

'Love,' said Miss Marple thoughtfully.

'By that you mean——' he hesitated.

'It's what Miss Temple said to me. I said "What killed her?" and she said "Love" and that love was the most frightening word in the world. The most frightening word.'

'I see,' said the Archdeacon. 'I see—or I think I see.'

'What is your solution?'

'Split personality,' he sighed. 'Something that is not apparent to other people unless they are technically qualified to observe it. Jekyll and Hyde are real, you know. They were not Stevenson's invention as such. Michael Rafiel was a—must have been schizophrenic. He had a dual personality. I have no medical knowledge, no psycho-analytic experience. But there must have been in him the two parts of two identities. One, a well-meaning, almost lovable boy, a boy perhaps whose principal attraction was his wish for happiness. But there was also a second personality, someone who was forced by some mental deformation perhaps—something we as yet are not sure of—to kill—not an enemy, but the person he loved, and so he killed Verity. Not knowing perhaps *why* he had to or *what* it meant. There are very frightening things in this world of ours, mental quirks, mental disease or deformity of a brain. One of my parishioners was a very sad case in point. Two elderly women living together, pensioned. They had been friends in service together somewhere. They appeared to be a happy couple. And yet one day one of them killed the other. She sent for an old friend of hers, the vicar of her parish, and said: "I have killed Louisa. It is very sad," she said, "but I saw the devil looking out of her eye and I knew I was being commanded to kill her." Things like that make one sometimes despair of living. One says why? and how? and yet one day knowledge will come. Doctors will find out or learn just some small deformity of a chromosome or gene. Some gland that overworks or leaves off working.'

'So you think that's what happened?' said Miss Marple.

'It *did* happen. The body was not found, I know, for some time afterwards. Verity just disappeared. She went away from home and was not seen again. . . .'

'But it must have happened *then*—that very day——'

'But surely at the trial——'

'You mean after the body was found, when the police finally arrested Michael?'

'He had been one of the first, you know, to be asked to come and give assistance to the police. He had been seen about with the girl, she had been noticed in his car. They were sure all along that he was the man they wanted. He was their first suspect, and they never stopped suspecting him. The other young men who had known Verity were questioned, and one and all had alibis or lack of evidence. They continued to suspect Michael, and finally the body was found. Strangled and the head and face disfigured with heavy blows. A mad frenzied attack. He wasn't sane when he struck those blows. Mr Hyde, let us say, had taken over.'

Miss Marple shivered.

The Archdeacon went on, his voice low and sad. 'And yet, even now sometimes, I hope and feel that it was some other young man who killed her. Someone who was definitely mentally deranged, though no one had any idea of it. Some stranger, perhaps, whom she had met in the neighbourhood. Someone whom she had met by chance, who had given her a lift in a car, and then——' He shook his head.

'I suppose that *could* have been true,' said Miss Marple.

'Mike made a bad impression in court,' said the Archdeacon. 'Told foolish and senseless lies. Lied as to where his car had been. Got his friends to give him impossible alibis. He was frightened. He said nothing of his plan to marry. I believe his Counsel was of the opinion that that would tell against him—that she might have been forcing him to marry her and that he didn't want to. It's so long ago now, I remember no details. But the evidence was dead against him. He was guilty—and he looked guilty.

'So you see, do you not, Miss Marple, that I'm a very sad and unhappy man. I made the wrong judgment, I encouraged a very sweet and lovely girl to go to her death,

197

because I did not know enough of human nature. I was ignorant of the danger she was running. I believed that if she had had any fear of him, any sudden knowledge of something evil in him, she would have broken her pledge to marry him and have come to me and told me of her fear, of her new knowledge of him. But nothing of that ever happened. Why *did* he kill her? Did he kill her because perhaps he knew she was going to have a child? Because by now he had formed a tie with some other girl and did not want to be forced to marry Verity? I can't believe it. Or was it some entirely different reason. Because *she* had suddenly felt a fear of him, a knowledge of danger from him, and had broken off her association with him? Did that rouse his anger, his fury, and did that lead him to violence and to killing her? One does not know.'

'You do not know?' said Miss Marple, 'but you *do* still know and believe one thing, don't you?'

'What do you mean exactly by "believe"? Are you talking from the religious point of view?'

'Oh no,' said Miss Marple, 'I didn't mean that. I mean, there seems to be in you, or so I feel it, a very strong belief that those two loved each other, that they meant to marry, but that *something* happened that prevented it. Something that ended in her death, but you still really believe that they *were* coming to you to get married that day?'

'You are quite right, my dear. Yes, I cannot help still believing in two lovers who wished to get married, who were ready to take each other on for better, for worse, for richer or poorer, in sickness and in health. She loved him and she would have taken him for better or for worse. As far as she had gone, she took him for worse. It brought about her death.'

'You must go on believing as you do,' said Miss Marple. 'I think, you know, that *I* believe it too.'

'But then what?'

'I don't know yet,' said Miss Marple. 'I'm not sure, but

I think Elizabeth Temple did know or was beginning to know what happened. A frightening word, she said. *Love*. I thought when she spoke that what she meant was that because of a love affair Verity committed suicide. Because she found out something about Michael, or because something about Michael suddenly upset her and revolted her. But it couldn't have been suicide.'

'No,' said the Archdeacon, 'that couldn't be so. The injuries were described very fully at the trial. You don't commit suicide by beating in your own head.'

'Horrible!' said Miss Marple. 'Horrible! And you couldn't do that to anyone you loved even if you had to kill "for love", could you? If he'd killed her, he couldn't have done it that way. Strangling—perhaps, but you wouldn't beat in the face and the head that you loved.' She murmured, 'Love, love—a frightening word.'

19. Goodbyes Are Said

THE COACH was drawn up in front of the Golden Boar on the following morning. Miss Marple had come down and was saying goodbye to various friends. She found Mrs Riseley-Porter in a state of high indignation.

'Really, girls nowadays,' she said. 'No vigour. No stamina.'

Miss Marple looked at her inquiringly.

'Joanna, I mean. My niece.'

'Oh dear. Is she not well?'

'Well, she says not. I can't see anything much the matter with her. She says she's got a sore throat, she feels she might have a temperature coming on. All nonsense, I think.'

'Oh, I'm very sorry,' said Miss Marple. 'Is there anything I can do? Look after her?'

'I should leave her alone, if I were you,' said Mrs Riseley-Porter. 'If you ask me, it's all an excuse.'

Miss Marple looked inquiringly at her once more.

'Girls are so silly. Always falling in love.'

'Emlyn Price?' said Miss Marple.

'Oh, so you've noticed it too. Yes, they're really getting to a stage of spooning about together. I don't much care for him anyway. One of these long-haired students, you know. Always going on demos or something like that. Why can't they say demonstration properly? I hate abbreviations. And how am *I* going to get along. Nobody to look after me, collect my luggage, take it in, take it out. Really. I'm paying for this complete trip and everything.'

'I thought she seemed so attentive to you,' said Miss Marple.

'Well, not the last day or two. Girls don't understand

that people have to have a little assistance when they get to middle age. They seem to have some absurd idea—she and the Price boy—of going to visit some mountain or some landmark. About a seven or eight mile walk there and back.'

'But surely if she has a sore throat and a temperature . . .'

'You'll see, as soon as the coach is gone the sore throat will get better and the temperature will go down,' said Mrs Riseley-Porter. 'Oh dear, we've got to get on board now. Oh, goodbye, Miss Marple, it's nice to have met you. I'm sorry you're not coming with us.'

'I'm very sorry myself,' said Miss Marple, 'but really you know, I'm not so young and vigorous as you are, Mrs Riseley-Porter, and I really feel after all the—well, shock and everything else the last few days, I really must have a complete twenty-four hours' rest.'

'Well, hope to see you somewhere in the future.'

They shook hands. Mrs Riseley-Porter climbed into the coach.

A voice behind Miss Marple's shoulder said:

'*Bon Voyage* and Good Riddance.'

She turned to see Emlyn Price. He was grinning.

'Was that addressed to Mrs Riseley-Porter?'

'Yes, Who else?'

'I'm sorry to hear that Joanna is under the weather this morning.'

Emlyn Price grinned at Miss Marple again.

'She'll be all right,' he said, 'as soon as that coach is gone.'

'Oh really!' said Miss Marple, 'do you mean——?'

'Yes, I do mean,' said Emlyn Price. 'Joanna's had enough of that aunt of hers, bossing her around all the time.'

'Then you are not going in the coach either?'

'No. I'm staying on here for a couple of days. I'm going to get around a bit and do a few excursions. Don't look so disapproving, Miss Marple. You're not really as dis-approving as all that, are you?'

'Well,' said Miss Marple, 'I have known such things happen in my own youth. The excuses may have been different, and I think we had less chance of getting away with things than you do now.'

Colonel and Mrs Walker came up and shook Miss Marple warmly by the hand.

'So nice to have known you and had all those delightful horticultural talks,' said the Colonel. 'I believe the day after tomorrow we're going to have a real treat, if nothing else happens. Really, it's too sad, this very unfortunate accident. I must say I think myself it *is* an accident. I really think the Coroner was going beyond everything in his feelings about this.'

'It seems very odd,' said Miss Marple, 'that nobody has come forward, if they were up on top there, pushing about rocks and boulders and things, that they haven't come forward to say so.'

'Think they'll be blamed, of course,' said Colonel Walker. 'They're going to keep jolly quiet, that's what they're going to do. Well, goodbye. I'll send you a cutting of that Magnolia highdownensis and one of the Mahonia japonica too. Though I'm not quite sure if it would do as well where you live.'

They in turn got into the coach. Miss Marple turned away. She turned to see Professor Wanstead waving to the departing coach. Mrs Sandbourne came out, said goodbye to Miss Marple and got in the coach and Miss Marple took Professor Wanstead by the arm.

'I want you,' she said. 'Can we go somewhere where we can talk?'

'Yes. What about the place where we sat the other day?'

'Round here there's a very nice verandah place, I think.'

They walked round the corner of the hotel. There was some gay horn-blowing, and the coach departed.

'I wish, in a way, you know,' said Professor Wanstead, 'that you weren't staying behind. I'd rather have seen you safely on your way in the coach.' He looked at her sharply. 'Why are you staying here? Nervous exhaustion or something else?'

'Something else,' said Miss Marple. 'I'm not particularly exhausted, though it makes a perfectly natural excuse for somebody of my age.'

'I feel really I ought to stay here and keep an eye on you.'

'No,' said Miss Marple, 'there's no need to do that. There are other things you ought to be doing.'

'What things?' He looked at her. 'Have you got ideas or knowledge?'

'I think I have knowledge, but I'll have to verify it. There are certain things that I can't do myself. I think you will help to do them because you're in touch with what I refer to as the authorities.'

'Meaning Scotland Yard, Chief Constables and the Governors of Her Majesty's Prisons?'

'Yes. One or other or all of them. You might have the Home Secretary in your pocket, too.'

'You certainly do have ideas! Well, what do you want me to do?'

'First of all I want to give you this address.'

She took out a notebook and tore out one page and handed it to him.

'What's this? Oh yes, well known charity, isn't it?'

'One of the better ones, I believe. They do a lot of good. You send them clothes,' said Miss Marple, 'children's clothes and women's clothes. Coats. Pullovers, all those sort of things.'

'Well, do you want me to contribute to this?'

'No, it's an appeal for charity, it's a bit of what belongs to what we're doing. What you and I are doing.'

'In what way?'

'I want you to make inquiries there about a parcel which was sent from here two days ago, posted from this post office.'

'Who posted it—did you?'

'No,' said Miss Marple. 'No. But I assumed responsibility for it.'

'What does that mean?'

'It means,' said Miss Marple, smiling slightly, 'that I went into the post office here and I explained rather scattily and—well, like the old pussy I am—that I had very foolishly asked someone to take a parcel for me and post it, and I had put the wrong address on it. I was very upset by this. The post-mistress very kindly said she remembered the parcel, but the address on it was not the one I was mentioning. It was this one, the one I have just given to you. I explained that I had been very foolish and written the wrong address on it, confusing it with another one I sometimes send things to. She told me it was too late to do anything about it now because the parcel, naturally, had gone off. I said it was quite all right, that I would send a letter to the particular charity to which the parcel had been sent, and explain that it had been addressed to them by mistake. Would they very kindly forward it on to the charity that I had meant to receive it.'

'It seems rather a roundabout way.'

'Well,' said Miss Marple, 'one has to *say* something. I'm not going to do that at all. *You* are going to deal with the matter. We've got to know what's inside that parcel! I have no doubt you can get means.'

'Will there be anything inside the parcel to say who actually sent it?'

'I rather think not. It may have a slip of paper saying "from friends" or it may have a fictitious name and address—something like Mrs Pippin, 14 Westbourne Grove and if anyone made inquiries there, there'd be no person of such a name living there.'

'Oh. Any other alternatives?'

'It might possibly, most unlikely but possible, have a slip saying "From Miss Anthea Bradbury-Scott"——'

'Did she——?'

'She took it to the post,' said Miss Marple.

'And you had asked her to take it there?'

'Oh no,' said Miss Marple. 'I hadn't asked anyone to post anything. The first I saw of the parcel was when Anthea passed the garden of the Golden Boar where you and I were sitting talking, carrying it.'

'But you went to the post office and represented that the parcel was yours.'

'Yes,' said Miss Marple, 'which was quite untrue. But post offices are careful. And, you see, I wanted to find out where it had been sent.'

'You wanted to find out if such a parcel had been sent, and if it had been sent by one of the Bradbury-Scotts—or especially Miss Anthea?'

'I knew it would be Anthea,' said Miss Marple, 'because we'd seen her.'

'Well?' He took the paper from her hand. 'Yes, I can set this in motion. You think this parcel will be interesting?'

'I think the contents of it might be quite important.'

'You like keeping your secrets, don't you?' said Professor Wanstead.

'Not exactly secrets,' said Miss Marple, 'they are only *probabilities* that I am exploring. One does not like to make definite assertions unless one has a little more definite knowledge.'

'Anything else?'

'I think—I think that whoever's in charge of these things, ought to be warned that there might be a second body to be found.'

'Do you mean a second body connected with the particular crime that we have been considering? A crime that took place ten years ago?'

'Yes,' said Miss Marple. 'I'm quite sure of it, as a matter of fact.'

'Another body. Whose body?'

'Well,' said Miss Marple, 'it's only my idea so far.'

'Any idea where this body is?'

'Oh! Yes,' said Miss Marple, 'I'm quite sure I know where it *is*, but I have to have a little more time before I can tell you that.'

'What kind of a body? Man's? Woman's? Child's? Girl's?'

'There's another girl who is missing,' said Miss Marple. 'A girl called Nora Broad. She disappeared from here and she's never been heard any more of. I think her body might be in a particular place.'

Professor Wanstead looked at her.

'You know, the more you say, the less I like leaving you here,' he said. 'Having all these ideas—and possibly doing something foolish—either——' He stopped.

'Either it's all nonsense?——' said Miss Marple.

'No, no, I didn't mean that. But either you know too much—which might be dangerous . . . I think I am going to stay here to keep an eye on you.'

'No, you're not,' said Miss Marple. 'You've got to go to London and set certain things moving.'

'You spoke as though you knew a good deal, Miss Marple.'

'I think I do know a good deal now. But I have got to be sure.'

'Yes, but if you make sure, that may be the last thing you do make sure of! We don't want a third body. Yours.'

'Oh, I'm not expecting anything like that,' said Miss Marple.

'There might be danger, you know, if any of your ideas are right. Have you suspicions of any one particular person?'

'I think I have certain knowledge as to one person. I

have got to find out—I have got to stay here. You asked me once if I felt an atmosphere of evil. Well, that atmosphere is here all right, an atmosphere of evil, of danger if you like—of great unhappiness, of fear. . . . I've got to do something about that. The best I can do. But an old woman like me can't do very much.'

Professor Wanstead counted under his breath. 'One—two—three—four——'

'What are you counting?' asked Miss Marple.

'The people who left in the coach. Presumably you're not interested in them, since you've let them go off and you're staying here.'

'Why should I be interested in them?'

'Because you said Mr Rafiel had sent you in the coach for a particular reason and sent you on this tour for a particular reason and sent you to The Old Manor House for a particular reason. Very well then. The death of Elizabeth Temple ties up with someone in the coach. Your remaining here ties up with The Old Manor House.'

'You're not quite right,' said Miss Marple. 'There are connections between the two. I want someone to tell me things.'

'Do you think you can make anyone tell you things?'

'I think I might. You'll miss your train if you don't go soon.'

'Take care of yourself,' said Professor Wanstead.

'I mean to take care of myself.'

The door into the lounge opened and two people came out. Miss Cooke and Miss Barrow.

'Hullo,' said Professor Wanstead, 'I thought you'd gone off with the coach.'

'Well, we changed our minds at the last moment,' said Miss Cooke cheerfully. 'You know we've just discovered that there are some very agreeable walks near here and there are one or two places I'm very anxious to see. A church with a very unusual Saxon font. Only four or five miles away and quite easily reached by the local bus, I think. You see, it's not only houses and gardens. I'm very interested in church architecture.'

'So am I,' said Miss Barrow. 'There's also Finley Park which is a very fine piece of horticultural planting not far from here. We really thought that it would be much pleasanter to stay here for a day or two.'

'You're staying here at the Golden Boar?'

'Yes. We were fortunate enough to be able to get a very nice double room. Really a better one than the one we have had for the last two days.'

'You will miss your train,' said Miss Marple again.

'I wish,' said Professor Wanstead, 'that you——'

'I shall be quite all right,' said Miss Marple urgently. 'Such a kind man,' she said, as he disappeared round the side of the house, 'who really takes so much care of me— I might be a great-aunt of his or something like that.'

'It's all been a great shock, hasn't it,' said Miss Cooke. 'Perhaps you may like to come with us when we go to visit St Martins in the Grove.'

'You're very kind,' said Miss Marple, 'but I don't think today I feel quite strong enough for expeditions. Perhaps tomorrow if there is anything interesting to see.'

'Well, we must leave you then.'

Miss Marple smiled at them both and went into the hotel.

20. Miss Marple Has Ideas

HAVING HAD LUNCH in the dining-room, Miss Marple went out on the terrace to drink her coffee. She was just sipping her second cup when a tall, thin figure came striding up the steps, and approached her, speaking rather breathlessly.

She saw that it was Anthea Bradbury-Scott.

'Oh, Miss Marple, we've only just heard, you know, that you didn't go with the coach, after all. We thought you were going on with the tour. We had no idea you were staying on here. Both Clotilde and Lavinia sent me here to say we do so hope you will come back to The Old Manor House and stay with us. I'm sure it will be nicer for you to be there. There are so many people coming and going here always, especially over a weekend and things like that. So we'd be very, very glad—we really would—if you would come back to us.'

'Oh, that's very kind of you,' said Miss Marple. 'Really very kind, but I'm sure—I mean, you know it was just a two-day visit. I meant originally to go off with the coach. I mean, after the two days. If it hadn't been for this very, very tragic accident but—well, I really felt I couldn't go on any longer. I thought I must have at least, well at least one night's rest.'

'But I mean it would be so much better if you came to us. We'd try and make you comfortable.'

'Oh, there's no question of that,' said Miss Marple. 'I was extremely comfortable staying with you. Oh yes, I did enjoy it very much. Such a beautiful house. And all your things are so nice. You know, your china and glass and furniture. It's such a pleasure to be in a home and not a hotel.'

'Then you must come with me now. Yes, you really must. I could go and pack your things for you.'

'Oh—well, that's very kind of you. I can do that myself.'

'Well, shall I come and help you?'

'That would be very kind,' said Miss Marple.

They repaired to her bedroom where Anthea, in a somewhat slap-dash manner, packed Miss Marple's belongings together. Miss Marple, who had her own ways of folding things, had to bite her lip to keep an air of complacency on her face. Really, she thought, she can't fold *anything* properly.

Anthea got hold of a porter from the hotel and he carried the suitcase round the corner and down the street to The Old Manor House. Miss Marple tipped him adequately and, still uttering fussy little speeches of thanks and pleasure, rejoined the sisters.

'The Three Sisters!' she was thinking. 'Here we are again.' She sat down in the drawing-room, and closed her eyes for a minute, breathing rather fast. She appeared to be somewhat out of breath. It was only natural, she felt at her age, and after Anthea and the hotel porter had set a fast pace. But really she was trying to acquire through her closed eyes what the feeling was she had on coming into this house again. Was something in it sinister? No, not so much sinister as unhappy. Deep unhappiness. So much so it was almost frightening.

She opened her eyes again and looked at the two other occupants of the room. Mrs Glynne had just come in from the kitchen, bearing an afternoon tea tray. She looked as she had looked all along. Comfortable, no particular emotions or feelings. Perhaps almost too devoid of them, Miss Marple thought. Had she accustomed herself through perhaps a life of some stress and difficulty, to show nothing to the outer world, to keep a reserve and let no one know what her inner feelings were?

She looked from her to Clotilde. She had a Clytemnestra

210

look, as she had thought before. She had certainly not murdered her husband for she had never had a husband to murder and it seemed unlikely that she had murdered the girl to whom she was said to have been extremely attached. That, Miss Marple was quite sure was true. She had seen before how the tears had welled from Clotilde's eyes when the death of Verity had been mentioned.

And what about Anthea? Anthea had taken that cardboard box to the post office. Anthea had come to fetch her. Anthea—she was very doubtful about Anthea. Scatty? Too scatty for her age. Eyes that wandered and came back to you. Eyes that seemed to see things that other people might not see, over your shoulder. She's frightened, thought Miss Marple. Frightened of something. What was she frightened of? Was she perhaps a mental case of some kind? Frightened perhaps of going back to some institution or establishment where she might have spent part of her life. Frightened of those two sisters of hers feeling that it was unwise for her to remain at liberty? Were they uncertain, those two, what their sister Anthea might do or say?

There was *some* atmosphere here. She wondered, as she sipped the last of her tea, what Miss Cooke and Miss Barrow were doing. Had they gone to visit that church or was that all talk, meaningless talk. It was odd. Odd the way they had come and looked at her at St Mary Mead so as to know her again on the coach, but not to acknowledge that they had ever seen or met her before.

There were quite a lot of difficult things going on. Presently Mrs Glynne removed the tea tray, Anthea went out into the garden and Miss Marple was left alone with Clotilde.

'I think,' said Miss Marple, 'that you know an Archdeacon Brabazon, do you not?'

'Oh yes,' said Clotilde, 'he was in church yesterday at the service. Do you know him?'

'Oh no,' said Miss Marple, 'but he did come to the Golden Boar and he came and spoke to me there. I gather he had been to the hospital and was inquiring about poor Miss Temple's death. He wondered if Miss Temple had sent any message to him. I gather she was thinking of paying him a visit. But of course I told him that although I did go there in case I could do anything, there was nothing that could be done except sit by poor Miss Temple's bed. She was unconscious, you know. I could have done nothing to help her.'

'She didn't say—say anything—any explanation of what had happened?' asked Clotilde.

She asked without much interest. Miss Marple wondered if she felt more interest than she expressed, but on the whole she thought not. She thought Clotilde was busy with thoughts of something quite different.

'Do you think it *was* an accident?' Miss Marple asked, 'or do you think there is something in that story that Mrs Riseley-Porter's niece told. About seeing someone pushing a boulder.'

'Well, I suppose if those two said so, they must have seen it.'

'Yes. They both said so, didn't they,' said Miss Marple, 'though not quite in the same terms. But perhaps that's quite natural.'

Clotilde looked at her curiously.

'You seem to be intrigued by that.'

'Well, it seems so very unlikely,' said Miss Marple, 'an unlikely story, unless——'

'Unless what?'

'Well I just wondered,' said Miss Marple.

Mrs Glynne came into the room again.

'You just wondered what?' she asked.

'We're talking about the accident, or the non-accident,' said Clotilde.

'But who——'

'It seems a very odd story that they told,' said Miss Marple again.

'There's something about this place,' said Clotilde suddenly. 'Something about this atmosphere. We never got over it here. Never. Never since—since Verity died. It's years but it doesn't go away. A shadow's here.' She looked at Miss Marple. 'Don't you think so too? Don't you feel a shadow here?'

'Well, I'm a stranger,' said Miss Marple. 'It's different for you and your sisters who've lived here and who knew the dead girl. She was, I gather, as Archdeacon Brabazon was saying—a very charming and beautiful girl.'

'She was a lovely girl. A dear child too,' said Clotilde.

'I wish I'd known her better,' said Mrs Glynne. 'Of course I was living abroad at that time. My husband and I came home on leave once, but we were mostly in London. We didn't come down here often.'

Anthea came in from the garden. She was carrying in her hand a great bunch of lilies.

'Funeral flowers,' she said. 'That's what we ought to have here today, isn't it? I'll put them in a great jar. Funeral flowers,' and she laughed suddenly. A queer, hysterical little giggle.

'Anthea,' said Clotilde, 'don't—don't do that. It's not —it's not right.'

'I'll go and put them in water,' said Anthea, cheerfully. She went out of the room.

'Really,' said Mrs Glynne, 'Anthea! I do think she's——'

'She's getting worse,' said Clotilde.

Miss Marple adopted an attitude of not listening or hearing. She picked up a small enamel box and looked at it with admiring eyes.

'She'll probably break a vase now,' said Lavinia.

She went out of the room. Miss Marple said,

'You are worried about your sister, about Anthea?'

213

'Well, yes, she's always been rather unbalanced. She's the youngest and she was rather delicate as a girl. But lately, I think, she's got definitely worse. She hasn't got any idea, I think, of the gravity of things. She has these silly fits of hysteria. Hysterical laughter at things one ought to be serious about. We don't want to—well, to send her anywhere or—you know. She ought to have treatment, I think, but I don't think she would like to go away from home. This is her home, after all. Though sometimes it's—it's very difficult.'

'All life is difficult sometimes,' said Miss Marple.

'Lavinia talks of going away,' said Clotilde. 'She talks of going to live abroad again. At Taormina, I think. She was there with her husband a lot and they were very happy. She's been at home with us now for many years, but she seems to have this longing to get away and to travel. Sometimes I think—sometimes I think she doesn't like being in the same house as Anthea.'

'Oh dear,' said Miss Marple. 'Yes, I have heard of cases like that where these difficulties do arise.'

'She's afraid of Anthea,' said Clotilde. 'Definitely afraid of her. And really, I keep telling her there's nothing to be afraid of. Anthea's just rather silly at times. You know, has queer ideas and says queer things. But I don't think there's any danger of her—well, I mean of—oh, I don't know what I mean. Doing anything dangerous or strange or queer.'

'There's never been any trouble of that kind?' inquired Miss Marple.

'Oh no. There's never been anything. She gets nervous fits of temper sometimes and she takes rather sudden dislikes to people. She's very jealous, you know, over things. Very jealous of a lot of—well, fuss being made over different people. I don't know. Sometimes I think we'd better sell this house and leave it altogether.'

'It is sad for you, isn't it,' said Miss Marple. 'I think I

can understand that it must be very sad for you living here with the memory of the past.'

'You understand that, do you? Yes, I can see that you do. One cannot help it. One's mind goes back to that dear, lovable child. She was like a daughter to me. She was the daughter, anyway, of one of my best friends. She was very intelligent too. She was a clever girl. She was a good artist. She was doing very well with her art training and designing. She was taking up a good deal of designing. I was very proud of her. And then—this wretched attachment, this terrible mentally afflicted boy.'

'You mean Mr Rafiel's son, Michael Rafiel?'

'Yes. If only he'd never come here. It just happened that he was staying in this part of the world and his father suggested he might look us up and he came and had a meal with us. He could be very charming, you know. But he always had been a sad delinquent, a bad record. He'd been in prison twice, and a very bad history with girls. But I never thought that Verity . . . just a case of infatuation. I suppose it happens to girls of that age. She was infatuated with him. Thought of nothing else, wouldn't hear a word against him. Insisted that everything that had happened to him had not been his fault. You know the things girls say. "Everyone is against him," that's what they always say. Everyone's against him. Nobody made allowances for him. Oh, one gets tired of hearing these things said. Can't one put a little sense into girls?'

'They have not usually very much sense, I agree,' said Miss Marple.

'She wouldn't listen. I—I tried to keep him away from the house. I told him he was not to come here any more. That of course was stupid. I realized that afterwards. It only meant that she went and met him outside the house. I don't know where. They had various meeting places. He used to call for her in his car at an agreed spot and bring her home late at night. Once or twice he didn't bring her

215

home until the next day. I tried to tell them it must stop, that it must all cease, but they wouldn't listen. Verity wouldn't listen. I didn't expect him to, of course.'

'She intended to marry him?' asked Miss Marple.

'Well, I don't think it ever got as far as that. I don't think he ever wanted to marry her or thought of such a thing.'

'I am very sorry for you,' said Miss Marple. 'You must have suffered a lot.'

'Yes. The worst was having to go and identify the body. That was some time after—after she'd disappeared from here. We thought of course that she'd run away with him and we thought that we'd get news of them some time. I knew the police seemed to be taking it rather seriously. They asked Michael to go to the police station and help them with inquiries and his account of himself didn't seem to agree with what local people were saying.

'Then they found her. A long way from here. About thirty miles away. In a kind of ditch hedgy spot down an unfrequented lane where anyone hardly ever went. Yes, I had to go and view the body in the mortuary. A terrible sight. The cruelty, the force that had been used. What did he want to do that to her for? Wasn't it enough that he strangled her? He strangled her with her own scarf. I can't—I can't talk about it any more. I can't bear it, I can't bear it.'

Tears rained suddenly down her face.

'I'm sorry for you,' said Miss Marple. 'I'm very, very sorry.'

'I believe you are.' Clotilde looked at her suddenly. 'And even you don't know the worst of it.'

'In what way?'

'I don't know—I don't know about Anthea.'

'What do you mean about Anthea?'

'She was so queer at that time. She was—she was very jealous. She suddenly seemed to turn against Verity. To

216

look at her as though she hated her. Sometimes I thought
—I thought perhaps—oh no, it's an awful thing to think,
you can't think that about your own sister—she did once
attack someone. You know, she used to get these storms of
rage. I wondered if it *could* have been—oh, I mustn't say
such things. There's no question of any such thing. Please
forget what I've said. There's nothing in it, nothing at all.
But—but—well, she's not quite normal. I've got to face
that. When she was quite young, queer things happened
once or twice—with animals. We had a parrot. A parrot
that said things, silly things that parrots do say and she
wrung its neck and I've never felt the same since. I've
never felt that I could trust her. I've never felt *sure*. I've
never felt—oh, goodness, I'm getting hysterical, too.'

'Come, come,' said Miss Marple, 'don't think of these
things.'

'No. It's bad enough to know—to know that Verity died.
Died in that horrible way. At any rate, other girls are safe
from that boy. Life sentence he got. He's still in prison.
They won't let him out to do anything to anyone else.
Though why they couldn't bring it in as some mental
trouble—diminished responsibility—one of these things
they use nowadays. He ought to have gone to Broadmoor.
I'm sure he wasn't r esponsible for anything that he did.'

She got up and went out of the room. Mrs Glynne had
come back and passed her sister in the doorway.

'You mustn't pay any attention to Clotilde,' she said.
'She's never quite recovered from that ghastly business
years ago. She loved Verity very much.'

'She seems to be worried about your other sister.'

'About Anthea? Anthea's all right. She's—er—well,
she's scatty, you know. She's a bit—hysterical. Apt to get
worked up about things, and she has queer fancies,
imagination sometimes. But I don't think there's any need
for Clotilde to worry so much. Dear me, who's that passing
the window?'

Two apologetic figures suddenly showed themselves in the French window.

'Oh do excuse us,' said Miss Barrow, 'we were just walking round the house to see if we could find Miss Marple. We had heard she'd come here with you and I wonder—oh, there you are, my dear Miss Marple. I wanted to tell you that we didn't get to that church after all this afternoon. Apparently it's closed for cleaning, so I think we shall have to give up any other expedition today and go on one tomorrow. I do hope you don't mind us coming in this way. I did ring at the front-door bell but it didn't seem to be ringing.'

'I'm afraid it doesn't sometimes,' said Mrs Glynne. 'You know, it's rather temperamental. Sometimes it rings and sometimes it doesn't. But do sit down and talk to us a little. I'd no idea that you hadn't gone with the coach.'

'No, we thought we would do a little sightseeing round here, as we had got so far, and going with the coach would really be rather—well, rather painful after what has happened just a day or two ago.'

'You must have some sherry,' said Mrs Glynne.

She went out of the room and presently returned. Anthea was with her, quite calm now, bringing glasses and a decanter of sherry, and they sat down together.

'I can't help wanting to know,' said Mrs Glynne, 'what really is going to happen in this business. I mean of poor Miss Temple. I mean, it seems so very impossible to know what the police think. They still seem to be in charge, and I mean the inquest being adjourned, so obviously they are not satisfied. I don't know if there's anything in the nature of the wound.'

'I shouldn't think so,' said Miss Barrow. 'I mean a blow on the head, bad concussion—well, I mean that came from the boulder. The only point is, Miss Marple, if the boulder rolled itself down or somebody rolled it.'

'Oh,' said Miss Cooke, 'but surely you can't think that

218

—who on earth would want to roll a boulder down, do that sort of thing? I suppose there are always hooligans about. You know, some young foreigners or students. I really wonder, you know, whether—well——'

'You mean,' said Miss Marple, 'you wondered if that someone was one of our fellow travellers.'

'Well, I—I didn't say that,' said Miss Cooke.

'But surely,' said Miss Marple, 'we can't help—well, thinking about that sort of thing. I mean, there must be some explanation. If the police seem sure it wasn't an accident, well then it must have been done by somebody and—well, I mean, Miss Temple was a stranger to this place here. It doesn't seem as if anyone could have done it—anyone local I mean. So it really comes back to—well, I mean, to all of us who were in the coach, doesn't it?'

She gave a faint, rather whinnying old lady's laugh.

'Oh surely!'

'No, I suppose I ought not to say such things. But you know, really, crimes are very interesting. Sometimes the most extraordinary things have happened.'

'Have you any definite feeling yourself, Miss Marple? I should be interested to hear,' said Clotilde, returning.

'Well, one does think of possibilities.'

'Mr Caspar,' said Miss Cooke. 'You know, I didn't like the look of that man from the first. He looked to me—well, I thought he might have something to do with espionage or something. You know, perhaps come to this country to look for atomic secrets or something.'

'I don't think we've got any atomic secrets round here,' said Mrs Glynne.

'Of course we haven't,' said Anthea. 'Perhaps it was someone who was following her. Perhaps it was someone who was tracking her because she was a criminal of some kind.'

'Nonsense,' said Clotilde. 'She was the Headmistress retired, of a very well known school; she was a very fine scholar. Why ever should anyone be trying to track *her* down?'

'Oh, I don't know. She might have gone peculiar or something.'

'I'm sure,' said Mrs Glynne, 'that Miss Marple has some ideas.'

'Well, I have some ideas,' said Miss Marple. 'It seems to me that—well, the only people that could be . . . Oh dear, this is so difficult to say. But I mean there are two people who just spring into one's mind as possibilities logically. I mean, I don't think that it's really so at all because I'm sure they're both very nice people, but I mean there's nobody else really logically who could be suspected, should I say?'

'Who do you mean? This is very interesting.'

'Well, I don't think I ought to say such things. It's only a—a sort of wild conjecture.'

'Who do you think might have rolled the boulder down? Who do you think could have been the person that Joanna and Emlyn Price saw?'

'Well, what I did think was that—that perhaps they hadn't seen anybody.'

'I don't quite understand,' said Anthea, 'they hadn't seen anybody?'

'Well, perhaps they might have made it all up.'

'What—about seeing someone?'

'Well, it's possible, isn't it?'

'Do you mean as a sort of joke or a sort of unkind idea? What *do* you mean?'

'Well, I suppose—one does hear of young people doing very extraordinary things nowadays,' said Miss Marple. 'You know, putting things in horses' eyes, smashing Legation windows and attacking people. Throwing stones at people, and it's usually being done by somebody young, isn't it? And they were the only young people, weren't they?'

'You mean Emlyn Price and Joanna might have rolled over that boulder?'

'Well, they're the only sort of obvious people, aren't they?' said Miss Marple.

'Fancy!' said Clotilde. 'Oh, I should never have thought of that. But I see—yes, I just see that there could be something in what you say. Of course, I don't know what those two were like. I haven't been travelling with them.'

'Oh, they were very nice,' said Miss Marple. 'Joanna seemed to me a particularly—you know, capable girl.'

'Capable of doing anything?' asked Anthea.

'Anthea,' said Clotilde, 'do be quiet.'

'Yes. Quite capable,' said Miss Marple. 'After all, if you're going to do what may result in murder, you'd have to be rather capable so as to manage not to be seen or anything.'

'They must have been in it together, though,' suggested Miss Barrow.

'Oh yes,' said Miss Marple. 'They were in it together and they told roughly the same story. They are the—well, they are the obvious suspects, that's all I can say. They were out of sight of the others. All the other people were on the lower path. They could have gone up to the top of the hill, they could have rocked the boulder. Perhaps they didn't mean to kill Miss Temple specially. They may have meant it just as a—well, just as a piece of anarchy or smashing something or someone—anyone in fact. They rolled it over. And then of course they told the story of seeing someone there. Some rather peculiar costume or other which also sounds very unlikely and—well, I oughtn't to say these things but I *have* been thinking about it.'

'It seems to me a very interesting thought,' said Mrs Glynne. 'What do you think, Clotilde?'

'I think it's a possibility. I shouldn't have thought of it myself.'

'Well,' said Miss Cooke, rising to her feet, 'we must be going back to the Golden Boar now. Are you coming with us, Miss Marple?'

'Oh no,' said Miss Marple. 'I suppose you don't know. I've forgotten to tell you. Miss Bradbury-Scott very kindly asked me to come back and stay another night—or two nights—here.'

'Oh, I see. Well, I'm sure that'll be very nice for you. Much more comfortable. They seem rather a noisy lot that have arrived at the Golden Boar this evening.'

'Won't you come round and have some coffee with us after dinner?' suggested Clotilde. 'It's quite a warm evening. We can't offer you dinner because I'm afraid we haven't got enough in the house, but if you'll come in and have some coffee with us . . .'

'That would be very nice,' said Miss Cooke. 'Yes, we will certainly avail ourselves of your hospitality.'

21. The Clock Strikes Three

MISS COOKE AND MISS BARROW arrived very promptly at 8.45. One wore beige lace and the other one a shade of olive green. During dinner Anthea had asked Miss Marple about these two ladies. 'It seems very funny of them,' she said, 'to want to stay behind.'

'Oh, I don't think so,' said Miss Marple. 'It is really quite natural. They have an exact plan, I imagine.'

'What do you mean by a plan?' asked Mrs Glynne.

'Well, I should think they are always prepared for various eventualities and had a plan for dealing with them.'

'Do you mean,' said Anthea, with some interest, 'do you mean that they had a plan for dealing with murder?'

'I wish,' said Mrs Glynne, 'that you wouldn't talk of poor Miss Temple's death as murder.'

'But of course it's murder,' said Anthea. 'All I wonder is who wanted to murder her? I should think probably some pupil of hers at the school who always hated her and had it in for her.'

'Do you think hate can last as long as that?' asked Miss Marple.

'Oh, I should think so. I should think you could hate anyone for years.'

'No,' said Miss Marple, 'I think hate would die out. You could try and keep it up artificially, but I think you would fail. It's not as strong a force as love,' she added.

'Don't you think that Miss Cooke or Miss Barrow or both of them might have done the murder?'

'Why should they?' said Mrs Glynne. 'Really, Anthea! They seemed very nice women to me.'

'*I* think there's something rather mysterious about them,' said Anthea. 'Don't you, Clotilde?'

'I think perhaps you're right,' said Clotilde. 'They seemed to me to be slightly artificial, if you know what I mean.'

'*I* think there's something very sinister about them,' said Anthea.

'You've got such an imagination always,' said Mrs Glynne. 'Anyway, they were walking along the bottom path, weren't they? You saw them there, didn't you?' she said to Miss Marple.

'I can't say that I noticed them particularly,' said Miss Marple. 'In fact, I had no opportunity of doing so.'

'You mean——?'

'She wasn't there,' said Clotilde. 'She was here in our garden.'

'Oh, of course. I forgot.'

'A very nice, peaceful day it was,' said Miss Marple. 'I enjoyed it very much. Tomorrow morning I would like to go out and look again at that mass of white flowers coming into bloom at the end of the garden near that raised up mound. It was just beginning to come out the other day. It must be a mass of bloom now. I shall always remember that as part of my visit here, you know.'

'I hate it,' said Anthea. 'I want it taken away. I want to build up a greenhouse again there. Surely if we save enough money we can do that, Clotilde?'

'We'll leave that alone,' said Clotilde. 'I don't want that touched. What use is a greenhouse to us now? It would be years before grapes would bear fruit again.'

'Come,' said Mrs Glynne, 'we can't go on arguing over that. Let us go into the drawing-room. Our guests will be coming shortly for coffee.'

It was then that the guests had arrived. Clotilde brought in the tray of coffee. She poured out the cups and distributed them. She placed one before each guest and then brought one to Miss Marple. Miss Cooke leaned forward.

'Oh, do forgive me, Miss Marple, but really, do you

224

know, I shouldn't drink that if I were you. Coffee, I mean, at this time of night. You won't sleep properly.'

'Oh, do you think so?' said Miss Marple. 'I am quite used to coffee in the evening.'

'Yes, but this is very strong, good coffee. I should advise you not to drink it.'

Miss Marple looked at Miss Cooke. Miss Cooke's face was very earnest, her fair, unnatural-looking hair flopped over one eye. The other eye blinked slightly.

'I see what you mean,' said Miss Marple. 'Perhaps you are right. You know something, I gather, about diet.'

'Oh yes, I make quite a study of it. I had some training in nursing, you know, and one thing and another.'

'Indeed.' Miss Marple pushed the cup away slightly. 'I suppose there is no photograph of this girl?' she asked. 'Verity Hunt, or whatever her name was? The Archdeacon was talking about her. He seemed to have been very fond of her.'

'I think he was. He was fond of all young people,' said Clotilde. She got up, went across the room and lifted the lid of a desk. From that she brought a photograph and brought it over for Miss Marple to see.

'That was Verity,' she said.

'A beautiful face,' said Miss Marple. 'Yes, a very beautiful and unusual face. Poor child.'

'It's dreadful nowadays,' said Anthea, 'these things seem happening the whole time. Girls going out with every kind of young man. Nobody taking any trouble to look after them.'

'They have to look after themselves nowadays,' said Clotilde, 'and they've no idea of how to do it, heaven help them!' She stretched out a hand to take back the photograph from Miss Marple. As she did so her sleeve caught the coffee cup and knocked it to the floor.

'Oh dear!' said Miss Marple. 'Was that my fault? Did I jog your arm?'

'No,' said Clotilde, 'it was my sleeve. It's rather a floating sleeve. Perhaps you would like some hot milk, if you are afraid to take coffee?'

'That would be very kind,' said Miss Marple. 'A glass of hot milk when I go to bed would be very soothing indeed, and always gives one a good night.'

After a little more desultory conversation, Miss Cooke and Miss Barrow took their departure. A rather fussy departure in which first one and then the other came back to collect some article they'd left behind. A scarf, a hand-bag and a pocket handkerchief.

'Fuss, fuss, fuss,' said Anthea, when they had departed.

'Somehow,' said Mrs Glynne, 'I agree with Clotilde that those two don't seem *real*, if you know what I mean,' she said to Miss Marple.

'Yes,' said Miss Marple, 'I *do* rather agree with you. They *don't* seem very real. I have wondered about them a good deal. Wondered, I mean, why they came on this tour and if they were really enjoying it. And what was their reason for coming.'

'And have you discovered the answers to all those things?' asked Clotilde.

'I think so,' said Miss Marple. She sighed. 'I've discovered the answers to a lot of things,' she said.

'Up to now I hope you've enjoyed yourself,' said Clotilde.

'I am glad to have left the tour now,' said Miss Marple. 'I don't think I should have enjoyed much more of it.'

'No. I can quite understand that.'

Clotilde fetched a glass of hot milk from the kitchen and accompanied Miss Marple up to her room.

'Is there anything else I can get you?' she asked. 'Anything at all?'

'No, thank you,' said Miss Marple. 'I have everything I want. I have my little night bag here, you see, so I need not do any more unpacking. Thank you,' she said, 'it is very kind of you and your sisters to put me up again tonight.'

'Well, we couldn't do much less, having had Mr Rafiel's letter. He was a very thoughtful man.'

'Yes,' said Miss Marple, 'the kind of man who—well, thinks of everything. A good brain, I should think.'

'I believe he was a very noted financier.'

'Financially and otherwise, he thought of a lot of things,' said Miss Marple. 'Ah well, I shall be glad to get to bed. Goodnight, Miss Bradbury-Scott.'

'Shall I send you breakfast up in the morning, you'd like to have it in bed?'

'No, no, I wouldn't put you out for the world. No, no, I would rather come down. A cup of tea, perhaps, would be very nice, but I want to go out in the garden. I particularly want to see that mound all covered with white flowers, so beautiful and so triumphant——'

'Goodnight,' said Clotilde, 'sleep well.'

2

In the hall of The Old Manor House the grandfather clock at the bottom of the stairs struck two o'clock. The clocks in the house did not all strike in unison and some of them indeed, did not strike at all. To keep a house full of antique clocks in working order was not easy. At three o'clock the clock on the first floor landing struck a soft-chimed three o'clock. A faint chink of light showed through the hinge of the door.

Miss Marple sat up in bed and put her fingers on the switch of the electric lamp by her bed. The door opened very softly. There was no light outside now but the soft footstep came through the door into the room. Miss Marple switched the light on.

'Oh,' she said, 'it's you, Miss Bradbury-Scott. Is there anything special?'

'I just came to see if you wanted anything,' said Miss Bradbury-Scott.

Miss Marple looked at her. Clotilde had on a long purple robe. What a handsome woman she was, thought Miss Marple. Her hair framing her forehead, a tragic figure, a figure of drama. Again Miss Marple thought of Greek plays. Clytemnestra again.

'You're sure there is nothing I can bring you?'

'No, thank you,' said Miss Marple. 'I'm afraid,' she said apologetically, 'that I have not drunk my milk.'

'Oh dear, why not?'

'I did not think it would be very good for me,' said Miss Marple. Clotilde stood there, at the foot of the bed, looking at her.

'Not wholesome, you know,' said Miss Marple.

'Just what do you mean by that?' Clotilde's voice was harsh now.

'I think you know what I mean,' said Miss Marple. 'I think you've known all the evening. Perhaps before that.'

'I have no idea what you are talking about.'

'No?' There was a faint satirical note to the questioning monosyllable.

'I am afraid the milk is cold now. I will take it away and get you some hot.'

Clotilde stretched out a hand and took the glass of milk from the bedside.

'Don't trouble yourself,' said Miss Marple. 'Even if you brought it me, I should not drink it.'

'I really cannot understand the point of what you're saying. Really,' said Clotilde, looking at her. 'What a very extraordinary person you are. What sort of a woman are you? Why are you talking like this? Who are you?'

Miss Marple pulled down the mass of pink wool that encircled her head, a pink wool scarf of the same kind that she had once worn in the West Indies.

'One of my names,' she said, 'is Nemesis.'

'Nemesis? And what does that mean?'

'I think you know,' said Miss Marple. 'You are a very well educated woman. Nemesis is long delayed sometimes, but it comes in the end.'

'What are you talking about?'

'About a very beautiful girl whom you killed,' said Miss Marple.

'Whom I killed? What do you mean?'

'I mean the girl Verity.'

'And why should I kill her?'

'Because you loved her,' said Miss Marple.

'Of course I loved her. I was devoted to her. And she loved me.'

'Somebody said to me not very long ago that love was a very frightening word. It *is* a frightening word. You loved Verity too much. She meant everything in the world to you. She was devoted to you until something else came into her life. A different kind of love came into her life. She fell in love with a boy, a young man. Not a very suitable one, not a very good specimen, not anyone with a good record, but she loved him and he loved her and she wanted to escape. To escape from the burden of the bondage of love she was living in with you. She wanted a normal woman's life. To live with the man of her choice, to have children by him. She wanted marriage and the happiness of normality.'

Clotilde moved. She came to a chair and sat down in it, staring at Miss Marple.

'So,' she said, 'you seem to understand very well.'

'Yes, I do understand.'

'What you say is quite true. I shan't deny it. It doesn't matter if I do or do not deny it.'

'No,' said Miss Marple, 'you are quite right there. It will not matter.'

'Do you know at all—can you imagine—how I have suffered?'

'Yes,' said Miss Marple, 'I can imagine it. I've always been able to imagine things.'

'Did you imagine the agony, the agony of thinking, of knowing you are going to lose the thing you love best in the world? And I was losing it to a miserable, depraved delinquent. A man unworthy of my beautiful, splendid girl. I had to stop it. I had to—I had to.'

'Yes,' said Miss Marple. 'Sooner than let the girl go, you killed her. Because you loved her, you killed her.'

'Do you think I could ever do a thing like that? Do you think I could strangle the girl I loved? Do you think I could bash her face in, crush her head to a pulp? Nothing but a vicious, depraved man would do a thing like that.'

'No,' said Miss Marple, 'you wouldn't do that. You loved her and you would not be able to do that.'

'Well then, you see, you are talking nonsense.'

'You didn't do that to her. The girl that happened to was not the girl you loved. Verity's here still, isn't she? She's here in the garden. I don't think you strangled her. I think you gave her a drink of coffee or of milk, you gave her a painless overdose of sleeping stuff. And then when she was dead, you took her out into the garden, you pulled aside the fallen bricks of the greenhouse, and you made a vault for her there, under the floor with the bricks, and covered it over. And then the polygonum was planted there and has flowered ever since, growing bigger and stronger every year. Verity has remained here with you. You never let her go.'

'You fool! You crazy old fool! Do you think you are ever going to get away to tell this story?'

'I think so,' said Miss Marple. 'I'm not quite sure of it. You are a strong woman, much stronger than I am.'

'I'm glad you appreciate that.'

'And you wouldn't have any scruples,' said Miss Marple. 'You know one doesn't stop at one murder. I have noticed that in the course of my life and in what I have observed of crime. You killed two girls, didn't you? You killed the girl you loved and you killed a different girl.'

'I killed a silly little tramp, an adolescent tart. Nora Broad. How did you know about her?'

'I wondered,' said Miss Marple. 'I didn't think from what I saw of you that you could have borne to strangle and disfigure the girl you loved. But another girl disappeared also about that time, a girl whose body has never been found. But I thought that the body *had* been found, only they hadn't known that the body was Nora Broad's. It was dressed in Verity's clothes, it was identified as Verity by the person who would be the first applied to, the person who knew her better than anyone else. You had to go and say if the body found was the body of Verity. You recognized it. You said that that dead body was Verity's.'

'And why should I do that?'

'Because you wanted the boy who had taken Verity away from you, the boy whom Verity had loved and who had loved Verity, you wanted him tried for murder. And so you hid that second body in a place where it would not be too easily discovered. When that was discovered, it would be thought to be the wrong girl. You would make sure that it was identified in the way you wanted. You dressed it in Verity's clothes, put her handbag there; a letter or two, a bangle, a little cross on a chain—you disfigured her face.

'A week ago you committed a third murder, the murder of Elizabeth Temple. You killed her because she was coming to this part of the world, and you were afraid of what she might have known, from what Verity might have written to her or told her, and you thought that if Elizabeth Temple got together with Archdeacon Brabazon, they might with what they both knew come at some appraisal of the truth. Elizabeth Temple must not be allowed to meet the Archdeacon. You are a very powerful woman. You could have rolled that boulder down the hillside. It must have taken some doing, but you are a very strong woman.'

'Strong enough to deal with you,' said Clotilde.

'I don't think,' said Miss Marple, 'that you will be allowed to do that.'

'What do you mean, you miserable, shrivelled up old woman?'

'Yes,' said Miss Marple, 'I'm an elderly pussy and I have very little strength in my arms or my legs. Very little strength anywhere. But I am in my own way an emissary of justice.'

Clotilde laughed. 'And who'll stop me from putting an end to you?'

'I think,' said Miss Marple, 'my guardian angel.'

'Trusting to your guardian angel, are you?' said Clotilde, and laughed again.

She advanced towards the bed.

'Possibly two guardian angels,' said Miss Marple. 'Mr Rafiel always did things on a lavish scale.'

Her hand slipped under the pillow and out again. In it was a whistle which she put to her lips. It was something of a sensation in whistles. It had the shrill fury which would attract a policeman from the end of a street. Two things happened almost simultaneously. The door of the room opened. Clotilde turned. Miss Barrow was standing in the doorway. At the same moment the large wardrobe hanging cupboard opened and Miss Cooke stepped out of it. There was a grim air of professionalism about them both which was very noticeable, in contrast to their pleasant social behaviour a little earlier in the evening.

'Two guardian angels,' said Miss Marple happily. 'Mr Rafiel has done me very proud! as one used to say.'

232

22. Miss Marple Tells Her Story

'WHEN DID YOU FIND OUT,' asked Professor Wanstead, 'that those two women were private agents accompanying you for your protection?'

He leaned forward in his chair looking thoughtfully at
the white-haired old lady who sat in an upright position
in the chair opposite him. They were in an official
Government building in London, and there were four
other persons present.

An official from the Public Prosecutor's Office; the
Assistant Commissioner of Scotland Yard, Sir James
Lloyd, the Governor of Manstone Prison, Sir Andrew
McNeil. The fourth person was the Home Secretary.

'Not until the last evening,' said Miss Marple. 'I wasn't
actually sure until then. Miss Cooke had come to St Mary
Mead and I found out fairly quickly that she was not what
she represented herself to be, which was a woman know-
ledgeable in gardening who had come there to help a
friend with her garden. So I was left with the choice of
deciding what her real object had been, once she had
acquainted herself with my appearance, which was
obviously the only thing she could have come for. When
I recognized her again on the coach, I had to make up my
mind if she was accompanying the tour in the rôle of
guardianship, or whether those two women were enemies
enlisted by what I might call the other side.

'I was only really sure that last evening when Miss
Cooke prevented me by very distinct words of warning,
from drinking the cup of coffee that Clotilde Bradbury-
Scott had just set down in front of me. She phrased it very
cleverly, but the warning was clearly there. Later, when
I was wishing those two goodnight, one of them took my

hand in both of hers giving me a particularly friendly and affectionate handshake. And in doing so she passed something into my hand, which, when I examined it later, I found to be a high-powered whistle. I took it to bed with me, accepted the glass of milk which was urged upon me by my hostess, and wished her goodnight, being careful not to change my simple and friendly attitude.'

'You didn't drink the milk?'

'Of course not,' said Miss Marple. 'What do you take me for?'

'I beg your pardon,' said Professor Wanstead. 'It surprises me that you didn't lock your door.'

'That would have been quite the wrong thing to do,' said Miss Marple. 'I wanted Clotilde Bradbury-Scott to come in. I wanted to see what she would say or do. I thought it was almost certain that she *would* come in when sufficient time had elapsed, to make sure that I had drunk the milk, and was in an unconscious sleep from which presumably I would not have woken up again.'

'Did you help Miss Cooke to conceal herself in the wardrobe?'

'No. It was a complete surprise when she came out of that suddenly. I suppose,' said Miss Marple thoughtfully, thinking it over, 'I suppose she slipped in there just when I had gone down the passage to the—er—to the bathroom.'

'You knew the two women were in the house?'

'I thought they would be at hand somewhere after they'd given me the whistle. I do not think it was a difficult house to which to gain access, there were no shuttered windows or burglar alarms or anything of that kind. One of them came back on the pretext of having left a handbag and a scarf. Between them they probably managed to leave a window unfastened, and I should imagine they came back into the house almost as soon as they left it, while the inhabitants inside were going up to bed.'

234

'You took a big risk, Miss Marple.'

'I hoped for the best,' said Miss Marple. 'One cannot go through life without attracting certain risks if they are necessary.'

'Your tip about the parcel dispatched to that charity, by the way, was entirely successful. It contained a brand new brightly-coloured man's polo-necked jumper in scarlet and black checks. Most noticeable. What made you think of that?'

'Well,' said Miss Marple, 'that was really very simple. The description that Emlyn and Joanna gave of the figure they had seen made it seem almost certain that these very bright-coloured and noticeable clothes were *meant* to be noticed, and that therefore it would be very important that they should not be hidden locally or kept among the person's own belongings. They must be got out of the way as soon as could be. And really there is only one way successfully of disposing of something. That is through the general post. Anything in the nature of clothes can be very easily dispatched to charities. Think how pleased the people who collect winter garments for Unemployed Mothers, or whatever the name of the charity, would be to find a nearly brand new woollen jumper. All I had to do was to find out the address where it had been sent.'

'And you *asked* them that at the post office?' The Home Secretary looked slightly shocked.

'Not directly, of course. I mean, I had to be a little flustered and explain how I'd put the wrong address on some clothes that I was sending to a charity and could they by any chance tell me if the parcel one of my kind hostesses had brought up there, had been sent off. And a very nice woman there did her best and remembered that it was *not* the address I was hoping it had been sent to, and she gave me the address that she *had* noted. She had no suspicion, I think, that I had any wish for the information apart from being—well, rather muddle-headed, elderly,

235

and very worried about where my parcel of worn clothes had gone.'

'Ah,' said Professor Wanstead, 'I see you are an actress, Miss Marple, as well as an avenger.' Then he said, 'When did you first begin to discover what had happened ten years ago?'

'To begin with,' said Miss Marple, 'I found things very difficult, almost impossible. In my mind I was blaming Mr Rafiel for not having made things clear to me. But I see now that he'd been very wise not to do so. Really, you know, he *was* extraordinarily clever. I can see why he was such a big financier and made so much money so easily. He laid his plans so well. He gave me just enough information in small packets each time. I was, as it were, directed. First my guardian angels were alerted to note what I looked like. Then I was directed on the tour and to the people on it.'

'Did you suspect, if I may use that word, anyone on the tour at first?'

'Only as possibilities.'

'No feeling of evil?'

'Ah, you have remembered that. No, I did not think there was any definite atmosphere of evil. I was not told who my contact was there, but *she* made herself known to *me*.'

'Elizabeth Temple?'

'Yes. It was like a searchlight,' said Miss Marple, 'illuminating things on a dark night. So far, you see, I had been in the dark. There were certain things that must be, must logically be, I mean, because of what Mr Rafiel had indicated. There must be somewhere a victim and somewhere a murderer. Yes, a killer was indicated because that was the only liaison that had existed between Mr Rafiel and myself. There had been a murder in the West Indies. Both he and I had been involved in it and all he knew of me was my connection with that. So it could not be any other type of crime. And it could not, either, be a casual crime. It must be a deliberate crime. It must be, and show itself definitely to be the handiwork of someone who had accepted evil. Evil instead of good. There seemed to be two victims indicated. There must be someone who had been killed and there must be clearly a victim of injustice. A victim who had been accused of a crime he or she had not committed. So now, while I pondered these things, I had no light upon them until I talked to Miss Temple. She was very intense, very compelling. There came the first link which I had with Mr Rafiel. She spoke of a girl she had known, a girl who had once been engaged to Mr Rafiel's son. Here then was my first ray of light. Presently she also told me that the girl had not married him.

'I asked why not, and she said "because she died". I asked then how she had died, what had killed her, and she said very strongly, very compellingly—I can hear her voice still, it was like the sound of a deep bell—she said *Love*. And she said after that "the most frightening word there can be is Love". I did not know then exactly what she meant. In fact the first idea that came to me was that the girl had committed suicide as a result of an unhappy love affair. It can happen often enough, and a very sad tragedy it is when it does happen. That was the most I knew then. That and the fact that the journey she herself was engaged upon was no mere pleasure tour. She was going, she told me, on a pilgrimage. She was going to some place or to some person. I did not learn then who the person was, that only came later.'

'Archdeacon Brabazon?'

'Yes. I had no idea then of his existence. But from then on I felt that the chief characters—the chief actors—in the drama, whichever way you like to put it, were not on the tour. They were not members of the coach party. I hesitated just for a short time, hesitated over some

237

particular persons. I hesitated, considering Joanna Crawford and Emlyn Price.'

'Why fix on them?'

'Because of their youth,' said Miss Marple. 'Because youth is so often associated with suicide, with violence, with intense jealousy and tragic love. A man kills his girl—it happens. Yes, my mind went to them but it did not seem to me there was any association there. No shadow of evil, of despair, of misery. I used the idea of them later as a kind of false pointer when we were drinking sherry at The Old Manor House that last evening. I pointed out how they could be the most easy suspects in the death of Elizabeth Temple. When I see them again,' said Miss Marple, punctiliously, 'I shall apologize to them for having used them as useful characters to distract attention from my real ideas.'

'And the next thing was the death of Elizabeth Temple?'

'No,' said Miss Marple. 'Actually the next thing was my arrival at The Old Manor House. The kindness of my reception and taking up my stay there under their hospitable roof. That again had been arranged by Mr Rafiel. So I knew that I must go there, but not for what reason I was to go there. It might be merely a place where more information would come to me to lead me onwards in my quest. I am sorry,' Miss Marple said suddenly becoming her normal apologetic and slightly fussy self, 'I am talking at much too great a length. I really must not inflict on you all that I thought and . . .'

'Please go on,' said Professor Wanstead. 'You may not know it but what you are telling me is particularly interesting to me. It ties up with so much I have known and see in the work I do. Go on giving me what you felt.'

'Yes, go on,' said Sir Andrew McNeil.

'It *was* feeling,' said Miss Marple. 'It wasn't really, you know, logical deduction. It was based on a kind of emotional reaction or susceptibility to—well, I can only call it atmosphere.'

'Yes,' said Wanstead, 'there is atmosphere. Atmosphere in houses, atmosphere in places, in the garden, in the forest, in a public house, in a cottage.'

'The three sisters. That is what I thought and felt and said to myself when I went into The Old Manor House. I was so kindly received by Lavinia Glynne. There's something about the phrase—the three sisters—that springs up in your mind as sinister. It combines with the three sisters in Russian literature, the three witches on Macbeth's heath. It seemed to me that there was an atmosphere there of sorrow, of deep-felt unhappiness, also an atmosphere of fear and a kind of struggling different atmosphere which I can only describe as an atmosphere of normality.'

'Your last word interests me,' said Wanstead.

'It was due, I think, to Mrs Glynne. She was the one who came to meet me when the coach arrived and explained the invitation. She was an entirely normal and pleasant woman, a widow. She was not very happy, but when I say she was not very happy it was nothing to do with sorrow or deep unhappiness, it was just that she had the wrong atmosphere for her own character. She took me back with her and I met the other two sisters. The next morning I was to hear from an aged housemaid who brought my early morning tea, a story of past tragedy, of a girl who had been killed by her boy-friend. Of several other girls in the neighbourhood who'd fallen victims to violence, or sexual assault. I had to make my second appraisal. I had dismissed the people in the coach as not being personally concerned in my search. Somewhere still there was a killer. I had to ask myself if one of the killers could be here. Here in this house where I had been sent, Clotilde, Lavinia, Anthea. Three names of three weird sisters, three happy—unhappy—suffering—frightened—

what were they? My attention was caught first by Clotilde. A tall, handsome woman. A personality. Just as Elizabeth Temple had been a personality. I felt that here where the field was limited, I must at least sum up what I could about the three sisters. Three Fates. Who could be a killer? What kind of a killer? What kind of a killing? I could feel then rising up rather slowly, rather slowly like a miasma does, an atmosphere. I don't think there is any other word that expresses it except evil. Not necessarily that any one of these three was evil, but they were certainly living in an atmosphere where evil had happened, had left its shadow or was still threatening them. Clotilde, the eldest, was the first one I considered. She was handsome, she was strong; she was, I thought, a woman of intense emotional feeling. I saw her, I will admit, as a possible Clytemnestra. I had recently,' Miss Marple dropped into her everyday tones, 'been taken very kindly to a Greek play performed at a well-known boys' public school not far from my home. I had been very, very impressed by the acting of the Agamemnon and particularly the performance of the boy who had played Clytemnestra. A very remarkable performance. It seemed to me that in Clotilde I could imagine a woman who could plan and carry out the killing of a husband in his bath.'

For a moment Professor Wanstead had all he could do to repress a laugh. It was the seriousness of Miss Marple's tone. She gave him a slight twinkle from her eyes.

'Yes, it sounds rather silly, does it not, said like that? But I could *see* her that way, playing that part, that is to say. Very unfortunately, she had no husband. She had never had a husband, and therefore did not kill a husband. Then I considered my guide to the house. Lavinia Glynne. She seemed an extremely nice, wholesome and pleasant woman. But alas, certain people who have killed have produced much that effect on the world round them. They have been charming people. Many murderers have been delightful and pleasant men and people have been astonished. They are what I call the respectable killers. The ones who would commit murder from entirely utilitarian motives. Without emotion, but to gain a required end. I didn't think it was very likely and I should be highly surprised if it was so, but I could not leave out Mrs Glynne. She had had a husband. She was a widow and had been a widow for some years. It could be. I left it at that. And then I came to the third sister: Anthea. She was a disquieting personality. Badly co-ordinated, it seemed to me, scatter-brained, and in a condition of some emotion which I thought on the whole was fear. She was frightened of something. Intensely frightened of something. Well, that could fit in too. If she had committed a crime of some kind, a crime which she had thought was finished with and past, there might have been some recrudescence, some raising up of old problems, something perhaps connected with the Elizabeth Temple inquiries; she might have felt fear that an old crime would be revived or discovered. She had a curious way of looking at you, and then looking sharply from side to side over one shoulder as though she saw something standing behind her. Something that made her afraid. So she too was a possible answer. A possibly slightly mentally unhinged killer who could have killed because she considered herself persecuted. Because she was afraid. These were only ideas. They were only a rather more pronounced assessment of possibilities that I had already gone through on the coach. But the atmosphere of the house was on me more than ever. That next day I walked in the garden with Anthea. At the end of the principal grass path was a mound. A mound created by the falling down of a former greenhouse. Owing to a lack of repairs and of gardeners at the end of the war it had fallen into disuse, come to pieces, bricks had been piled up surmounted with earth and turf, and had been planted with a certain creeper. A creeper well known when you want to hide or cover some rather ugly piece of building in your garden. Polygonum it is called. One of the quickest flowering shrubs which swallows and kills and dries up and gets rid of everything it grows over. It grows over everything. It is in a way a rather frightening plant. It has beautiful white flowers, it can look very lovely. It was not yet in bloom but it was going to be. I stood there with Anthea, and she seemed to be desperately unhappy over the loss of the greenhouse. She said it had had such lovely grapes, it seemed to be the thing she remembered most about the garden when she had been a child there. And she wanted, she wanted desperately to have enough money so as to dig up the mound, level the ground and rebuild the greenhouse and stock it with muscat grapes and peaches as the old greenhouse had been. It was a terrible nostalgia for the past she was feeling. It was more than that. Again, very clearly, I felt an atmosphere of fear. Something about the mound made her frightened. I couldn't then think what it was. You know the next thing that happened. It was Elizabeth Temple's death and there was no doubt, from the story told by Emlyn Price and Joanna Crawford, that there could be only one conclusion. It was not accident. It was deliberate murder.

'I think it was from then on,' said Miss Marple, 'that I knew. I came to the conclusion there had been three killings. I heard the full story of Mr Rafiel's son, the delinquent boy, the ex-jailbird and I thought that he was all those things, but none of them showed him as being a killer or likely to be a killer. All the evidence was against him. There was no doubt in anyone's mind that he had killed the girl whose name I had now learned as being Verity Hunt. But Archdeacon Brabazon put the final crown on the business, as it were. He had known those two young people. They had come to him with their story of wanting to get married and he had taken it upon himself to decide that they should get married. He thought that it was not perhaps a wise marriage, but it was a marriage that was justified by the fact that they both loved each other. The girl loved the boy with what he called a true love. A love as true as her name. And he thought that the boy, for all his bad sexual reputation, had truly loved the girl and had every intention of being faithful to her and trying to reform some of his evil tendencies. The Archdeacon was not optimistic. He did not, I think, believe it would be a thoroughly happy marriage, but it was to his mind what he called a necessary marriage. Necessary because if you love enough you will pay the price, even if the price is disappointment and a certain amount of unhappiness. But one thing I was quite sure of. That disfigured face, that battered-in head could not have been the action of a boy who really loved the girl. This was not a story of sexual assault. In this love affair the love was rooted in tenderness. I was ready to take the Archdeacon's word for that. But I knew, too, that I'd got the right clue, the clue that was given me by Elizabeth Temple. She had said that the cause of Verity's death was Love—one of the most frightening words there is.

'It was quite clear then,' said Miss Marple. 'I think I'd known for some time really. It was just the small things that hadn't fitted in, but now they did. They fitted in with what Elizabeth Temple had said. The cause of Verity's death. She had said first the one word "Love" and then that "Love could be the most frightening word there was". It was all mapped out so plainly then. The overwhelming love that Clotilde had had for this girl. The girl's hero-worship of her, dependency on her, and then as she grew a little older, her normal instincts came into play. She wanted Love. She wanted to be free to love, to marry, to have children. And along came the boy that she could love. She knew that he was unreliable, she knew he was what was technically called a bad lot, but that,' said Miss Marple, in a more ordinary tone of voice, 'is not what puts

243

any girl off a boy. No. Young women like bad lots. They always have. They fall in love with bad lots. They are quite sure they can change them. And the nice, kind, steady, reliable husbands got the answer, in my young days, that one would be "a sister to them" which never satisfied them at all. Verity fell in love with Michael Rafiel, and Michael Rafiel was prepared to turn over a new leaf and marry this girl and was sure he would never wish to look at another girl again. I don't say this would have been a happy-ever-after thing, but it was, as the Archdeacon said quite surely, it *was* real love. And so they planned to get married. And I think Verity wrote to Elizabeth and told her that she was going to marry Michael Rafiel. It was arranged in secret because I think Verity did realize that what she was doing was essentially an escape. She was escaping from a life that she didn't want to live any longer, from someone whom she loved very much but not in the way she loved Michael. And she would not be allowed to do so. Permission would not be willingly given, every obstacle would be put in their way. So, like other young people, they were going to elope. There was no need for them to fly off to Gretna Green, they were of sufficiently mature age to marry. So she appealed to Archdeacon Brabazon, her old friend who had confirmed her—who was a real friend. And the wedding was arranged, the day, the time, probably even she bought secretly some garment in which to be married. They were to meet somewhere, no doubt. They were to come to the rendez-vous separately. I think he came there, but she did *not* come. He waited perhaps. Waited and then tried to find out, perhaps, why she didn't come. I think then a message may have been given him, even a letter sent him, possibly in her forged handwriting, saying she had changed her mind. It was all over and she was going away for a time to get over it. I don't know. But I don't think he ever dreamt of the real reason of why she hadn't come, of why

244

she had sent no word. He hadn't thought for one moment that she had been deliberately, cruelly, almost madly perhaps, destroyed. Clotilde was not going to lose the person she loved. She was not going to let her escape, she was not going to let her go to the young man whom she herself hated and loathed. She would keep Verity, keep her in her own way. But what I could not believe was—I did not believe that she'd strangled the girl and had then disfigured her face. I don't think she could have borne to do that. I think that she had re-arranged the bricks of the fallen greenhouse and piled up earth and turf over most of it. The girl had already been given a drink, an overdose of sleeping draught probably. Grecian, as it were, in tradition. One cup of hemlock—even if it wasn't hemlock. And she buried the girl there in the garden, piled the bricks over her and the earth and the turf——'

'Did neither of the other sisters suspect it?'

'Mrs Glynne was not there then. Her husband had not died and she was still abroad. But Anthea was there. I think Anthea did know *something* of what went on. I don't know that she suspected death at first, but she knew that Clotilde had been occupying herself with the raising up of a mound at the end of the garden to be covered with flowering shrubs, to be a place of beauty. I think perhaps the truth came to her little by little. And then Clotilde, having accepted evil, done evil, surrendered to evil, had no qualms about what she would do next. I think she enjoyed planning it. She had a certain amount of influence over a sly, sexy little village girl who came to her cadging for benefits now and then. I think it was easy for her to arrange one day to take the girl on a picnic or an expedition a good long way away. Thirty or forty miles. She'd chosen the place beforehand, I think. She strangled the girl, disfigured her, hid her under turned earth, leaves and branches. Why should anyone ever suspect her of doing any such thing? She put Verity's handbag there and a little chain Verity used to wear round her neck and possibly dressed her in clothes belonging to Verity. She hoped the crime would not be found out for some time but in the meantime she spread abroad rumours of Nora Broad having been seen about in Michael's car, going about with Michael. Possibly she spread a story that Verity had broken off the engagement to be married because of his infidelity with this girl. She may have said anything and I think everything she said she enjoyed, poor lost soul.'

'Why do you say "poor lost soul", Miss Marple?'

'Because,' said Miss Marple, 'I don't suppose there can be any agony so great as what Clotilde has suffered all this time—ten years now—living in eternal sorrow. Living you see, with the thing she *had* to live with. She had kept Verity, kept her there at The Old Manor House, in the garden, kept her there for ever. She didn't realize at first what that meant. Her passionate longing for the girl to be alive again. I don't think she ever suffered from remorse. I don't think she had even that consolation. She just suffered—went on suffering year after year. And I know now what Elizabeth Temple meant. Better perhaps than she herself did. Love *is* a very terrible thing. It is alive to evil, it can be one of the most evil things there can be. And she had to live with that day after day, year after year. I think, you know, that Anthea was frightened of that. I think she knew more clearly the whole time what Clotilde had done and she thought that Clotilde knew that she knew. And she was afraid of what Clotilde might do. Clotilde gave that parcel to Anthea to post, the one with the pullover. She said things to me about Anthea, that she was mentally disturbed, that if she suffered from persecution or jealousy Anthea might do anything. I think—yes—that in the not so distant future—something might have happened to Anthea—an arranged suicide because of a guilty conscience——'

'And yet you are sorry for that woman?' asked Sir

Andrew. 'Malignant evil is like cancer—a malignant tumour. It brings suffering.'

'Of course,' said Miss Marple.

'I suppose you have been told what happened that night,' said Professor Wanstead, 'after your guardian angels had removed you?'

'You mean Clotilde? She had picked up my glass of milk, I remember. She was still holding it when Miss Cooke took me out of the room. I suppose she—drank it, did she?'

'Yes. Did you know that might happen?'

'I didn't think of it, no, not at the moment. I suppose I could have known it if I'd thought about it.'

'Nobody could have stopped her. She was so quick about it, and nobody quite realized there was anything wrong in the milk.'

'So she drank it.'

'Does that surprise you?'

'No, it would have seemed to her the natural thing to do, one can't really wonder. It had come by this time that she wanted to escape—from all the things she was having to live with. Just as Verity had wanted to escape from the life that she was living there. Very odd, isn't it, that the retribution one brings on oneself fits so closely with what has caused it.'

'You sound sorrier for her than you were for the girl who died.'

'No,' said Miss Marple, 'it's a different kind of being sorry. I'm sorry for Verity because of all that she missed, all that she was so near to obtaining. A life of love and devotion and service to the man she had chosen, and whom she truly loved. Truly and in all verity. She missed all that and nothing can give that back to her. I'm sorry for her because of what she *didn't* have. But she escaped what Clotilde had to suffer. Sorrow, misery, fear and a growing cultivation and imbibing of evil. Clotilde had to live with all those. Sorrow, frustrated love which she could never get back, she had to live with the two sisters who suspected, who were afraid of her, and she had to live with the girl she had kept there.'

'You mean Verity?'

'Yes. Buried in the garden, buried in the tomb that Clotilde had prepared. She was *there* in The Old Manor House and I think Clotilde *knew* she was there. It might be that she even saw her or thought she saw her, sometimes when she went to pick a spray of polygonum blossom. She must have felt very close to Verity then. Nothing worse could happen to her, could it, than that? Nothing worse. . . .'

23. End Pieces

'THAT OLD LADY gives me the creeps,' said Sir Andrew McNeil, when he had said goodbye and thanks to Miss Marple.

'So gentle—and so ruthless,' said the Assistant Commissioner.

Professor Wanstead took Miss Marple down to his car which was waiting, and then returned for a few final words. 'What do you think of her, Edmund?'

'The most frightening woman I ever met,' said the Home Secretary.

'Ruthless?' asked Professor Wanstead.

'No, no, I don't mean that but—well, a very frightening woman.'

'Nemesis,' said Professor Wanstead thoughtfully.

'Those two women,' said the P.P.D. man, 'you know, the security agents who were looking after her, they gave a most extraordinary description of her that night. They got into the house quite easily, hid themselves in a small downstairs room until everyone went upstairs, then one went into the bedroom and into the wardrobe and the other stayed outside the room to watch. The one in the bedroom said that when she threw open the door of the wardrobe and came out, there was the old lady sitting up in bed with a pink fluffy shawl round her neck and a perfectly placid face, twittering away and talking like an elderly school marm. They said she gave them quite a turn.'

'A pink fluffy shawl,' said Professor Wanstead. 'Yes, yes, I do remember——'

'What do you remember?'

'Old Rafiel. He told me about her, you know, and then he laughed. He said one thing he'd never forget in all his life. He said it was when one of the funniest scatter-brained old pussies he'd ever met came marching into his bedroom out in the West Indies, with a fluffy pink scarf round her neck, telling him he was to get up and do something to prevent a murder. And he said, "What on earth do you think you're doing?" And she said she was Nemesis. Nemesis! He could not imagine anything less like it, he said. I like the touch of the pink woolly scarf,' said Professor Wanstead, thoughtfully, 'I like that, very much.'

2

'Michael,' said Professor Wanstead, 'I want to introduce you to Miss Jane Marple, who's been very active on your behalf.'

The young man of thirty-two, looked at the white-haired, rather dicky old lady, with a slightly doubtful expression.

'Oh—er—' he said, 'well, I guess I have heard about it. Thanks very much.' He looked at Wanstead. 'It's true, is it, they're going to give me a free pardon or something silly like that?'

'Yes. A release will be put through quite soon. You'll be a free man in a very short time.'

'Oh.' Michael sounded slightly doubtful.

'It will take a little getting used to, I expect,' said Miss Marple kindly.

She looked at him thoughtfully. Seeing him in retrospect as he might have been ten years or so ago. Still quite attractive—though he showed all the signs of strain. Attractive, yes. Very attractive, she thought he would have been once. A gaiety about him then, there would have been, and a charm. He'd lost that now, but it would come back perhaps. A weak mouth and attractively shaped eyes that could look you straight in the face, and probably had been always extremely useful for telling lies that you really wanted to believe. Very like—who was it?—she dived into past memories—Jonathan Birkin, of course. He had sung in the choir. A really delightful baritone voice. And how fond the girls had been of him! Quite a good job he'd had as clerk in Messrs Gabriel's firm. A pity there had been that little matter of the cheques.

'Oh,' said Michael. He said, with even more embarrassment, 'It's been very kind of you, I'm sure, to take so much trouble.'

'I've enjoyed it,' said Miss Marple. 'Well, I'm glad to have met you. Goodbye. I hope you've got a very good time coming to you. Our country is in rather a bad way just now, but you'll probably find some job or other that you might quite enjoy doing.'

'Oh, yes. Thanks, thanks very much. I—I really am very grateful, you know.'

His tone sounded still extremely unsure about it.

'It's not me you ought to be grateful to,' said Miss Marple, 'you ought to be grateful to your father.'

'Dad? Dad never thought much of me.'

'Your father, when he was a dying man, was determined to see that you got justice.'

'Justice.' Michael Rafiel considered it.

'Yes, your father thought Justice was important. He was, I think, a very just man himself. In the letter he wrote me asking me to undertake this proposition, he directed me to a quotation:

"Let Justice roll down like waters
    And Righteousness like an everlasting stream." '

'Oh! What's it mean? Shakespeare?'

'No, the Bible—one has to think about it—I had to.'

Miss Marple unwrapped a parcel she had been carrying.

'They gave me this,' she said. 'They thought I might like to have it—because I had helped to find out the truth of what had really happened. I think, though, that you are

251

the person who should have first claim on it—that is if you really want it. But maybe you do *not* want it——'

She handed him the photograph of Verity Hunt that Clotilde Bradbury-Scott had shown her once in the drawing-room of The Old Manor House.

He took it—and stood with it, staring down on it. . . . His face changed, the lines of it softened, then hardened. Miss Marple watched him without speaking. The silence went on for some little time. Professor Wanstead also watched—he watched them both, the old lady and the boy. It came to him that this was in some way a crisis— a moment that might affect a whole new way of life.

Michael Rafiel sighed—he stretched out and gave the photograph back to Miss Marple.

'No, you are right, I do not want it. All that life is gone —she's gone—I can't keep her with me. Anything I do now has got to be new—going forward. You—' he hesitated, looking at her—'You understand?'

'Yes,' said Miss Marple—'I understand—I think you are right. I wish you good luck in the life you are now going to begin.'

He said goodbye and went out.

'Well,' said Professor Wanstead, 'not an enthusiastic young man. He could have thanked you a bit more enthusiastically for what you did for him.'

'Oh, that's quite all right,' said Miss Marple. 'I didn't expect him to do so. It would have embarrassed him even more. It is, you know,' she added, 'very embarrassing when one has to thank people and start life again and see everything from a different angle and all that. I think he might do well. He's not bitter. That's the great thing. I understand quite well why that girl loved him——'

'Well, perhaps he'll go straight this time.'

'One rather doubts that,' said Miss Marple. 'I don't know that he'd be able to help himself unless—of course, the thing to hope for is that he'll meet a really nice girl.'

'What I like about you,' said Professor Wanstead, 'is your delightfully practical mind.'

'She'll be here presently,' said Mr Broadribb to Mr Schuster.

'Yes. The whole thing's pretty extraordinary, isn't it?'

'I couldn't believe it at first,' said Broadribb. 'You know, when poor old Rafiel was dying, I thought this whole thing was—well, senility or something. Not that he was old enough for that.'

The buzzer went. Mr Schuster picked up the phone.

'Oh, she's here, is she? Bring her up,' he said. 'She's come,' he said. 'I wonder now. You know, it's the oddest thing I ever heard in my life. Getting an old lady to go racketing round the countryside looking for she doesn't know what. The police think, you know, that that woman committed not just one murder but three. Three! I ask you! Verity Hunt's body was under the mound in the garden, just as the old lady said it was. She hadn't been strangled and the face was not disfigured.'

'I wonder the old lady herself didn't get done in,' said Mr Broadribb. 'Far too old to be able to take care of herself.'

'She had a couple of detectives, apparently, looking after her.'

'What, *two* of them?'

'Yes, I didn't know that.'

Miss Marple was ushered into their room.

'Congratulations, Miss Marple,' said Mr Broadribb, rising to greet her.

'Very best wishes. Splendid job,' said Mr Schuster, shaking hands.

Miss Marple sat down composedly on the other side of the desk. 'As I told you in my letter,' she said, 'I think I have fulfilled the terms of the proposition that was made to me. I have succeeded in what I was asked to do.'

'Oh I know. Yes, we've heard already. We've heard from Professor Wanstead and from the legal department and from the police authorities. Yes, it's been a splendid job, Miss Marple. We congratulate you.'

'I was afraid,' said Miss Marple, 'that I would not be able to do what was required of me. It seemed so very difficult, almost impossible at first.'

'Yes indeed. It seems quite impossible to me. I don't know how you did it, Miss Marple.'

'Oh well,' said Miss Marple, 'it's just perseverance, isn't it, that leads to things.'

'Now about the sum of money we are holding. It's at your disposal at any time now. I don't know whether you would like us to pay it into your bank or whether you would like to consult us possibly as to the investment of it? It's quite a large sum.'

'Twenty thousand pounds,' said Miss Marple. 'Yes, it is a very large sum by my way of thinking. Quite extra-ordinary,' she added.

'If you would like an introduction to our brokers, they could give you possibly some ideas about investing.'

'Oh, I don't want to invest any of it.'

'But surely it would be——'

'There's no point in saving at my age,' said Miss Marple. 'I mean the point of this money—I'm sure Mr Rafiel meant it that way—is to enjoy a few things one thought one never would have the money to enjoy.'

'Well, I see your point of view,' said Mr Broadribb. 'Then your instructions would be that we pay this sum of money into your bank?'

'Middleton's Bank, 132 High Street, St Mary Mead,' said Miss Marple.

'You have a deposit account, I expect. We will place it to your deposit account?'

'Certainly not,' said Miss Marple. 'Put it into my current account.'

'You don't think——'

'I do think,' said Miss Marple. 'I want it in my current account.' She got up and shook hands.

'You could ask your bank manager's advice, you know, Miss Marple. It really is—one never knows when one wants something for a rainy day.'

'The only thing I shall want for a rainy day will be my umbrella,' said Miss Marple.

She shook hands with them both again.

'Thank you so much, Mr Broadribb. And you too, Mr Schuster. You've been so kind to me, giving me all the information I needed.'

'You really want that money put into your current account?'

'Yes,' said Miss Marple. 'I'm going to spend it, you know. I'm going to have some fun with it.'

She looked back from the door and she laughed. Just for one moment Mr Schuster, who was a man of more imagination than Mr Broadribb, had a vague impression of a young and pretty girl shaking hands with the vicar at a garden party in the country. It was, as he realized a moment later, a recollection of his own youth. But Miss Marple had, for a minute, reminded him of that particular girl, young, happy, going to enjoy herself.

'Mr Rafiel would have liked me to have fun,' said Miss Marple.

She went out of the door.

'Nemesis,' said Mr Broadribb. 'That's what Rafiel called her. Nemesis! Never seen anybody less like Nemesis, have you?'

Mr Schuster shook his head.

'It must have been another of Mr Rafiel's little jokes,' said Mr Broadribb.